How, Upon Reflection, To Be Amorous

Marvin Cohen

EDITED BY COLIN MYERS

Sagging
Meniscus

Parts of this book previously appeared in:

Ambit #32 (1967), *Ambit* #44 (1970), *Ambit* #49 (1971), *Ararat Quarterly* #38 (1969), *Third Assembling* (1967), *The Avant-Garde Today* (1981), *Books Magazine* (April 1968), *Broadsides From America* (1965), *Chelsea* #32 (1973), *Exacting Clam* #6 (2022), *Hyn Poetry Quarterly* #1 (1969), *Loves Etc* (1973), *Panache Magazine* (1971), *PreRealism* #1 (1975), *Saint Louis Literary Supplement* vol 2/#1 (1978), *Trace* #72/73 (1970), *Umbral* #3 (1978), *West Branch* #1 (1977), *Wormwood Review* #65/66 (1977), youtu.be/dShkonHqDgo (2018)

Set in Janson with LaTeX.

ISBN: 978-1-952386-72-5 (paperback)
ISBN: 978-1-952386-73-2 (ebook)
Library of Congress Control Number: 2023942883

Sagging Meniscus Press
Montclair, New Jersey
saggingmeniscus.com

PREFACE

Marvin Cohen, born in 1931, has been writing about love for as long as he remembers. This anthology samples his writing across a variety of formats; from dramatic dialogue to essay, prose poem to verse, epigram to novella.

The title of this anthology reflects the multiple aspects of love. On the serious side, Elmer Suderman has observed: "Marvin Cohen is concerned with some very profound, even if commonplace themes of our time: relationship of the artist to reality and words, . . . loneliness, frustration, meaninglessness in an artificial society, love degenerating into lifeless sex . . . and many others."[1]

By contrast, Frank Allen in an article titled "Rejoicing Harlequin," reflected that Marvin "descends into a comedy of manners, parodying contemporary cultural and sexual mores, . . . composing a comic Platonic conception of the American Dream."[2]

One recurring theme is the Don Juan legend. This anthology extends the exploration undertaken in Marvin's novels *Inside the World: As Al Lehman* and *Women, and Tom Gervasi* (both 2018), his tales "The Don Juan of East Eighty-Ninth Street" (in *Five Fictions*, 2018) and "Bill Cole's Soul's Sole True Pure Love" (in *Questions to be Asked*, 2021, and his anthologies, especially *The Monday Rhetoric of the Love Club*, 1973 and *Fables at Life's Expense*, 1975, and particularly in the play *The Don Juan and the Non Don Juan*, 1980 (in *Plays on Words*, 2020), of which he wrote:

"I am unimpressed with the banality of everyday life and want to give it zest and a new angle. I have found surrealism is a way of looking at life differently while imposing your own personality on

---

[1] Elmer Suderman, "Monday Rhetoric of the Love Club" (*[Studies in Short Fiction]*, Winter 1974)
[2] Frank Allen, "Rejoicing Harlequin: The Comic Art of Marvin Cohen" (*Menu*, 1985)

it. Don Juan has always interested me particularly from the point of view of the power he has over other people.

"This time it's power in an amorous vein. It's a matter of who comes out on top, who submits and who demands. It can be likened to sport—one side demands and the other side tries with all its might to win. Ultimately no-one wants to lose.

"There's a lot at stake and the person who loses can be humiliated and suffer as a result. In all of us there is the Don Juan and the Non-Don Juan and these two aspects of our character are to be reconciled." [3]

Most of the pieces in this book come from Marvin's big box of unpublished typescripts; the rest are from his previously published but unanthologized work or his recently emailed poems and dialogues. Marvin says he is pleased to see them in print as he loves all of his literary offspring. He hopes you love them too.

—*Colin Myers*

---

[3] quoted in Stella Saunders, "The Don Juan in All of Us" (*[Kensington Post]*, February 20th 1981)

LOVE PARTNERS

LOVE

How, Upon Reflection, To Be Amorous

FOR CANDACE WATT

**LOVE'S FEELING
IN CANDID REVEALING.**

To love is to feel close,
and it must be kept that way,
not to withdraw.
You really need that person,
and desperately hope likewise
that she requites you
with similar desperation
or approximately so.
You really can't do without her,
and count that she feels the same way.
Being with her is not monotonous,
but is full of meaning
that never quite dulls;
an addiction without poisoning,
that approximates wonderful fiction
of superb interestingness
that never really grows any less.
Having her within your sight
increases your powerful might
to fulfill your reassurance
that there she is for you:
a stable state of affairs.
It's real, she's there,
as needed as constant breath
to keep guard against death.
Within you, she's quite concealed
as your private "must."
You're helpless without that trust.

Your love is a happy blessing
that shouts pride in confessing.

**PRAISING CANDACE WATT
TO SUCH SUFFICIENCY, IT'S A LOT.**

Who or what
charms like Candace Watt?
She's the opposite to a blood clot
that dooms the vessels to be shot.
If you love her, it's quite a lot
for her to bear, no matter what.
I signed our marriage pact to every dot,
and look at my sweet darling whom I got!

**TYPES OF NATURE'S LOVE
FROM DEEP BELOW OR FROM ABOVE,
THE WAY THE FINGERS FIT IN A GLOVE
AND THE LADY BIRD LOVES HER DOVE.**

Loving Candace is easy.
The tree loves the wind if it's breezy.
Trees love their roots in the ground,
barking that "roots are profound."
The birds love the air to fly in,
with gifted wings to do the job,
and have enough space to avoid the mob.
The squirrel loves the tree to climb up
from branch to slimmer twigs,
the better to search for figs.
Bald men naturally take to wigs.
The flowers love insects with pollen,
whether the leaves bloom or have fallen.
The fish love the sea to swim in.

Obesity loves diet to slim in.
Candace is easy to love.
Nature reigns on us from above
and from the ground level too.
Loving Candace is automatic.
She won't let me be autocratic.

LOVE'S DEFINITION
THAT STICKS TO ITS POSITION
AND RESISTS ALL OPPOSITION.

Of all things, what's love?
The state of being above,
because of the other.
Otherwise, why bother?
It's as easy to love Candace
as to stifle a wound with a bandage,
or at least feast when you're famished,
so your relationship won't be damaged.
And somehow you'll both manage,
even resorting to carnage,
but smoothing it over with varnish.

MY TWO CANDACE WATTS.
WHICH IS WHICH, AND WHO'S WHAT'S?

First there was the real you,
and then the memory came to life.
Which was which and who was who?
Time danced in between us:
The real you was the one I loved.
But memory stood in for you
like an actress playing a role.
She did a reasonable facsimile

and owned my double stage:
my passion roused to a rage.
Now I have you both, back and forth.
You take turns; my love is reinforced.
I take a double scoop, I take a double course.
I can't do without either:
the healthy germ and the healthy fever:
the original, and the continual retriever.
So memory serves a good purpose:
I get the depth, and I get the surface.
The memory provides the essence,
and then there's the real presence.

MY LOVE OF CANDACE WATT
BEGS THE QUESTION OF WHAT'S WHAT.

When I look at my wife, Candace Watt,
I seem to adore her a lot.
But that's between me and her:
the mystery of what makes the cat purr.
Having been with her a long time
completes the puzzle of the necessary rhyme.
Having enjoyed her acquaintance much
gives us both a familiar touch.
Whenever we come face to face,
the clock roars and we rush to grace.
Like truck drivers on the long haul,
we've circumnavigated the familiar ball
of minutes, days, and years
to find out how life appears
and also what's its essence.
We've become dependent on each other's presence.
It's still full of wholesomeness
that rescues us from dolefulness.

When each one enters the room,
we're glad we had once been wife and groom,
and allow each other to generously assume
what nature, art, and politics are
under our common living star.

FAREWELL TO A GREAT COUPLE
WHOSE MARRIAGE PROVED SO SUPPLE,
IT PERSISTED WITHOUT DISRUPTAL,
BUT WITH AN OCCASIONAL GRUMBLE
WITHIN THE MARITAL FOREST OR JUNGLE.

My love of Candace Watt
is dearly deep in upshot.
She has a slim, cute figure,
but mine is appropriately bigger.
We met and launched a later romance,
as each took a breathless, hesitant stance.
Was it inevitable that we married, perchance?
Possibly. So we're in for the long haul,
like truck drivers whose far away distances never appall.
From past to future we've stretched afar,
so brevity was not a factor in our eternal star.
Were Candace and I made for each other?
Life together was great. Could we have another?
No. Our mutual greed would smother.
So it's nearly time that we have to die.
Whose tears come first, taking turns to cry?
The one who mourns will say "Good night,"
as the other takes their leave in perilous flight.
Let's bid farewell to both,
to honor their long-ago troth
wherein they took persuasive oath
too late for vigorous youth,
but enough to convey their double-edged truth.

WOOING CANDACE WATT,
BUT TOO POOR TO OWN A YACHT.

Such a lovely woman is Candace Watt
that I'd like to take her on a yacht,
but alas I've insufficient money
to so indulge my sweet dear honey.
So cancel that unused trip
on the yacht, and skip
all the preliminaries of going to sea
for the ostentatious purpose of boasting a yacht
just to impress Candace Watt.
Can't I impress her by myself alone
as a simple loving human being
feeling fit and exerting charm?
That's what I humbly offer. Would it do her harm?
Now she knows that money isn't everything,
we'll seek cheaper methods for joy to bring.
The glittering fascinations of enormous wealth
dissolve to nothing compared to two people's health.

TO CANDACE AN EPISTLE
WHICH IF SHE GRANTS, I'LL WHISTLE
NOT TO TURN ON MYSELF A PISTOL.

When Candace takes me for granted,
I'll mention a sculptor who sculpted in granite,
but also sculpted in marble.
As a sculptor, he was a marvel.
So don't you ever take me for granted.
In your mind I've often planted
the idea of what a great guy I am.
Believe me literally, or else I'll scram
and punish you by not giving a damn.

So if you want to retain my love,
join me at the heights here above,
and condescend to so kiss me true and true
to convey not only my love for you,
but also your love sublime
that sweetly I may dearly call mine.
Such motivation is this bottom line.

LET ME BE CANDID
ABOUT HOW I MET CANDACE.
WHAT LUCK! IT WAS THE GRANDEST.

Having known Candace Watt,
I really hit the jackpot!
I met her right on the spot,
by accident at a party
which was somewhat arty.
She gave me a platter of food
that requited my hungry mood.
I ate up her shining presence,
and this was fortune's greatest present.
I still enjoy her in the present.
She really had me smashed.
The party? I had crashed,
not knowing the host or hostess.
But Candace proved to be the mostest.
Compared to her, others are the grossest.
Our meals are furnished at the grocer's.
Between us, I eat the mostest.
Love itself has become our new hostess.
We're worn out, and need the most rest.
But time itself will do the arrest,
due to death's earnest quest.

**HERE'S ALL THE WHAT'S WHAT
OF ME AND CANDACE WATT,
NEGATING PEOPLE'S NEED TO ASK WHAT.**

Loving Candace Watt
is not a load of rot.
We never had a tot,
being married late,
and slow off the gate.
An ancestry like a Scot
gave her strawberry blond hair.
But that's neither here nor there.
Her soul is big as the globe.
No wonder we had to elobe,
and then were soon to grobe.
Thus all romances evolve,
like plumbers know their valve
of faucets hot or cold.
Knowledge makes us bold
with complete authority,
akin to enlightened morality.
We can dispense with formality
and get on with nitty gritty,
taking excursions into being witty
while keeping up with feeding the kitty.
How privileged, living in the City!
Sophistication is our product
as a real grown-up adult,
thus determining our conduct.
Enjoying life together
occurs independent of weather.
We're not freaky. (We don't wear leather.)
We're frequently apart,

but never threaten to part,
and unlikely ever to start.
Love has deepened
through the years,
and its volume is never in arrears.

FOREPLAY

(Prime Title:)

A PLEA TO A PUBLISHER; WITH THE URGENCY OF UN-WILLING CHASTITY THAT CRAVES VIA FAME TO BE DE-STROYED BY LOVE.

(Sub Title:)

TO MAKE PUBLIC MY PRIVATE PROVEN WORTH, AND BALANCE MY INSIDE WITH THE COMMENSURABLE OUTSIDE. A PLEA FOR JUSTICE; FOR THE ROMANTIC ENHANCEMENTS OF GLORY.

(UnderSub Title:)

STOP DEBARRING ME FROM LOVE, WHICH WOULD BE-COME MINE UPON THE LITERARY RECOGNITION I DE-SERVE: WHICH DEPENDS ON YOUR SOON PUBLISHING ME SO I CAN BOAST AT COMPETITIVE SOCIAL PARTIES (ROMANCE'S OPEN MARKET FLAUNTING WARES AND ASSETS) THAT I'M WELL ACKNOWLEDGED IN WORLDLY VALUE FOR MY POETIC PRODUCTS, AND DESERVE ALL THE ACCLAIM I CAN GET, SO LOVE ME PLEASE. LOVE ME. I'M PUBLISHED. LOVE ME.

(Body of text itself (for which the above titles were made in the first, second, and third place):)

There's such a disproportion between my status and my stature. My stature is immense with golden works unpublished. But their being unpublished means my status is kept low. This inequity between my actual merit and my undeserved social unrecognition, makes me miserable, for I long frustratedly to live up in role out-wardly to the work I've produced from private worth. I crave appreciation, please.

And the delay is killing me. I'm alone, the girls don't bother with me. I'm getting into middle age, and unfamous. If I only had the measure of fame I deserve, in my remaining virile lifetime yet, then girls who would be attracted to an intellectual hero, a literary "figure" would come into my ken, and from them I'd find a loved one. That would make me less lonely. Oh if this could only be so! Then please hasten publication.

I wait, and wither. I wilt, and decline. Alas! Is *posthumous* glory all I'm to get? That wouldn't bring me the delights of love. Let me enjoy love, and let my fame, open the way to love. Let Recognition smile female favors upon me. May I be soon and well published. Then, at parties, I'll not be a "no one."

DESIRE

HOW WANTS CAN FEEL, WANTS *ARE* FEELING. WHAT DO THEY WANT?

Each want sets up a sadness condition. Each want signifies potential unhappiness. Yet each want is eagerness for a happiness. Each want is a gamble; "do I dare?" The reward is there, potentially, for risking the want; but also the potential penalty is there, in the want, depending on what follows the want, to satisfy it or to disappoint it,

"Want" is a looking for a state, and acute sensitivity to the failure of attaining it, should the want not be realized. The want becomes the standard of comparison. It's the eager emotional "set," leading to joy or pain.

But the want isn't arbitrarily determined: each want follows from something lacking, or felt to be lacking; some discomfort and dissatisfaction. Things must get better: and want anticipates it, expresses a lack, denotes what "something is wrong," which could be set right. A want means a lack of resignation to an unsatisfactory state: the feeling that "it could be better"; "it must improve"; "things can't go on, this way." It's an-action-inclination, to "make things right." While we have the want (meaning feel it), we can't rest, till there be a solution, somehow, which seems "only just," which we have a right to, it's just in the offing, if only we can effect it. We act and act, or plan or plot or think, till we substitute resignation for the want, or bring about sufficient relief so that the want stops.

Want stems from something unpleasant, and is potential of more unpleasantness, if the condition that the want *is*, is not met. A want goads; it plagues us, irritates us, won't let us alone; it craves its own demise, being succeeded by a diversion from it, or a relief, or *some* more pleasant feeling, that either directly solves the want, or makes us forget it, or in some way provides comfort.

A want, in proportion to its being a want (degree of intensity), can't bear itself: it wants a better state to drown it out. It sets us in motion, at thought, puts us active, looking for a better feeling to succeed that damnable feeling which is our damn want; which can't go on: so we take steps. We find something better, to follow. We look for a rest.

Hopeful want can be pleasant, if prospects improve. An optimistic, confident want, glowing with expectation, can be very pleasant. We seem just about to—.

Therefore, some wants *can* bear themselves, but they're pleasant wants, and anticipate pleasant feelings to follow the pleasant feelings that these wants are.

So they're not *damn* wants, but they feel good; and they enjoy the promise of what's to be.

How we *feel* is a state of want. Some feelings want just to perpetuate themselves; others, to alleviate themselves. They all look forward, to the next moment, in some way. What will the next moment bring? What imminent prospect is there?, the very near future. We pleasantly anticipate being pleased. Or we unpleasantly anticipate the end of that unpleasant anticipation. What's just ahead, is what our feeling points to,

We want to feel good. And what's next?

We feel pleasantly toward what's next, or unpleasantly desperate. There *will be* a "next"; but what?

AN UNTAMED INTERIORITY, THAT TURNS DOWN ALL INSTITUTIONAL CIRCUMSCRIBING AND RESISTS THE NAME PLATES FOR THE SYSTEMATICALLY DEFINED, AS THE WORLD CAN'T SWALLOW IT DOWN.

Clogged with food, rippling on the swell of anxiety, undulating with the roar of drink, bitter with hope, lyrical with terror, paralyzed by memory, lurching between unknowns, I became suddenly blind with love.

The cluttered instant can't recognize itself. It's packed with a squabble of contradictions. Its rippling interiority is all unrelieved discord. It's a resisting wilderness to our civilized principle of consistency, and offers no neck to the collar of domestication. It sprawls unstill, and keeps no steady figure for the branding measure to chart into the known. But it has its own felt existence, however unprocessed to worldly terms outside, where instants are immediately parceled off the historical.

It's been living. Let its chaos go undisturbed. It's forgone itself, when understood.

(The explanatory title, as text-interpretation:)

STUCK WITH BEING ONLY HIMSELF, HE LOOKS TO BE LOVED FOR HIMSELF. TO CONFIRM HIMSELF; AND TO LOVE, TO LEAVE HIMSELF, TO EXPAND, TO JOIN, TO SHARE. A WHOLE SMALL THING WANTS TO BE A SMALL THING THAT'S *PART* OF A LARGER WHOLE. IT LOOKS OUTSIDE FOR LOVE—FOR THE SELF IS NOT ENOUGH. TO PUT THAT SELF IN WITH *ANOTHER* SELF, WOULD BE PREFERABLE. LONELINESS HAS GONE ON LONG ENOUGH. NOW, TO LOOK.

(Characters:) Two men, both of the same sex. Though their identities might differ, and do, they must be identical in gender, to engender an identical viewpoint to expand their mere male selves, or male cells, in which each is imprisoned. They look for love, for the lack of which they're as lonely as hell. The lonely will look. The single-self animal wants to pair

with another self, with gender in mind, engendering a role of sharing a whole instead of being a lonely and smaller whole. To be not merely a self-contained self, but part. *To play a principal role, as* part of. *Love is required—from and to the other "part"-ner. Part and partnership. A self is all alone, by the self. But* with *an* other *self—ah!*

I like you well enough to want you to be like me.

That's condescending. I'd rather you dislike me enough to respect me *as* me.

Why insist on being *you?*

I *prefer* me.

You have no choice; you're stuck to the being of you; but you pretend to *choose* it. That's putting on airs: to affect free will, in so personal identity-matter.

The "truth" is, I'm tired of being me, and would like to escape. Yet, too, I'm addicted to the *habit* of being me: and would never relinquish it.

You affect free will. Like it or not, you're doomed always to remain you. It's your *fate*. So you're you by *fatalism*, not by choice.

You make me feel helpless.

But you *are* helpless.

But I don't want to *feel* it. I'd rather imagine I have some power over myself.

Self-deception, self-delusion—that's your auxilliary state, annexed to your state of being helplessly you.

Why strip me of illusion?—you make me feel worse.

Oh, you're sensitive to how you "feel?"

Yes. Feeling, to me, is more important than "truth."

Oh, you're so human—you prefer pleasure to displeasure. How common!

Yes; *so* common, that that's *you*, as well.

Yes; but I'd rather harp on *you*: then I feel omnipotent, and released from my too-human subjective frailty.

You're more confident when you bait me? And you feel weaker, the closer to *yourself* you get?

Yes. So let me bully you, it does me good.

Since it does *me bad*, I won't let you.

Then you put your self before me?

Yes, my priority is self-interest. So far as I'm concerned, I'm first. No one else cares, so *I* must care, for me.

That's sad. You must be unattractive, undesirable, if no one but yourself can care for you.

It's a lonely condition. But everyone's caring for themselves— for the same reason. Ah, I want love.

Yes, *to be loved* would be wonderful.

To be loved by someone whom you love well enough to want to be loved by—is ideal. Let's look for that.

Yes, let's look. Where will *you* look?

Wherever I can. I'll look for love, to leave a lonely life. To find love from one whom I love. To love the one whom I want love from. To be part of the same love, shared by another. I'll look, lonely, for it. I'll look and look, till I die.

What hopes have you, or chances for, or odds on, success?

I'll look my lonely look. I'll look and look.

Good look.

Was that a pun on "good luck?"

Yes; you'll need it.

The pun?

No, the luck. (Good.)

WHAT I FEEL IS IMPORTANT, MEANINGFUL, SIGNIFICANT—WHEN *YOU* ROUND IT OUT, WITH YOUR LOVING CONCERN, WITHOUT YOU, MY FEELINGS DROP PALE, OUTSIDE THE CIRCUIT OF COMPLETE RADIANCE.

How important am I to myself? Very, I must stay alive.

How important are the things that happen to me? Very, for it's to *me* that they happen.

Yes, but it's not enough that they happen to me. Someone must *bear witness*, someone who's not me, but to whom what happens to me is of concern. She *cares* about what happens to me.

Now, without you, when I try to eat my soup and it's too hot, there's only, there's merely, me in my solipsistic ego feeling the annoyance and impatient at the delay.

There's no you to feel sympathy, to even share my fate, and, compassionately, to offer the suggestion of diluting the soup with cold water by which *you* solved your own simultaneous predicament.

When I feel tired, now, the meaning of the tiredness is limited and incomplete. What does it really matter that *I* feel tired? *I* feel many things.

But with *you* there, with *you* to complain to, with you to feel sorry and to offer solace, my tiredness takes on an unlimited, complete meaning. It's not merely just another subjective self-indulgence of an unwitnessed vapor. It takes on importance because *you* notice it, you care, you want me to sleep or to otherwise revive my energy. You *bless* my tiredness, like a saint who blesses the leper's hurting place or the wounded one's wound or the lame man's lameness or the grief of the recently bereft. *You*'re there. My tiredness *exists*. I'm not just imagining it. Or I am imagining it, but in a proud and *confirmed* way. It's *real*, because your eyes acknowledge it and it's important to you. What I feel is important to you. This affects the importance to *me* of what I feel. My life is quickened with significance. It *matters*.

If I have good luck, a boost in fortune's prospect, it's no longer just *selfish*, if you *also* rejoice. It's *real*, not selfish, if you also rejoice.

That's part of what you mean to me. You make my meanings specially meaningful. You reinforce them by what meanings they have for *you*. My meanings take on extra meanings, you're the means, of this extension.

What these meanings mean is more life. *Your love* gives me more life—or more fulfilled life.

I have such *potential* life—all my events, all my feelings, my states, my ideas, are all fraught with potential meaning, laden with potential significance: your love *delivers* these meanings, *delivers* these significances, converts the bare barren potential into the full-ness of the deeply shared, the bond of sympathy, which redeems suffering into transcendence and wholeness.

This can only happen by the condition of being dwelled on lovingly with concern by the one whom one himself loves. Two loves make one whole. Within that whole, a radiant significance blesses the most minor events.

Your absence leaves me unattended. If my soup is too hot, so what? It's merely *my* pain, *my* inconvenience.

In your absence, if I say something fanciful and inventively whimsical, I risk receiving from the unloving listener, "Oh, don't be ridiculous; you're talking nonsense."

But if it were said to you, you would understand. I wouldn't feel like a fool, I'd feel confirmed, complete, proud, and whole. What I would say would reflect our shared radiance.

I miss all this. Lacking your presence, I lack my fullest self, my total being.

And I miss not making *your* world complete for *you*. I miss not endowing your annoyances with the comfort and blessing of my understanding. I miss not endowing your spoken words with the stature of *words truly heard*. For I hear your words with big, re-membering ears. I make your words quotable weeks after they're said. I make all your mental expressions important. I make your feelings *worth communicating*. I make *you* terrific, by being loved by me. I make you as big as you can possibly be. I make your life *flash out*, in splendid waves and beams, I'm your loving auditor. What goes through your head lands into my reflector, and you get it all back, specially enhanced, given the magnification of the emphasis that makes you proud, in your loved state.

I miss all this between us. For only *between* us, could all this exist.

Your absence makes this impossible, for the present. It takes the life out of the doubling of our lives. It reduces my life to plain-ness, to the barren, thin, one-dimensionality of the undoted-on.

Not that *anyone* can transfigure my events by doting on them. It needs the special flourishing flowering condition of *your* care.

Your care, because I love you. But why do I love you? Because *your care counts*. Anyone else's won't do.

I care for you. I care for your care. Your care cares for me. And you have my care. My care completes our embrace.

A BEWILDERED LOVER SPEAKS OUT HIS MUTENESS

Of course, you are magic. The indefinable things about you are, exasperatingly, the ones that most compel preoccupation. Thus there is never a linkage between what you provoke in me and what I'm equipped or qualified to communicate it with. For all that you do to me, I must remain awkwardly mute about it. And when you most compel my passion, articulation is severely muffled by failure. No external event can measure the immensity you create in me. Since you have more effect on me than anyone else, my dumbness to you is most conspicuous.

You're like a butterfly that can't be caught. You instill the magic potion of joy in my incredulous bones, joy taken from your ecstatic wing. The sunlight flashes more brilliant than before: even the shade is mottled with your perfumed shape. I throb, caught in your quivering net. You're my afternoon's solitary Muse. I quicken with desire to express something to you: but the result is naught. I can account for nothing, though inspiration enlarges your butterfly image to the benign semblage of a dragon.

Though you confront me with the provocation of the best that's in me, there's nothing I can produce worthy of what you kindle. I'm impaled with the power of helplessness; I'm drunk, but blabberingly incoherent. You're like a stimulant that distracts the stimulated from a direct focus on so elusively singular a cause. You incapacitate my endeavor to serve you to a thrilling reward: I'm made ineffectual by those palpitations you've put to motion in the structure you so disturbingly unsettle. You make me powerless, and reduce my balance by slicing dizzy lengths of ground under my uneven basis. Then when I'm seen as awkward, seize some blame and pardon my heightened vulnerability to your most inflaming properties, spiritual ineffables, and mystery-driven fascinations of the invisible. Never can I pin you to definition, since all that you are moves in a realm inaccessible to the demons that seek to define.

If your influence is to disturb, yet what you unsettle in me goes to create a far further satisfaction than anything neat and settled can impose in some explained order of symmetry. While I flail on helpless pinions, you sizzle my motion so out into jungles of eternity that I'm lost most momentously found.

So, simply, let me insert here that what I've arrived to say is that I love you. And let "love" gain, by these perplexities.

HOW TO ATTRACT THE ONES YOU'RE ATTRACTED TO, TO REMEDY THE BAD SITUATION OF BEING ATTRACTED TO THE ONES WHO ARE NOT ATTRACTED TO YOU, AND ATTRACTING THE ONES YOU'RE NOT ATTRACTED TO. HOW TO MAKE LOVE SHARED, AND GAIN FRIENDSHIPS AS WELL—BENEFITS OF *MUTUAL* ATTRACTION, FEELINGS RESPONDED TO IN LIKE VEIN. UNIMPORTANT THINGS LIKE THAT.

(Written in dialogue form, for two voices of the same sex and gender, both male. They alternate, as in all dialogues. Hear them.)

I only attract the people I'm not attracted to.

Are the others repelled by you?

Or repulsed—whichever means attraction's opposite.

That's a bad coincidence—for all concerned.

How to correct matters so that I love whom I'm loved by, and like whom I'm liked by? For time is going by, soon it's too late and I won't care anymore. I want to *enjoy* love and friendship. Please help.

Mutual attraction would be the solution, I think.

To what extent, or degree?

So mutual, that you and the other will requite and reciprocate each other's warm feelings for each other. Making a complete cycle enclosing you both warmly inside.

Oh; that would be ideal.

And you want to make it happen?

Dearly. And soon.

Then don't be too eager and desperate which is how you sound.

You mean that "puts off" the ones I'm interested in, since it makes me seem undesirable?

Yes. You must act as if you don't *lack* love—that you don't *need* it too desperately, being used to having it. Otherwise, the ones you're attracted to will feel there's something lacking *in* you—and they'll be right.

Oh, why must I play a game? I'm too sincere to!

You're too impatient to. You want the "real thing," right at once. So your approach to people would be simultaneously self-demeaning and aggressive, pleading and demanding, supplicating and presumptuous defensive and bold, brash but timid, shy but lunging. What an awkward figure you'd cut—and probably do.

Instead?

Be casual, patient. Wait.

That's dishonest. I don't *feel* it.

Then *pretend*, *affect* it. It's for your own interest I advise you strongly. You're getting older. Your sexual prime is waning—you feel urgency. *Act* calm. Wait, but alertly.

I'll try it. You explained why I don't attract those I'm attracted to. So now can you explain how sometimes I *do* attract people, but only those I'm *not* attracted to?

Because you're not putting the same pressure on *them* that you do on the ones you're attracted to but who are not attracted to you. That's a clue, now. Act—or pretend to—toward the ones you're attracted to in the same way that you naturally act towards the ones you slight and would dispense with and dispose of: with indifference and mild disdain.

Then, when I have the ones I'm attracted to "hooked" by that method—what then?

Then, love them—and feel secure or being responded to in like vein—or love vein; and enjoy with them the bliss of *shared* love: the supreme goal, romantically speaking, of the whole human heart at all times, but especially at secret moments when tenderness wells up and is bursting with pearly poignance. Ah, the heart is lonely. Cure it, with love.

Of what variety?

Shared love. Received for given, given for received. Reality with the dream, in combination.

Oh, that's ideal.

Ah, it may be yours. Some night; enchanting.

LOVING CAPTAIN DARING-DAUGHT—FROM AFAR

Doris was too literal-minded for her own good, in this instant. She was reading a long novel written over a century ago or almost, that had a handsome character in it. With him, she *literally* fell in love! It was so self-defeating, on her part!

Even if he had really been an actual person at the time the novel was written, enough time had elapsed since then as to cause him to be dead by now *anyway*. He was old enough to be her great-grandfather, at least! In fact, old enough to be dead, if he had ever lived.

But somehow, inexplicably, Doris had fallen for him. What an impractical choice! She could never *ever* hope to marry him.

As it turned out, her love object, Captain Daring-Daught (it was an English novel), had been a purely fictional creation. Never once had any actual feet of his (of which he had had none, at any rate) touched this actual terrestrial terra cotta, our own earth, symbol of the closeness-at-hand of our humanity-enclosed universe. This atmospheric air, no nose of his had breathed the tiniest ounce. Nor had he discharged from his mouth the least heard word, upon airwaves. He had purely lacked existence, at all.

But to *Doris*, his characterization was real. Hers, however, was a hopeless passion. Doomed, to all romantic eternity.

Captain Daring-Daught was a semi-major character in this rambling old novel. He himself was depicted as having conceived an undying love for Lady Lacklorn, who—though the captain was dashing—rejected him stubbornly at first, then slowly yielded, to his passionate—importunities. They were to be married, but complications ensued. She was aristocratically out of his class. Her father, an imperious lord, had made other plans for her. The plot was heartbreaking, and labyrinthine.

Doris wept at certain parts: copiously, but unashamed.

Her copy of the novel was thumbworn, by now. She shelved it, and borrowed library copies. In each copy, whatever edition, Captain Daring-Daught was just as dashing. Her love grew, with each re-reading.

Did Doris consider Lady Lacklorn to be her rival? Yes, but she forgave Captain Daring-Daught for being heartlessly unfaithful to Doris—loved him all the more for it, so fatal, unearthly, was her pure passion for him.

Yes, she did love, and from a great distance. The impossibility enhanced the idealism, the purity. She despaired of attaining. But she *had* won him: for heaven in afterlife. They'd be married angels, by the Catholic hierarchy. All that waited was for *her* to die, and she'd join him.

Even now, he was waiting for her. Had been, for a long time. But what's time, in heaven? He can wait much longer. Doris will die of old age: many, many years from now. She'll be preserved, for him. She will have wasted herself on no-one else. She'll be no second-hand Doris, no hand-me-down, when finally their union takes place. Captain Daring-Daught is preparing for this event.

First, he asked his novelist-creator's permission to marry Doris once she dies. The old author, himself an angel, and famous in the latter part of his lifetime as an internationally celebrated novelist, consents, graciously, yes.

And what of Lady Lacklorn? In the novel, she tragically failed to unite with the captain. Her cruel father had her married to another. (That passage was the weeping point for the novel's many fans.) Lady Lacklorn then died soon after—of a broken heart. A little while later, the novel was ended, after resolving some knots of other characters. Doris was worried that maybe the author had intended Captain Daring-Daught and Lady Lacklorn to unite forever in heaven. But the novel was too realistic—thank God. Only in real life, is there sufficient unreality for Doris to gain her afterlife wish. She waits that day, in quiet confidence, and in serene bliss.

HOW COMMUNICATIVITY CAN INTERGENDERALLY BE DOSED BY HABIT-FORMING INSTALLMENT HEAPED ON THE CONTINUUM OF FIRST ONCE HAVING BEEN INITIALLY INSTIGATED

(Characters: Boy and girl. However, latter becomes first to speak, with concluding word left to former.)
(Action: Attempted seduction, vocally.)
(Plot: Negligible, if perfunctory.)
(Scene: The pair of them.)
(Outcome: Issue unknown.)
(Result: Actively uncertain, vocally done.)
(Conclusion: No moral implied. But where's the immoral?)

(She): Communicativity: ever between us, will that be?

Let's kiss and see.

That's only a rub, and outward friction.

The *true* rub lies in some *inner fiction.*

Your enigmas only riddle me. Try to woo to win.

I'm kept dangling on the side of *out*: Admission must be gained, in the name of the whim of *in.*

No sophistry may you *pull* on me. Nor will I let you *push* either.

Then we have no mental accord, nor physical commerce neither.

What will bridge our souls together?

It all hangs leadenly, on a slim feather.

Depending on *what*, for chance?

For love's durable habit, the first event must happen once.

Is this your crude notion of a proposition?

Live and learn. I'll teach you the proper position.

The liberties you take are enough to alarm.

Why should city folks be barred from the elementary compoundings on a farm?

Are you leading me through the hazardous valleys of harm?

I'll soothe your whimpering outcry by pouring on some fire balm.

And what would heal the wound you'd have me have?

One such another wound: packed in with loaves of love.

CREATING LOVE BY SPEECH

(Just having met: young man and young woman. Latter speaks first.)

Why are you so shy?

Because you're so pretty.

Oh. Should I become ugly, then? Your shy embarrassment must be uncomfortable, in the face of all my beauty, and I must spare your feelings and ease you into relative unconcern, into indifference, which homeliness would inspire. I'll wrinkle and broaden my face into mismatched bones and incomplete features which the lack of a center clutters with irregularity or the gaps of unsightly unseemliness. Wouldn't you be less nervous, then?

Yes; and you wouldn't matter.

No. *(Romantically)* Then we could come to terms.

(Callously) I wouldn't bother.

Oh. *(Insulted)* You *are* choosy, aren't you? Your taste is only for special girls.

Yes, such as what you are *now*, before you would disfigure yourself.

Oh. Those were confident tones. Are you less nervous now? Is your masculine aggressiveness unruffled by a tender regard for my face's sweet lines?

Yes. I could thrust boldly forward.

You *are* audacious! You may take no liberty! Respect me, first!

I do, I will. Love *automatically* confers respect.

Have your feelings leaped to *love*, then? I'm unprepared!

Have I been hasty?

Yes, quite inconsiderately premature! Take a step backwards. I'm a *lady* and will be treated accordingly!

Now your coyness has turned haughty.

You presume, and impetuously slur me.

My intention is only to woo.

May your demeanor be graceful at it: which is, to make it easy for me to accept the overtures of your courtship, with no loss of pride on *my* part.

That's quite a lot, that you expect.

My expectations equal my merit. I wouldn't so immodestly exceed my worth, as to demand the due I don't deserve. Play the attentive gallant, in this respect.

Why do you premium *dignity*, when your beauty redundafies it?

Beauty may be demeaned and cheaply ravished, unless dignity prudently chaperone.

Your beauty being already established, let me pay homage to it.

I'm greatly pleased that you should say this.

My feigned love is evolving into genuinity.

Artful honesty is what touches me most. Your sincere tactics shall undoubtedly win me.

Yet you're difficult of access.

I wouldn't have you think me easy.

My attempts are so arduous, that their fruit is ardor.

Stripped of ease, your task is harder.

The right degree of assertion, in a narrow margin, may help me succeed.

Deeds of effort define the greatness of their goal.

Our talk is fanning me into love.

And what we play at, becomes the overwhelmingly serious need. Has desperation pitched your love to a high note?

Its urgency overcomes speech's exertions.

Now I feel suitably desirable.

Have I become your favored suitor?

I see no other around. Sure, you'll do.

THE MAN WOOING

I'll drink you in with my eyes.

That's a fancy expression. Do you really like me that much?

I like you more than I can say.

Oh, you're tongue-tied. Are you shy?

No, just "smitten."

Oh, I've made a conquest?

I'm yours entirely.

Oh, you're a pushover!

I fall down at your feet.

On your knees: are you proposing?

It's more serious than a mere proposition.

Is it for "keeps?"

Forever . . . and a day.

You're so romantic.

My heart is yours.

Aren't your expressions lacking originality?

For me, they're real.

Does being real confer on your words a unique expressive meaning?

It's from my heart.

I've heard of that one before.

Then answer me.

I love you too.

Have I overwhelmed you?

No. The more the merrier.

A BUSINESS CORRESPONDENCE REGARDING LOVE

As incomplete as one volume of a ten-volume encyclopedia, my heart without your love is completely lacking in something, which only you, dear soul, could fully provide. Therefore, please love me. I promise to desperately appreciate it. In exchange for my gratitude, grant me the extravagant bargain of your love. I'll kiss you many times over, consume your use, and absorb your perishing goodness in the full economy of my delight; and when you're gone, I'll file away the profit of your love's memory among the inactive papers that I cherish, and watch my heart's business turn bankrupt. I love you. Willing to exchange. Make a deal, and let the commerce flow. In one pair of lips, out the other, and through the heart from the sacred profanity of the body's corporate entrance, where central heating lights up the office hours and private transactions are clinched, sealed, and delivered, Friday's salary earned on a working Monday, love's wages bought and paid, the heart's lifetime in employment.

LOVE OR MONEY

THE SOLVED PROBLEM

Love makes the world go round.

No, I thought it's *money* that makes the world go round.

Give them both credit. They're both heavyweight factors, and the world can still stand, getting pushed around by both.

But what if love pushes the world one way, and money counter-pushes the world in the opposite direction?

As long as it's the same world, it'll rectify itself with recovery and revolve accordingly.

Is the world that adjustable?

It's a tough old globe.

Yeah. Space makes room for it.

It better.

DOES LOVE OR MONEY HAVE THE GREATER INFLUENCE?
LOVE DEPENDS ON THE HEART, BUT MONEY ON THE PENCE.
HOWEVER, WE TRY NOT TO CREATE OFFENSE.

Love makes the world go round.

No. Money is more profound,
and covers much more financial ground.
Love, of course, is all very well.
But money rings a more rambunctious bell,
dealing with almighty dollars and cents.
Use your nose and follow its scents.

But love is infinitely more romantic.

But money it is that makes the world tick
despite love's ever lustful trick.

It's up to you, so take your pick.

No. Both are necessary,
and need not be an adversary
to each other. Let them be friends
and if gave offense, now make amends.

To decide, let's see where the wind will wend.

If the world goes crazy, let's make the two blend.
Love and money: Give them a bond,
and both wind up equally fond.

THE OUTSIDE PERSON OR THING LACKING, TO COMPLETE THE INSIDE FEELING

I

As he did on other mornings, a man woke up. But his span of sleep had been an emotional escort from apathy that began the night, to a phase newly emerged: Love's beam floated about him. This man had arrived at love's estate. But the mood had no local attachment; the girl was not in view to surrender an existence to his suppositions. Love was air-borne, the formless hovering of an image. It took no corner of reality for its own, and for nourishment was consumed in a glow. A more specific fulfillment would be a greedy sacrilege. Outlines melted into one diffusion; this loveliness was heaven-sent.

This innocence soon died. It was imperative to find *some*one. The general crumbled; the particular was directed to arrive at a focal center. *One* girl, where all roads of the absolute end.

Where was romance to strike? On whose fertile bank would the heart pitch its permanent tent?

There had been a party invitation. The search mustn't be too frantic; re*lax*ed desperation would brave the tide: an affable willingness to meet all and sundry. Selectivity must expand the heart's honest art.

The party surged on drink's foamy splash. Girls with glittering eyes were there. But on each was the possessive shadow of an escort.

Love drained from the man: no actual girl completed the potential metaphor.

Should he join a lonely hearts club? No; it would strew his feet with muddy rejects. He wanted no dregs at the bottom of the hideous barrel of availability.

II

Though he took out hundreds of new different girls on various dates, no decisive commitment emanated from necessity. Solitude was merely crowded with numbers; hordes of unsuitable girls drowned that spontaneous outburst of love; frustration crushed the desire. Unfed, love had wilted. *Hate* was his newest customer. It caressed him, lovingly.

Loosely rattled in a package of generality, the hatred needed to be nurtured at some specific venomous breast. This poison was bloated into a bulging power. Where could malice streak a target? A scapegoat must slake this rare brew of thirst.

Like love, hatred also failed to find an object to fix on. Was there no correlative, in all the world outside, to the thing which emotion felt inside? Then insulation was the true fact about a lone man. A moat, minus a drawbridge, stifled him off, without engagement to yield the surroundings in. For what he felt on the interior, he lacked the vehicle to accomplish the gratification of a contact. Rather than expand, he'd dwindle to nothing. This scope was the vast fate to greet him.

Thus he did dwindle, into nothing's specific. It was only an unruly blur. Even there, nothing definite.

A CAPSULE AFFAIR

A girl thought to herself, "Why are my legs being stared at by that man? Sitting across from me on this bus, he sags in his seat with poor posture, chin lowered into his coat, to study me down up my up; what have I up there, to appeal to him?"

She stopped crossing her legs, discreetly placed her knees together, and demurely lowered her dress tight down on them; this did not discourage her observer.

"Perhaps he loves me," she thought; "for a stranger, that's romantically quick."

She tried to envisage what their baby would look like; to estimate more accurately, she covertly (on the sly) noted the man held captive to her lower charms.

She tossed her head, in derisive triumph: "We've nothing in common," she finally decided to conclude. A pang of regret flared in pity for the rejected stranger. Had she a sister, or girl friend, she might introduce him to?— for his loneliness was so *stubbornly* sensual.

Her bus stop approached. She displayed some flesh while getting up: the brute across from her squirmed: was he in pain?

The bus lurched, so she wriggled out with protruding haunches. She had once taken a psychology lesson in school: on this basis, she dismissed that optical intruder from her vainglorious head of hair with the notion, "Obviously oversexed."

The bus waited for a red light; walking on the sidewalk, she passed the window that depicted her fascinated admirer's eyes lost soulfully in the contemplation of her departing self. The bus moved off. "He's gone. But he understood me." It was her final tribute.

THE BARBARA IN MY LIFE. SHE KILLED FOREVER WHAT SHE CAUSED: LOVE

Being in love with Barbara was no fun. She was mean to me. Instead of saying "no" right away, so that I could recover quickly before the trap kept springing the wound deeper, malice made her decide to make use of my love, exploiting my extreme vulnerability, attacking my very weakness and taking me captive to her spoiled, perverse, and capricious dictates; toying with fondness and squeezing bitterness from my sweetness of heart.

Barbara tempted me into a glorious hell, where the more I fell the better was its worse in its best attraction toward the worst I could bear. I'm well out of it now, for I can recall how it wasn't exactly a picnic on a bed of roses. Barbara pulled me deep in; the pain tried to push me out, but the pull was too much; and the more complaining the pain did the more her tug on me tightened to its white-red extremity, proving the physical conviction of mere mental pain. Such was the effect Barbara had on me. It lasted as long as it did. The proof of survival is my telling of it. I'm congratulated to be out of it. I'm talking about love. Nothing can be so terrible as love. Barbara put a puncture in my life, of such depth that the juicy meat of the heart is all *emptied* out. I subsist on the numbness that remains. I have my pet name for it: Barbara.

FLIRTATIONS

THE BRIEFEST AFFAIR
PLUCKED OUT OF THE AIR,
ENDING UP IN HER LAIR.

A realistic flirtation
can get you an invitation
to where temptation
provides the occasion
for erotic persuasion.
You easily succumb
and make yourself numb
when so much sperm
manages to squirm
between her thighs,
culminated by romantic sighs.

You're one of the luckier guys.
I asked her for another date.
But she cautioned: "I'm not your mate.
My husband is away tonight.
Leave now, to avoid fright."
I quickly abandoned the joint
because I easily got her point.

**ADVICE FOR MEN
TO TURN THEIR SEXUAL DRIVE
INTO WELCOME ON ARRIVAL,
OUTPACING ANY RIVAL.**

If you flirt, that increases the chances
for interesting romances.
Even if you slightly tease,
good luck may get you a squeeze.
So take a chance and be forward,
and you may latch on to something torrid.
But if timidity holds you back,
you may get off on the wrong track
and find your arms embracing emptiness
instead of an intoxicating temptress.
So good luck on your elaborate cautions
which could contradict opportunities.
Does every good man get his portions?
No, distribution is uneven
with fickle results, even.
So fortune favors the bold.
Get in there, before you're too old.
Give attractive propositions
to increase same favorable positions
in how you can ever make out
in your big dreams for an amorous bout.

Be handsome and have money
to spend on your fresh honey.
Failure is hardly considered funny.
Pretend passion if you can,
requiring the victim to reply, "Amen"
and give herself to you, now and then.
But she's in charge of saying when.

REJECTED FIDELITY ADVICE

If I love my wife, but a new woman is flirting suggestively with me, how can I succumb to the latter without jeopardizing my hitherto successful marriage?

Resist temptation with the new one to maintain loyal fidelity with your loving wife. Play it safe while avoiding complications.

But aren't I sacrificing a potentially thrilling adventure?

A successful marriage is too high stakes to risk foolish ruining. Why be a rat to your wife and invite potential divorce?

But we have no children whose lives could be hurt. A new adventure beckons. This new one is a beaut. She's hot to wrest me into a second marriage.

But wouldn't you grieve to wreck your current bliss?

Chance-taking is the key to a romantic life.

Do you think of yourself as a conquering movie hero?

I'm vain enough to lust for vanity's rewards. A new relationship invigorates energy into throbbing novelty's wild unknown.

You two-timer! Your morality stinks!

So does your cautionary advice. How's your own marriage?

I never had one.

You cheap little coward! You spineless creep!

FLIRTING DIALOGUE (JUST MET)

(MAN:) Hello. What's your topic?

(WOMAN:) Love makes the world go round.

(MAN:) No, money does.

(WOMAN:) But love generates reproduction to get babies.

(MAN:) No, lust does.

(WOMAN:) You're so contradictory!

(MAN:) That makes conversation possible. Too much agreement can make conversation stagnant.

(WOMAN:) Then I'll contradict you.

(MAN:) Don't. Let's be in harmony.

(WOMAN:) Too much harmony can lull people to sleep.

(MAN:) Then let's be in harmony dynamically.

(WOMAN:) That can liven things up.

(MAN:) Then let's have a date.

(WOMAN:) Are you propositioning me?

(MAN:) Yes, let's seduce each other.

(WOMAN:) But it's too sudden.

(MAN:) Well, let's be gradual.

(WOMAN:) You take the initiative.

(MAN:) But that's old-fashioned.

(WOMAN:) But if I'm too aggressive, that might make you shy.

(MAN:) We'll arrive at a compromise.

(WOMAN:) But too much neutrality might cancel each other out.

(MAN:) All right. Let's make a fresh start.

(WOMAN:) Will it lead to love?

(MAN:) Why not? Why waste this beginning?

(WOMAN:) Oh, you're parsimonious.

(MAN:) Stop being critical.

(WOMAN:) I wasn't. It was only a comment.

(MAN:) We shouldn't bicker. Are we in a clash?

(WOMAN:) I have an appointment. I must dash. *(Abruptly leaves.)*

FLIRTATION'S FUTURE

Flirtation has different attitudes. A light flirtation is when you don't care if you succeed or not in manipulating the other to get interested in arranging another meeting.

And what's a heavy flirtation?

That's when you're very interested in influencing the other to strongly respond to the possibility of another meeting, which you plan to make into a major if not decisive event.

Can flirtation lead into—

Into the unborn lives of the children who get born because your flirtation succeeded in a crucial mating: with children to result, and then maybe even grandchildren, influencing the future to include a virtual dynasty of personal family affiliations.

Flirtation is dangerous in fraught possibilities.

Watch out—they could backfire.

Be careful about what you want.

Also watch out about your methods of succeeding or failing to attain it, including to what extent—

Enough already! No more! Let me stay within the safety of the present, without sticking my gambling or withholding nose out into a devastating unknown.

What cowardly caution!

WHAT CAN FLIRTATION LEAD TO?

If you start to flirt, what can come of it?

Who knows? It's an adventure. It's between what *you* are at the time, and what *she* is at the time, in your different circumstances.

Well, some flirtations show promise as a *match*, while others fizzle out.

There's a certain suspense going on. How far will it go?

Maybe into a match of "true love." Maybe into nowhere, as a "mistake" for one or both of the prospective partners. ("It's just one of those things," set to music.)

How to get romance started?

It depends on who's already involved with somebody else, or not. What's *her* history of relationships, up to the current date? What's *yours*?

There are too many problematicals. Love is a mystery. Sex is the big reproductive factor, the "elephant in the room." It can be neither ignored nor overlooked.

What decisions are potentially building up for you? For her?

The suspense can be breathtaking. Two lives are at stake.

And maybe unborn children's potential lives, as well.

Well, the negotiations go on. Is it a "cat-and-mouse" game?

Oh, don't be simplistic. Must everything be dramatic, like a play?

If so, mainly youthful people are real actors in it.

The drama is a free-for-all.

With loads of problematics. What are the odds?

Incalculatingly complex.

Does "love make the world go round?"

Is sex a factor?
Does lust rear its head?
Stop! Too much!
We're just started.

**MUTUAL INFIDELITY,
INCURRING NO LIABILITY.**

I sneaked a letter in an envelope
to my secret woman, with whom to elope
without my wife ever knowing.
Then we'd fly to Brazil
to get a South American thrill
and also learn Portuguese,
and in Spanish mutually tease
to flirtationally please.
When my wife would find out,
tears of delight will sprout
to get a quick divorce
without a show of force.
Would it lead to remorse?
Not for my wife:
She's enjoying Henry, the man of her life.
So wife and I trade infidelities,
opportunistically to seize
the balls of temptation and squeeze.
With such the same genitalia,
how could new sex be a failure
with a new woman in exchange
for the former wife in arrange?

ME AND ADELLE:
EXCITING, FOR A SPELL.

Guess who flirted with me? Adelle!
Temptingly, it rang a bell,
since her sexy beauty was nothing to ignore.
Her regular boyfriend must have been away,
so here was my opportunity to play
with fire, since her boyfriend would kill me if he knew
that I stole Adelle for a harmless screw.
Well, *not* so harmless! He found out,
and confronted me with a shout
to lay off Adelle, whom he planned to marry.
I cowered. (He was a big lug.)
I told him: "It never got beyond a hug,
since she'd vowed fidelity to you,
and refused outright to let me screw."
The boyfriend apologized for being suspicious.
Adelle was lost, but it would have been delicious;
but dangerous. I was a guest at their wedding,
and imagined enviously about their bedding.
"It could have been me," I thought.
But I would have been killed if I had been caught.
"Don't play with fire," my mother had always taught.
As a wedding guest, I got inebriated.
My career with Adelle had been abbreviated.

WOOING BERTHA

I OFFERED MYSELF TO BERTHA,
FEELING I WAS FULLY WORTH HER.
BUT SHE REJECTED ME OUT OF HAND,
SO MY ERECTION STOPPED ITS STAND.

How I loved Bertha!
I intended to go further
to become introduced to her
for intimacy's cozy sake.
How her breasts would shake
and how her hips would swirl
when her whole body would unfurl,
proving her to be a remarkable girl!
So we went out on a date,
with me as a candidate
to be her future married mate.
Imagine! I was hardly sedate!
Right away, I presented my case
as an ideal husband to be.
All Bertha had to do
was only say "yes"
to confer her bless-
ing on my suit.
However, it didn't suit her,
and off I had to go
with her rejection in hand
as though practically signed
officially: She wouldn't be mine.
Why did she refuse me?
I don't know. Please excuse me.

BERTHA AND THE SWAN
WERE WHAT MY EYES LIGHTED UPON.
NOT TO GET THEM MAKES ME SAD AND WAN.

Bertha's wide groin section
caught my esteem and affection.
Her hips and ass were to ponder on,
but better still were to *get* on.
I was like a lake full of the swan
that dashed about in a merry flush
splashing along and asked for a push
deeply felt within its wing-ed bush.
The water of course roared and twirled,
and I was simply in another world.

I LOST MY CHANCE
WHEN MY INVITATION TO THE DANCE
GOT LOST, PERCHANCE.

I really had hoped to marry Bertha.
But too shy, I had to go further
to boldly propose.
But I was afraid of getting rejected,
so I didn't yet have my proposal projected.
Was she getting tired of waiting?
I delayed so long,
that now she had five kids
and a dead husband.
So after that loss of time,
I had to atone for my crime
by finally proposing.
But she said it was too late,
and released me to my lonely fate.
My not marrying Bertha

was my death certificate.
But in Heaven I met her again,
to drop a hint. She replied, "When?"

I WOOED BEAUTIFUL BERTHA,
WHO COULD MAKE MY FINANCES GO FURTHER.
BUT SHE INTERPRETED MY PLOY
AS LOVE'S PRETENSE, WHICH SHE'D DESTROY.

How could I ever go further
than to marry beautiful Bertha?
She was rich and I was poor,
so I poured out my allure
as a legitimate marriage candidate
by asking her for a crucial date
with the idea, of course, to be her mate,
and act as if it was ordained by fate.
But Bertha, alas, said "no,"
and told me where to go:
She advised me: Hell was my place
to hide there and save face
to punish me for my phony wiles
with pretense to seductive styles
of persuading a fair lady
with me to get a matrimonial baby.
My offering had been a bit shady
to arouse her suspicion
that I would use as ammunition
my bulging cock in my trousers
with big balls as arousers.
She refused to be seduced
by my slick moustache that was juiced
with perfume as to entrance
her gullible senses to romance.

She accused me of being a phony
to propose marriage for her money,
and refused outright to be my honey.
Thus, being told where to go,
I embraced Hell, which was my soul's foe.

**BERTHA'S SUDDEN BETRAYAL
BUSTED OUR PLANS AND MADE THEM FAIL,
WHEN ABRUPTLY OUR WEDDING BECAME STALE.**

Love is the big full blast,
and we hope it will last.
But Bertha instead
from our wedding fled,
with a stranger to elope,
betraying my marital hope.
So my plans with Bertha,
being stuck, could go no further.
So I married her sister,
the better to assist her
to somewhat reduce the scandal.
But her sister couldn't hold a candle
compared to darling Bertha.
(Her sister would never be worth her.)
This is the end of the saga
with Bertha. I'd angrily flog her,
but her sudden groom will prevent it.
This is a weird tale. You couldn't invent it.
Some day I'll re-unite with Bertha.
I search in vain. I can't unearth her.
I'll ask her mother to rebirth her
if her mother is still alive,
with old reproduction to thrive
like a bee happy to rejoin her hive.

MY LIFE'S TRAGEDY CENTERED ON BERTHA.
BUT REALISTICALLY, WAS IT WORTH HER?

Bertha rejected my proposal.
I had put myself at her disposal,
so she found me disposable,
and rejected me with stern tenacity
in New York, our favorite city,
where I tried to woo her by being witty.
It succeeded in making her laugh,
but not enough to draft
a mutually signable marriage contract
that would promptly wed us upon contact.
So Bertha alas was never my bride,
a fact that I could never hide,
so I couldn't point to her with justifiable pride
as my lawfully allowed married wife
with whom to compete in marital strife.
So our whole future I had planned for Bertha
dismally came down to eartha,
and dropped aimlessly out of sight,
converting hopeful day to failure's night,
assigning my love and lust
to the dismal fortune of being a bust,
and like the cowboys, biting the dust.
I wanted a whole meal, but only got a crust
from our early affair
that danced upon impermanent air.
So between us, there'll never be an heir.
I wondered what he would look like
if fortune had enabled him to come down the pike.
Like me, visualized as his "father."
But such an unrealized dream went no farther.

Bertha-less, how could I bother?
But Bertha became my imaginary bride,
when insane fantasy with me would ride,
enhanced by lonely tragedy
that would sadly grapple with me
and ultimately topple me.
Thus I came a cropper
with this horrible stopper.
For Bertha, I could never be a shopper.
Our tragedy was a whopper.
So if you have a tear to spend,
shed it now at my poem's end.

FITTING THE LOVE TO THE OBJECT

As it turned out, I found out that the girl I was in love with was really the wrong girl!

(A similarity would be that at a maternity hospital a mother gives birth and the baby is pulled out and filed away till the mother revives, and finally when she does revive she clamors for her kid; but the nurse; had an inaccurate filing system and were careless about the child's identity in relation to the given mother. So finally the mother *is* given a child, but it's not hers. Does she *know* it's not hers? Or does she ignorantly bathe in bliss? Different cases, different results. Let tragedy breathe not lightly, upon our frosted window-pain.)

What could I do to rectify the error of having the wrong girl to be in love with? Simply to confess cleanly to her, and hope she would understand.

"Martha," I began, with a gentle tug of ominence, "I love you, but all the time I'm loving you I see that my love is mistaking you for the one it really loves, and so I'd like to pull out and place my love on the right horse—I mean girl. The error is all mine, I assure you. I just misplaced my love on you, through an oversight I'm to be pardoned for, since you do closely resemble the *real* object of my love—in fact, you seem *identical* with her."

That explanation, or apology, got me nowhere. Martha was loath to relinquish the pleasure of being loved by me, and scathed me with this: "You've reposed your love in me, so I have it. It may have been a mistake at first; but time and habit have corrected that mistake, if indeed mistake it was. Well, not *corrected* it, so much as sloughed it over, or flurred it by. Anyway, I'm keeping it, your love for me. It pleases me now, and it ought to please you. I even *depend* on it, for my emotional well-being. Too late to change, at this stage of the game."

That was Martha rebutting, or rebuffing, me, I forget which. Well, I was her property, she claimed me. Or rather, what she possessed was my love for her, rather than me who was loving her. It pleased her to keep it.

So she offered an alternative, or rather imposed it, to wit, that, I should change the *true* object of my love from the Martha I mistook Martha for (namely herself) to the Martha she really was (namely herself, just as before). She recommended this solution as being most likely to content us both.

Then I recognized her as the one I *really* loved. "At last!, it's been worth waiting for!," I exclaimed, and enthusiastically embraced her, as only befit the occasion (as well as her person).

"Are you sure I'm the right one?" she replied, making up, by becoming cautious herself, for my abandoning caution to, as the free saying goes, the wind, the wind that lives up in the air.

"Sure I'm sure," I reassured her: "If my love is real, then I really love you. You're the one. Are you you?"

"If your love for me is love," she said, "and the love is for me, the *me*, as distinguished from 'me', then it's mine, your love, I own your love, and I'm the one you love."

I couldn't refute such logic. So I made sure she was the right one I loved. I trained it full-blast on her, my love, like a whirring fan upon a heat-drenched face. It blew up her hair, but she kept claiming it. It was hers by virtue of receiving, mine to give.

What would *I* get? Now I ought to consider getting love from her. If she had it, was I the right one?

THE RIGHT AND WRONG OF LOVE; AND THE PREDOMINANCE OF THE LATTER, EVEN TO THE EXTENT OF FATAL EXCLUSIVITY. LOVE MISAPPLIED, MISDIRECTED, MISSPENT. LOVE ETERNALLY IN ERROR.

I loved the wrong person! It was a case of mistaken identity. I must now take pains to rectify such a "gaffe." It's like when the baby is jerked or whisked out of the laboring mother in the maternity ward and then put out to dry in the room marked "born babies only," the wrong identification tag is attached to the natural necklace, linking that tiny tot with a different mother altogether than the one who had carried it rent-free in a nine-months swollen womb.

I must love *personally*, not anonymously, just like a baby's own *personal* mother *is the* only true natural mother, the real one, that that baby should ever call "mother." Otherwise, it's an unnatural world, when *any* baby can call *any* mother "mother," when any mother can claim any baby for her own. Interchangeability is a defiance of strict and unique possession. A baby is non-transferable, nor is the mother: they're each other's own: deemed, therefore, "dear": "dear" mother, "dear" child: meaning rare: the only.

And so it is, I must love the *right* girl. I must throw away the wrong one. Lust deranged my mind into the illusion that she was the right one: a natural act of self-deception, at the service of permitting the physical act of love to "go through" sanctioned by the authority of romance. Lust must have sentimental backing to strip it of guilt, sin, embarrassment, baseness, vulgarity, grossness, obscenity, crudity, and other allegations of deficiency in the sense of lyrical and throbbing beauty. Romance glimmers, love sings in a choir, and all that effort must be for the *right girl*: otherwise, a glaring mistake is made, and I'm accused of hypocrisy and opportunism in the mere service of lust, that base deed.

Discarding the wrong one, I look for the right one, but time runs out, now I'm too old, I'm nearly dead. I should have started sooner, when I had potent power to raise the act of sex into romance's supreme blunder.

I'll go unloved to the grave unloving. Time ran short, and my cock crept inward to sleep there forever. The charms are unresponded to. So love has fled. I attached love to the wrong girls, having been eluded by the right one, or having omitted to recognize her when availability flashed her by for an instant like a dangling plum outside the window of a passing bus. The bus does pass, with me at the window seat. I look back, see what I missed. Another plucked it, who merely strolled.

The bus dumps me off, at the end. I'm my own luggage cargo-excess baggage. I'm carried down the ladder into the earth. There I'm deposited, and put to rest. My body grows too cold for love. The seat of the affections—that heart, with its fondness for rambling, and its stray fondnesses—is now a tired old useless pump. My life is covered up, in mounds of earth. The *possibility* of love is also buried: interred with me. It's corrupted underneath, decays, and blunders out of existence.

It left unfound the right one. *She* must be dead, *too*, somewhere. An afterthought: Could our graves ever meet? Via an *underground* passageway, the true tunnel of love? Unsentimental answer: No. So love gives up hope. And that's love's true death. Hope *was* its life, to the last burst.

A SERIES OF RESPONSES TO SOMEONE

I made a mistake, and here's how. I met someone and a part of him was liked by me. I confused that part for all of him, and so said, "I like him." ("Him" being "all of him.")

Next time I met him with glowing expectations from the above. What a falling there was! A part of him was disliked by me, which became confused for all of him, making me say, "I don't like him," and by "him" I meant "all of him." The same fallacy as the first one, only in reverse.

Later on, I got to see that the parts were parts, and so was able to see the whole: man.

Now I'm not so sure about him. I don't care, one way or the other.

TWO COMPLAINTS

COMMON COMPLAINT

I was in love, but with the wrong girl. I was in it too thick to extricate myself, too late would struggle avail. To be in love, itself was wonderful. But being in love with the wrong girl made it intolerable. Such was the state of my affairs—show mercy on yourself by refraining from envy. *Any* love is not good; but we *must* love. The luck of the circumstance of *which* girl then becomes crucial—for well or for ill. Ill was the state of the case of me, or rather, with *that* girl. Why *that* one? She was *just the wrong one!*

THE COMPLAINT I CAN MAKE TO NO ONE ELSE

You kept touching me and teaching me how to love you more and more—and I kept learning—I learned so well, my love kept mounting—this went on, all the time we were together—I kept learning and learning only too well—my expectations were being optimistically educated—even long after we had temporarily had to part due to an outside accident having nothing to do with us—and suddenly you cut me off—suddenly I was lost—suddenly all the love that had been built up in me was choked and smothered with nowhere to go—my nights are nightmares of loneliness and love for you. Can you uneducate me; can you unlearn me, and unwind the process, so that my love may be reversed into your present indifference?

The love that had been trained and developed in me with such persistent excelling innocence and strength is suddenly left flat without a function—what was it trained for? To be let down drastically and told that the game will never start—that its preparations had risen and risen toward its great future fulfillment, and now when the fruition should be slowly exulting, I find myself precisely in nowhere?

You led me into an unending process—then you stepped out of it, and I hurtle on.

THE LOST DATE

My girl and I had a secret date. The secrecy was so special, we neither knew about it.

And we kept the secret so well hidden, not one of us two showed up at the trysting spot where our assignation was to have been. (Or let's say that our being late has kept up perpetually.)

So we're both in the dark about our date. Meanwhile, we've had others, to while away the time.

REJECTION

THE EROTIC TENSION IN THE KEPT-APARTNESS OF THOSE WOULD-BE SELF-SUBJUGATORY, SELF-SURRENDERING-TO-THE OTHER, ENVIOUS ANTAGONISTS OF TRADITIONAL ENMITY THAT YEARN IN VAIN TO BE EACH OTHER; THE HUMAN VERSUS THE RATIONAL: EQUALLY DISCONTENT.

Why are the rational and the "human" such enemies?

Rationally, I can't explain why. Nor can I *humanly* explain it. They just *are*, that's all.

Passion is irrational. So is boredom. So is anything,

What *is* rational? I'm not rational enough to know.

But I know that *everything* is human. My humanity tells me that.

Love and hate—human, not rational.

I live, humanly.

Maybe, when I cool down, and get mellow with resignation, I can be rational instead of rationalizing.

But still, the rational is rationed, but there's no rationing of the human: it soars irrationally, or plunges, far out of bounds—past all limits. It's excessive, irrationally human—humanly irrational.

Irreconcilable, mutually contradictory, inherently antagonistic: the rational and the human.

And I'm human enough to find the rational fascinating: I'd betray, overturn, my humanity, if the rational would let me join it—but it spurns my offer, finding me unfit.

There I am, a potential convert, willing to defect—and the rational rejects me, so I become more patriotically human, as a reaction; and more hostile, bitter, vengeful, against the rational that has insulted me so.

I'm defiantly human—and unreasonably anti-rational. I'm hurt, and I strike back.

But my feeling is irrational. *All* feelings are.

There's no fight. For we're in two distinct worlds, I and the rational, We sneer and snarl, from our separated dimensions, at what we think is the other.

But I mistake my opponent, and my opponent mistakes me. Even for an argument, even to disagree at a safe remove, there are no grounds. Our terms differ, our spheres, and frames of reference; there's no point at which we may even fight: for we're held apart, on swirls that never cross. We hear only rumors of each other—remote, untrue.

If ever we *do* come to grips—then watch out!

I dream of the rational: but only in *my* terms—irrational. Similarly distorted is *its* view of me. I can't see past myself, to the other. Is the other self-bound, as well?

Two prison camps, well separated. I yearn to escape my prison and find imprisonment in the other; it, bored of being its rational self, wishes to be me. It's rejected my offer to defect to join it, since it doesn't need any more of itself; on the contrary, it offers to join me. But then it wouldn't be itself anymore—for which I value my enemy. For were my enemy to annex itself to me, it would be subdued in my flame, and its worth I wanted would be unusable.

I want to lose myself in it; it in me. We're both willing to be self-destructive. But our posture is to destroy each other. Maybe it's no idle posture. Maybe one of us *will* down the other— reluctantly; for whoever the victor is, will feel inferior to the vanquished, whom he envied, and wished to join, in self-annihilation, prostrate at the other's feet, if only it could be "taken in."

But a thing can't absorb what it's not. The rational couldn't absorb me *as* me—and I would be useless to it otherwise. Nor could the human me devour the rational, without undermining and emasculating it to the point where it wouldn't do me any good.

So kept apart, we look and year, and snarl and sneer. Neither's content, while the other's "being" so self-sufficiently *is*. Each is debarred, from the envied other. They're enemies, in love.

REJECTION IN LOVE: A SCIENTIFIC INQUIRY

Everybody is always rejecting somebody else's love and at the same time *being* rejected by somebody whom he loves. Why is that? It's odd that it happens so frequently. Is it a natural perversity built in us? Or a symptom of something gone wrong in the world? It's hard to figure out. My own life history can cite numerous examples of it. And all the people I know, friends and acquaintances, have revealed multiple cases of it in *their* lives. It's as common as the air we breathe and the water we drink. We've all learned to tolerate it. How can we possibly fight it?—or we can fight it, but how overcome it?

I refuse to accept it. It's not ideal. Only the ideal is acceptable, for me. That stamps me as an idealist, Which is what I am. It also means that I find almost everything unacceptable.

Instead of being a complainer (which is what an idealist is almost always), let me be scientific and try to discover why is it is that, as I first pointed out at the start, "everybody is always rejecting somebody else's love and at the same time *being* rejected by somebody whom he loves."

I intend a composite investigation of all my experiences in that regularly recurring sphere of dissatisfaction, from both sides (rejector and rejected); I'll come up with an explanation that would help to solve and cure the problem. Without exception, all humanity would esteem me with gratitude, like they would the scientist who rids human tissue of its long-fatal nemesis, cancer. So here I go. If I succeed, I'll achieve popular fame. If not, at least I tried. There's no waste, to fail at something that important. It's the crucial romantic problem of all time, by consensus. It's something truly big, that I'm undertaking. Is my capability equal to it? If not, perseverance will take up the gap. I'll keep up a heroic toiling. I'll labor like a *working* idealist, not a theoretical one. It will be painstaking, at personal sacrifice. I'll give all I have. The cause is bigger than anything I risk personally. What a benefaction, should I succeed, on every fellow creature! Up will flow happiness. Despair, grief, and woe will subside substantially; with me the hero. Wow!, here I go.

I woo a girl, and get rejected. Meanwhile, I reject a girl who's been passionately flirting with at me. It's all even up, the score is tied.

No, it's not. The one who rejected me I value much higher than the one I rejected. So I'm on the *losing* end, now.

But why is rejection going on? It's hard to care equally as you're being cared about. Or it's hard to as *not* care as the one who relatively ignores *you*. A greater shade of indifference to you than yours to the other one is just as unequal as a greater shade of *desire* for you than yours for the other one. But where are we going from here? The problem is set, not solved. Is it necessary to overcome human nature? Love should have an interchangeable equality: reciprocation should be mutual from both ends, in evenly portioned requital.

What *should* be, isn't. How?, why? I don't know.

I try again, I fall in love, she says no. I'm coveted, but I don't care. Same thing, same results. Still no closer to the answer.

It's painful to try all over again, or to let it spontaneously happen to you. What a dreary sameness of futility! It becomes like an inevitable law. What can only I do? Can I change the sun, alter the weather? What happens, does. There's no controlling it. To get to the bottom of it, beats me. I'm going to give up. Trying has earned despair. My ambition has lost confidence.

I only partly understand, but not why. I've been frustrated of my reward. I wasn't able to penetrate deeper. It's forbidden to me, or anyone. It's a bad mystery. We can't cure it.

Or so I assume, having myself failed. But someone *else* may find out why; in time to come.

Another experiment, to confuse the issue more. Someone whom I *formerly* rejected, I now pursue. It's *her* turn now, so she rejects *me*. There's something hilarious about that. I'm always being confounded. To be enlightened by a single explanation would get me somewhere. I'm denied it. Let me *accept* failure. I only seek distraction. My work on the problem is finished. There had been no work, really. Only blunders, and self-delusion.

From here, where? My experiments have led nowhere. They prove only what's known before. Confirmation doesn't help. Progress is blocked up.

Suddenly, something happens. I've met a girl whom I like very much. And *she* likes *me*, very much!

It's wonderful, it's taking place now. How long will it last? There's only one lifetime.

It's a mutual romance, and we're married.

The honeymoon is over. *Some*one is disenchanted:

She, me: does it matter?

We're divorced, and that's final.

She rejected *me*. Oh, well. If she hadn't, wouldn't I have rejected *her*?

We can't turn back to find out. Let's *assume* so; our lesson is cynical. Till otherwise proven, it remains so.

Rejection. Love's inequality. No ideal romantic democracy, never.

Alone! Unshared. Solitary.

Oh where, oh where, is the one?—who'll return what I give?— who *I*'ll turn to, if *she* gives?

It's in the Land of Never. It's a forbidding land. It won't contain creatures of time.

BARBARA PROBST LOFTILY APART IN AN EXALTED SPHERE FROM THE MERE ME WHO'S DREAMING HER

One day, Barbara Probst was walking in my mental heaven, which was light on her feet. She swam in air, raised to any feeling she wished,

I was there too, but not quite on the same level. I was more bound lumpen to a ground of rock and earth and dirt, of stubbles, pebbles, weeds, and grass, and the growing things issuing there below: grub, slug, worm, and the dark mechanism of insect military society, whose effective practicality relegated consciousness to that formula of nonsense, Man.

Barbara Probst was light in the air, I was solid in my chained dungeon. I wished to reach her,

But if I did reach her, this double-level edifice would collapse; and the dream and the sordid would become indistinguishably one. That would do damage to the Barbara Probst image. So better this double-level life. Can you call it a life? It's frustration-bound romance,

NOT BEING LOVED DUE TO INSUFFICIENT SELF-LOVE

I'm in love with myself; won't you help?

Isn't yours enough?

Oh, I'm *used* to *that*. But you would add a fresh slant to my self-love, by reinforcing it from another angle. In my position, I can never have too many mirrors to reflect my original self-love as external confirmations and assorted endorsements.

But why isn't your self-love self-sufficient? Perhaps your self-love is weak, riddled with doubt, which is why it requires help from the outside.

At core, you're right. So I desperately beg you for your love. I need *you* to love me, to compensate for my deficient love of my own self.

I'd only love you if you set me a good example by your self-love. Since you show yourself unworthy of even self-love, then you're unworthy for mine, as well. So don't come badgering me. I turn you down.

Your rejection *further* weakens my self-love. Finding myself unworthy of your love increases my self-contempt. What a cycle!

Then have recourse to others. One of several may love you, to set you a fine social example.

I LOVE FRANCES, WHO LOVES ART. BUT I HATE ART. WILL FRANCES LOVE ME IN SPITE OF MY NOT LOVING ART WHICH SHE LOVES? I'LL ARTFULLY TRY TO BRING THIS ABOUT. BY BUILDING A NEW LOVE, IN HER ART-DEVOTED HEART.

Frances loved art, and I loved her. She didn't love me—yet. But I'd try to arrange it. I'd contrive, in time, to get her—with justification—to link her interest in art with an admiration of me, and thus, by extension, her love of art (already so long going on) with, finally, a new love: me.

It would be hard work, for me to make that crucial association of art and love and me in her mind—I'd have to deserve it, to bring it about. I'd have to bone up on art. It had always bored me. But for Frances' sake now—or rather, for my sake (winning her love)—I'd diligently apply myself to art. I'd educate my taste for it. That would bring me in line with hers (though hers was longstanding, and mine would be new); we'd have that sublime passion and refined appreciation in common. From that exalted, giddy height, it's but a short step to mutual love for *each other*, two devotees inspired by the same god. And art would bind our lives together. We'd be doubly drunk on it. It would, in effect, "marry" us.

Which was my literal ambition, toward Frances! To marry her, sleep with her (she remained chaste to me so far), have her as my precious work of art, the true masterpiece to culminate my arduous art education.

In order to impress her with my worthiness to share her love of art, I had to earn this equality by genuinely loving art myself. Fine, that's a good goal. I'd strive with all my might, to attain it. But it's artificial. The truth is, I *hated* art, with a passion—a passion of the same intensity with which I proposed to love it.

I hated art, with all my heart. Ah, but I loved Frances. And Frances rejected me as a lover and husband-candidate on the grounds of a basic incompatibility: her worship of the art goddess, and my desecration of the same shrine. Thus, I wouldn't do, for her. Not until I reformed radically, and acquired a devotion to that mystic cult on a par with hers. I'd have to come around, to *her* way of looking at it. *I* had to adjust, not she; since I loved her, and she didn't love me. So mine was the effort; the toil; the test. She remained, and would judge me. By art's cold standards, alone.

Cold standards, from *my* view. Warm, pure, natural, by hers. Oh, we were poles apart: Frances with her art; me, with my artless love, for her. *I'd* have to bridge the gap: join her on *her* shore. *If* I wanted her. And I did. But at what a price! To perfume my loathing for art, with an artificial love for it. But she'd *see* that my love for it was artificial, contrived, put-on; that it was for her sake—my winning her—would offend her the more.

Art guarded her heart. I had to woo art, first, to lure the key to her heart away. But what I'd have to woo was ugly to me. And Frances, with her finely attuned sensibilities to this fateful subject, was well placed to see straight through my false wooing, and expose me for violating the dear she loved, being a blasphemer in the guise of a pilgrim.

So I was caught. I couldn't fake it. Pretense was out of the question. I'd have to play my cards straight. No more subterfuge, at this point.

I begged Frances for an interview. She granted it. I said, "You love art enough for both of us. I couldn't even hope to match it. So love art, but love me separately. Can you so divide yourself?"

Her answer I'll never forget: "No."

A LOPSIDEDLY PAINFUL TERMINATION OF CORRESPONDENCE

(Two characters, of indeterminate sex. Either could be man, the other could be woman. Each obviously straightly heterosexual, despite indeterminateness and even interchangeability of literal sex. They are at opposite sides of stage: each may be lighted alternately as focus is on what he's writing and simultaneously articulating in speech, while his counterpart is in turn dimmed or blacked out.)

(First character, sitting at writing table, profile to audience, writing letter, mouthing each word or phrase out loud as it's being written:) Your obvious deep love for me flatters, but doesn't sustain. Henceforth *desist*, and leave me unsolicited, spare yours truly embarrassment, resign your passion to go unrequited. Hoping you'll forgive . . .

(Second character, sitting at different writing table in different room or different apartment—other side of stage—three quarters front to audience, head sadly bowed at writing task, mouthing out-loud phrases as they flow from reluctant pen:) Are you sure? Earnestly beg you to

reconsider. Shall you ever-again be so loved, by any other mortal? I'm respectful to your wish, but implore you, open up your heart: please *receive* what I have to offer . . . But my desperation is most gentle, and sadly subdued . . . I'm dumb with adoration, at your side . . . You darling Otherness of my soul . . . I intimate an imminent yet infinite and undimmed intimate twin intimacy for your infinity; persistent, unwitting, unwitty . . .

Your eloquence moves, but does not convince. I feel pity: this correspondence must *desist*, it's getting out of hand . . . henceforth refrain; be brave, you noble soul . . . This is the last letter penned from this hand . . . let it console you . . . brutal, unpretty, tripping plainly out, to persuade: Give up; grieve no more . . .

I'm numb . . . And now the stoic turns to silence.

(The stage dims, an awful silence is heard: a heart has died. Insufferable pathos. Romance excruciatingly gone to death. The suffering of a spirit folded up in pain. The tragedy destructive to one heart: causing the other to mourn, as well; but more comfortably, relived by the wholesome air of independent detachment.)

Alternative Titles:

— **AN UNBALANCED RELATIONSHIP**
— **A DIRGE FOR UNREQUITED LOVE**
— **AN UNCOMPLICATED TRAGEDY**
— **A TRITE BUT OBVIOUS MELODRAMA**
— **THE WAY THINGS GO, UNFORTUNATELY**
— **INTENSITY UNREWARDED**
— **LOVE WITHOUT HAPPINESS**
— **ONESIDEDNESS AS HELL FOR ONE**

(Characters: A woman and man, inside her apartment. (At the end, a solo offstage chorus commentating a conclusion.) Woman speaks first:)

The more I want from you, the more I love you, the more hurt and disappointed I'm capable of being by you, the more I love you; the more expectant and forward-dependent I am on you, the more I love you, the more angry in vindictive wrath I'm capable of being to you, the more I love you, the more intensely and emotionally affected I'm capable of being by you, the more I love you, the more my needs increase with you, the more I love you, the more I'm in your power, the more I love yes, the more everything you do concerning me is crucial to me, the more I love you, the more every intonation in your attitude is excruciatingly crucial to me, the more I love you, the more I need you to love me, the more I love you, the more I want to possess you powerfully, the more I love you, the more I need to powerfully reside in you, the more I love you, the more my identification with you is thoroughly possessive, the more I love you, the more your whole being is a vital necessity to my life, the more I love you, the more what you are is what I am, the more I love you, the more what I am must be what you are, the more I love you, the more your life is more precious than my own, the more I love you, the more my life without you would be unspeakably barren and tragic, the more I love you, the more that anything you are is all and everything to me, the more I love you, the more whatever is completely you outshines the rest of the world, the more I love you, the more of the total world is involved in anything that's you, the more I love you, the more grief it would be to lose you, the more I love you; and what do *you* think of *me*?

You're all right, fine. I like you.

But compared to what *I* feel—

What you feel can't dictate to me or impose on me the necessity to feel to you in mere obligation the way you'd like me to feel to you with spontaneous initiative out of my own heart. I'm not passionate about you, but I like you.

It's not enough, I need so much more from you than that—

That's because you love me.

But once loving you, I can't easily stop.

You have a difficult problem of the heart, since I don't seem to cooperate.

(Piningly, mournfully, with plaintive regret:) If only you could!

The fact remains,—

But I *hate* that fact: it's my destruction!

It's impossible for me to correct it. *Liking* you is the most I can do.

Then what can *I* do?

Suffer yourself out of it.

How?—It's too painful.

Patiently undergo, endure—

You're breaking—

Yes, I'm breaking your heart. *(Angrily, self-defensively:)* I didn't *mean* to be a criminal.

Oh, but I love you.

I'm well aware of it!

Please, don't be callous, be compassionate. Your icy indifference acerbates my plight.

I don't know what "acerbates" means; but I don't *mean* to harm you. I didn't *try* to cause the downfall of your feelings.

Not the downfall, but the uprise. You made my feelings soar, and they're suspended way up there—

I didn't "*make*" them—you reacted to me;—it wasn't my fault.

I'm helpless, the pain is too much.

What can I do?—leave you?

That would be worse.

But I'm simply not inclined to reciprocate.

If only you could ease my torment. Can't you *try* to treat me with pity, and concede to me—

—By so doing, I'd go against my grain—

—By marrying me?! I *beg* you to propose.

What!, and ruin my life that way, marrying someone I don't love?!

In time, you might *learn* to love me.

I can't wait that long. I'm a creature of immediate impulse. My responsibility doesn't extend further.

Then my life is simply a death.

Your despair will eventually give way; and gradual forgetfulness, leading to indifference—

—That would be *true* death. Not only cannot I foresee it, but I don't want to. Holding on to my love for you is my sole method of identity now. If only you can give it its happy outcome, that I so agonize for—!

It's not in the stars. There's nothing I can give you.

Do you love another?

Yes. She's away now. But she's due back in a few months.

Jealousy clamps down and represses any curiosity I might have about her—I *rage* in it.

If only you can *tone down* your intensification—

—Of my emotional state? No, it feeds on itself, and grows.

Well, I feel sorry for you.

If only you could feel more—or *convert* your sorrow, transform it, to—

—No, not to love. If I don't feel it, I don't feel it.

Then my disappointment is becoming angry—

I must leave. Don't *pour* your emotions over on me. You let yourself go, very sloppily. To drench *me* with your mess. Let me *be*, in peace.

But what you may *be*, is inside *me*, as well.

Then dislodge it! I demand my liberty, and find captivity too oppressive—

I feel suicide.

(Correcting:) Suicid*al*?

Yes.

Don't give way. Just hold together. Keep in. Restrict. Take a tight hold.

It's my only outlet, the suicide; what else is there?

Your grief-stricken state ls unhealthy, morbid, excessive—

But what am I to *do*? What can I resort to, what recourse can give just *slight* satisfaction?

Just endure a little more heroically, less self-pityingly with unbecoming pining, whining, wailing, and a pride-destructive, wanton, lavish demonstration of self-indulgently ignoble self-disrespect. Keep what you feel in to yourself more stoically, though it tastes bitter.

But my love invades me, it permeates, it radiates, it soaks through all my pores, in and out. I'm wild, irrational—

Obviously, I can't preach logic to you *now*. I must leave. *(Ironically:)* Thank you for receiving me. Next time, if there *is* one, don't be so tiresome.

Oh, you're cruel!

(Defensively:). It's *easy* to be, with you: you *ask* for it.

(In dramatic, steely tone:) I could really *murder* you.

Now, control your fury. You're becoming unbearable.

That's what *you* are!

Then exorcise me, got rid of my spell, smoke it out.

I'm just too passionate—

And now it's rearing its negative form. With me as victim!

Who else!? Tell me, who else? I can give you everything, so you must *receive* what I can give—whatever it turns into, away from my original tenderness.

It's my privilege to choose not to. You've gone too far, so now it's farewell, not goodbye.

Please don't say that.

You compelled me, My back was to the wall. I demand independence, and that you don't harass me.

I can't stop bothering you! I just *need* you!

Stop imploring! Your dignity has been compromised forever; and I can only punish your disgrace.

I had no alternative. What I feel, I feel.

I realize that. And what *I* feel is to leave you, and never see you again.

That would destroy me, more completely than you already have.

(Resignedly:) Then it must be. It's your fate. Accept it.

(Horrified:) Don't ask that of me!

I'm desperate! Release me; don't smother me.

(Desperate whining:), I'm drowning for lack of air myself. *You* can rescue me; *please*.

(The man opens the door, leaves the apartment, and shuts the door.)

(A solo voice from offstage, directing effects and commentating like a chorus, delivering the conclusion:) The woman is a total figure of aloneness,, in such stage-lighting effect—visual relief—that her isolation is complete, and grows looming to dominate the whole stage, like an animal enlarging by rapid degrees into a monolithic monster that devours all the air for herself and leaves everything outside a vacuum; all is absorbed into her appetite's vast and merciless consuming. This is love, festering from within by being deprived of its nourishment. Love doomed to the enormity of its ravenous starvation. The total terror, grief in sheer starkness. Suffering as the ultimate nakedness of fact. *(Final visual pre-curtain scene in keeping with solo chorus' description.)*

BOY DESIRES GIRL, NOT DESIRED IN RETURN, THEY CLASH IN SUCCESSIVE FITS OF ANGER, BOY CONTRITE, GETS MIXED UP, GIRL LEAVES, BOY REMAINS, WITH THAT THING JUST SEETHING IN HIS MIND. *ONE* LOVE CROSSED OFF. AND ALL IN ONE MEETING-EPISODE. NEVER MET BEFORE, NOR EVER AGAIN.

"When I look at you, I feel like making love to you," blurted the sincere, deeply-struck young man to a girl he had only just met. "Then don't look and you won't be disappointed," the girl suggested, "since you don't interest me."

The man got angry. His pride was hurt. His glow of lustful tenderness, being rebuffed, turned into bitter, resentful aggression. Mentally, he "killed" this interesting girl. But only mentally, so that she still stood there, breathing defiantly. He "took it out," with hostile, cruel words, soaked in irony, which exploded at her tear-ducts and "reduced" her to tears, or "increased" her to them. She was caught off-guard, and for a retort was at a loss. He had seized the offensive with such a sudden shock, it immobilized her. She wept copiously. He was glad to have struck blood, at first. Then, when he had her helpless, he felt contrite, reproached by guilt. He would have to atone, or make amends. How?, but.

The ideal way to apologize for his malicious outburst would be to express love to her; ideal for *him*. However, she had already told him she wasn't interested—or, more potently, *didn't want* that sentiment from him: would in fact, to put it more intensely, *dislike* that from him. So that avenue of atoning for his cruelty was blocked off. That avenue had in fact *brought about* his cruelty, for having earlier been blocked off, by his overture being against her wishes,

Damn her contrary wishes! He had denounced her scathingly for having rejected him; then he saw how unfair he had been, and wanted to atone for his bad behavior by making love to her—the very thing she had forbade him. So, what to do? Though his anger had just been spent in his indignant, "self-righteous" outburst, his frustration had only complicated itself. He had become confused, and the girl was still there. Her sobbing had stopped. She was preparing stormy words for him.

And they landed, on his head. He took it all, head bowed. He was still waiting to take more, when, looking up, he saw she had left. And he never saw her again. Well, that's *one* love out of his life, gone. There had been those before, there would be those after. This one had started off bad, and ended up worse. And it all happened in one episode, in one meeting, This was no chain sequence of events. It was one "action," whose general impact was a "blow" on him. He'd recover, but he was damaged now,

"I only wanted to make love to her. But she didn't want to with me, then or ever, as she strongly implied. It wasn't wrong of me to want to make love to her. It was just unfortunate that she didn't wish to reciprocate, or have any like feeling for me. Then I really hurt her, with words. Then she hurt me back, and left. It'll all rankle in me; but not, I suppose, in her. For she never *did* care for me, while I did for her. What a difference that makes; caring. A world's difference, in fact. That caring should be requited is the big issue. When that doesn't happen—I turned irrational, I lashed out. My generous impulse toward her—when turned down—turned into venom. From high positive, it went to high negative. She didn't deserve it, I deserved it. I got what my guilt craved for, when she really blasted me. So I'll really remember this. There were more feelings in it for me— a cycle, a gamut. She *won't* remember it too well, or too deeply. It was less complicated for her. She rejected me, having no feeling for me, and then got seared by my hurt retort. Then she seared me back, got revenge, and left. Well, I'm left, 'holding the bag.' It's now in my memory, where it will live, with emotional bubbles rising and falling from it, like in a boiling cauldron or huge kettle of the stove. Well, it really happened. It did."

TO DEPRIVE DAVID, AND CALL IT CURING HIM; TO CONVERT DAVID TO TRIVIAL REALITY'S TIME, WHILE HIS SAD DREAM FANTASY COMES TRANSFERRED TO US, IN THE LOFTY BARGAIN WE STRIKE AGAINST HIS REMOTENESS TO OUR ABHORRED WORLD OF FACT WE'LL SEEK REDEMPTION FROM IN DAVID'S DOWNFALL

He and his sense of reality are always miles apart.

What fills up all that space in the middle?

Their dispute does. Their rancor, and animosity, the blended asymmetry of their enmity.

How did himself and his own sense of reality ever reach a falling of the ways?

Once, his sense of reality had the upper hand in directing his whole path, until its guidance ultimately misled him into the warping of his fantasy life, on whose pre-eminence he had spiritually come to depend. His sense of reality was put to the blame, and they parted with bitterness, and now they keep to separate ways, himself on the one side, and far away his disenfranchised sense of reality, set adrift but hoping to be reclaimed when the tug between them would give way to convergence and unity once again. That's what his sense of reality had hoped. Himself reckoned, stubbornly, the opposite; and to bring the tussle up to date, today they're still at odds, he rejecting reconciliation or overtures of patching up peace. That's how their current situation stands, for he's taken leave of his senses, and dreams alone sustain him.

He lives in a fantasy world? Then his hair must surely be red,

But the pallor of his face is beyond compare. His inverted eyes reach past his actual circumstance, fishing beyond memory for some pleasing distortion to dandy on his wandering lap, or an infant's playboy to pull and stretch to a destruction of his whimsical tatters, according to the precision of his freedom from logic. David is his name, but when called that, he doesn't heed.

Is he locked up deafly inside?

He only converses with *former* friends, on past days and years. He lives at a younger time.

Shouldn't David be taken under psychiatric care?

Cure is what he least desires. He wants his sickness to establish its pseudo-health on a settled self-willed government, free of compromising trade and commercial tarnishing with crude reality's barter. His refinement of an inner life produces a dreamy heaven for his amusement, and at times he plucks forth some poetic images for his spiritual dallying. He's even been scrawling verses of late, and touched up a canvas with some very personal paint. David, the despair of his mother, is, you see, an artist of his own proclaiming, and a dabbler at elusive poetry; for he watches an inner horizon of clouds shift their film effects, as though attending a private movie under his own immediate direction of all-in-one actor-in-audience. He's the only viewer on that screen. Such a distraction leaves him out of touch. Reality, including other people, is tendered the slight and insult of his ignoring it, in the harmless preoccupation of an indwelling innocence that never emerges to pluck the outer truth from any obliging branch in the dense rich woodland and rooted tree-life of Reality's unhampered growth. David misses the whole forest of experienced fact and truth, for he dares not interrupt his introspection that glides after a fabricated twig of menial artifice, fertile to planted idea, but barren in solid existence. By this evidence it would appear that David is lost to this world, and we must give him up. He would fascinate you as a case history, if you were a specialist in pathology. A girl dropped out of his life, and the wake of such a vacuum suctioned all reality out, evacuating his lonely island of grief that then grew walls to block misery in and keep relief out. It's an old romantic tale of woe, one of literature's traditional mainstays of Tristram and Isolde lineage, of Montague and Capulet saga, and the stuff that Verdi turned to La Traviata. That's what fate dished out for David's legacy, so he withdrew from the world, to retire his hurt in perpetuity like a well-moneyed racehorse sent out to clover when its earnings are stopped by an injury to only one of four legs. David's retreat keeps an old love "intact," where change can't corrupt it or newness give itself in exchange for it by substituting fresh life or perhaps another girlfriend who could repair the damage by becoming a Mrs David and keep him well-supplied with kisses. In effect, David has died. He relies only on a dreaming head that starves on former sustenance, oblivious to fresh tissue below and opportunities for meeting girls next Friday or Saturday and the healing possibility of forming an all-replacing attachment, just the alliance that can banish his loyalty to a remote affair by affording him the consoling sensations of the present, a bonding absorption in an immediate new girl with dates to know her better and the health of getting engaged. That would put forlorn grief to rest, given a rich feminine remedy to restore reality. Then David would put behind his strangeness, and join us in normal rhythm, on active terms of society, as one of use, easy to know, not distant. He would reacquaint himself with the same familiar patterns we all conduct ourselves by, by which we confidently know others as our fellow men. He would accept humanity again, and be a person himself, accessible to speech or look. He wouldn't be the peculiar recluse of melancholy, but contribute to the general happiness, as a participant rehabilitated in communal life. To this end, should we rescue him, and drag his feet back to earth? Break his fantasy spell? Remove him from our remove, and dose him full with a vivid reality injection? Return David to himself?

Let's save him at once! Where is he?

Brooding in his room. We'll go there and knock down the door if necessary. We'll restore him by shock, if need be. And re-capture him for time's twisting turns, out of his stagnant rut. Wash him upstream, where he'll join the flow of a natural course, and not be stuck where life's hazard tricked him at an awkward bank and the goal slipped away and he was wrenched to disaster and went into a mental rot. We'll release him; loose and free, he'll overtake the quickening years, and come back new. In reality's swim, he'll get a companion, forgot what he lost before, and de-cline in years by gathering ripeness among reality's daily wayfares, with their rewarding abundance. Let's unlock David, if he lets us, for the wholesome welfare of his instant rejubilation; and watch his morbid spectres dwindle as his soul and sense come out rushing to embrace, that have been paired apart for so long now. And reality will have regained the lost David, who will be seen to have found a lovely and real girl, one he can touch with more than his faculty of a sad lost dream, for life is more than the mind alone. Life is bodily submission to future light. So rear up David, from the dead.

But hasn't his death gone to his head, and his redemption is too late?

No, he might still awake; let's inspire him: *we*'re examples of what might be.

Are we the models to his enlightenment? Are we the launching to his revival?

Let that be our worthy function. Though we be only false myth, be can direct David to truth; an instructor doesn't need to be what he instructs. We'll salvage him: and raise our dreams in his stead, while he falls to mere truth. We'll acquire his fault: a trade for what we teach. He'll sink to low reality; and we'll take his exalted perch, the lover doomed never to forget. To hell with outside life! There's an internal world to conquer yet!

We'll become Davids, ourselves; and, rejoicing, leave this world; while he must tumble down to it, sacrificing his fantasy to the impoverishment of our crude earth of fact. It's true we envy David. By reconstructing him, we'll change places with him, and gain his favored unreality, the most special weapon against life's abuse. First we cure him; and when he's reformed, the transference of his illness will complete our lifelong license to dream. David will be narrowed down to now. While, in *our* loftiness, we'll turn time inward, and glide on its stately dream.

WHO'S CARING FOR ME? NOT YOU?

I hope you'll feel responsibility and worry for me. Not worry but just responsibility. But worry is a way of having responsibility for the responsibility.

You daily want me to *care* for you, then.

Sure. Feel concerned.

But what if my feeling for you isn't strong enough?

Then increase it, through time,

What if in time it *decreases*?

Till your attitude becomes indifference?

Yes. Pardon me.

Then I'll feel neglected. Overlooked. Ignored, in fact.

But others—surely others could give you what I don't.

But what they give me won't be *yours*, I'll be concretely deprived of your special attention.

But *general* attention, abstractly from others, will come.

I'll be you-deprived; however rich, otherwise.

SHE REFUSES TO FILL HIS LIFE'S DREAM-VACANCY, SINCE SHE'D RATHER BE HERSELF THAN TO SERVE HIM SO IDEALLY

(Characters: A wooing young man; an idealized, therefore cautious and rejecting, young woman. He speaks first, in breathless hope:)

My dream has a vacancy; Would you like to fill it?

I'm uncertain whether my qualifications are suitable, or whether my background shows the sort of experience that has prepared me for such an undertaking. What role *is* it? What am I required to do?

Do nothing, merely be. For once you have the being, the doing will follow in character. As you are, you're just right. You'd fill my dream's vacancy the way a foot fills its year-old shoe: snugly but not too tight; comfortably, but not too loose. My dream has been dreaming about you, without knowing that you were the one it was all about. You've had the charm to appear; now have the wise mercy to enter, at the spot where my dream has made room for you all these years. And once you've done that, I'll wear a completed soul, at last. Life will have totalled itself into the dream, and the two be one.

That's a large order to ask of me. The responsibility scares me somewhat. Can't you give me a more modified place in your scheme?: a function more in modest keeping with my awe and inadequacy in the face and onslaught of your exacting, imperious, and demanding, and self-fatal post you've assigned me to? I'd rather take care of myself and enjoy a lonely, detached freedom, than enter so irrevocably, so crucially, so self-sacrificially, into the fulfilling depth of your hard core's dream. I would be vitally serving you: but what would I be to myself?

Toss away such a petty qualm: only *noble* scruples should deserve your worried head. My dream needs your finishing touch, to be one with life. Your function would be life-giving, to an exalted generosity you'd never chance upon again. Never would the romantic heroine's role of superb necessity in the hero's life, ever come so perfectly your way, as now. The power you have, to redeem, inspire, uplift, and fulfill me! To meet my dream head-on, and see yourself as what it craved for in its finest enactment. *Other* girls only strike *adequately* on fellows' lives, or obliquely figure in them, or overlap with the mating opportunity. But here the door has opened once in my life, and to you alone, as personification ideal, and reality. The door is about to close, if you don't enter now. Hasten, don't hesitate. My glory calls to you. You'll be enriched with my depth.

It's out of my measure, it's too deep for me. I feel more comfortable in shallower circumstances. Thanks anyway. I was touched by your offer. But to oblige would mean my stepping off my level, out of my ken, contrary to *my* nature, though serviceable to yours. I'll put a flattered memory on your invitation, and mull with regret, some future day; over my not having accepted. My current fear will feed my later remorse. Having refused you, I'll be a spinster to the soul forever, though undoubtedly I'll marry at least once. We turn down what's too strong for us. That's what I've just done.

IS THERE NO WOMAN TO FIT MY IDEAL? THEN LOVE GOES BEGGING. MY IDEAL SCARES THEM OFF. IT MIGHT REPLACE THEIR *OWN* SELVES, IN AN UNEASY FIT.

The loved woman struggles free of my love, killing it. She resumes her unloved self—into which she fits easily. Had I meant to trap her in an unreal cage? To tie her into falsity romance-dictated? My love drops off; she rises out, off and down, into her unsoaring level. Freely unidealized, her reality romps off to play promiscuous fickleness into no and all shapes, at will. I had exalted her out of existence. She broke the stranglehold of my love, to step into the void's modesty, and whirl everlastingly; lonely, but at liberty. Pressed down into no image, thrust up on no high perch; evading my grip, she goes infinitely loveless— flirting with an inhuman love out of man's harmful reach. Good luck up there—or down. I've lost you. What have you gained? The All of the unloved. Such unconfinement—don't you miss being trapped? You're free to pursue a true self—in a void? You're not to be imperialized—

you have your *own* empire to own: to achieve that open range of possibilities limited to no scope; but open ever. Love was to pin a particular on you and close down your horizons. You evade it and fly under the ground, escaping that star-hunting gaze in my love-bejewelled eyes that go fishing for a slave on the lure of idealizing bait, on all of heaven's sea to pluck you out and confine you in fantasy's zoo. That won't do for you. A lonely oasis for you, not the loving sands of my clutching desert. I who sought you—but you seek death; which is the figurative definition of the large unloved state. Go, I withdraw my love—and plunge it elsewhere. There *are* slaves willing. Bondage is of *human* sweat; some give in, and enjoy it. Some even live larger, that way. To shrink narrowly into life, not to expand into that enormous infinity of death—whose scale, frankly, is inhuman. You're so immodest, as to seek a loveless Everywhere, rather than locally to be roped in to a narrow post of love—by one man's projecting. Everyone's a slave to *some*thing—by being liberated to the opposite. There is no *total* freedom. Freedom is *conditional*. The conditional is too committing? Fidelity must be placed *some*where. Anything that *is*, is by limitation. Even running away is to run *some*where. Why not *here*, to spare you all that running? Come, these arms want to clamp down on your freedom; bend it, brand it, stamp it, compress it—own it into bondage. I plead you submit. Run away from running away. Hold still, I must have you. As *I* see you, idealizing. Adoring your image, but ignoring you.

Her reply is pure negative. So my loving has no holding; holds no having. She tugs loose; and hides everywhere in her disappearance. Faced with her absence, I look for a new presence, on whom to attach my usually misappropriating ideal. Will the fit come closer this next time? Will the girl like being clad in her illusory semblance? I have an ideal garment; to be worn *inside*. Who will assume it; and not have her "other" identity threatened? Who defends no identity? Then let her take mine.

My salesmanship slips. No one to buy my ready-made ideal of her, I'm peddling unwelcome goods. But I offer them with love,

BEING REJECTED

I love Anna, but she loves me less.

You mean she doesn't requite you?

I try to woo her, but she pushes me aside.

Maybe she'll come around.

I'm tired of waiting.

Have you tried prayer?

No, I'm an atheist. It's up to Anna herself, not to a higher power.

Can you convince her by boasting your credits and boosting your merits? Through the advertising technique?

No. Her mind seems made up: I'm not worthy.

Then you just have to give her up. Face reality. She owns the power to reject you, and that's that. Let loving her dwindle into nothing, and date other women who may be more willing.

That's heartlessly matter-of-fact.

Isn't reality fact-based?

It's reality's fault. Why can't reality co-operate?

You're the stubborn one. Give her up as a lost cause. Get a first-rate substitute.

You're so logical and pragmatic.

This is the world. It overpowers your imagination.

But that's where Anna dwells.

Prod her loose. Then fill up the sorrow vacuum.

With an inferior product?

Lower your standards. Let mediocrity rule.

Get an unworthy for my shrinking tool?

Or else go to a different school.

SEX IS FOR THE YOUNG, DEATH FOR THE OLD

I knew a girl for all my life, as a chaste friend, then when my life was edging to its close as a man too old to live much longer, I saw that the girl was the same age as when I first met her, young and beautiful at barely twenty-two. In a belated attempt to make amends, I (as they say) "fell" in love with her, which was too romantic to be without its spice of lust as well. "But you're my old friend," the girl shouted to my dismal hearing, bodily decrepitude, and my celluloid process of decay. "I want you *now*, to make up for lost time," I flatly maintained, determined to make the end of my life the model for my beginning to imitate, if not too late. "But our ages are too far apart," said the young girl whom half a century ago I had known in my youth as a young girl, the same one as today. "Our sexes are far apart too," I hinted, while chasing her. On her young feet she outsped me, and I stopped, panting. If only I was younger, I didn't have to die so soon. Too much time had gone by, and I couldn't have stopped it. Instead of seeing what I could in the street scene, I saw the whole world in one sight. That was enough.

SADNESS AS THE TRUTH AND REALITY OF LOVE

I had such love for Cathleen, Anne had such love for me. That's the way it goes. Cathleen finally discouraged me. It took a long time, before she could convince me to abandon all my futile hopes to unsag her sunken love. In *my* turn. I had to repeatedly disappoint Anne, till her heart lost faith.

Why is passion wasted?

Why is sadness romance's answer?

Why is loving doomed?

And *being*-loved no less poignant?

No answers. A tragic rhetoric has molded these questions. Love was put in life: the smaller-doomed, in the larger-doomed one. No way out.

NOT TAKING HOLD

A man saw a woman from a distance. This increased his interest, since it had a long way to go between himself and the girl. His imagination was given wide room for infinite projecting, seeing how far away the woman herself actually stood.

Lust seized him; providing him with the euphemism of desiring her. He approached, like a hunter bold, towards his prey.

The woman saw him coming. She knew she was his object. It thrilled her, till he grew closer. Then she could see, clearer and clearer, that she didn't want him. So she readied her "no" for when he drew close enough to hear her rejection.

The time had come, he was near. She said no. But by then the man was seeing *her*. Now that he could see her, he didn't *want* her. So he said no too. He had come a long way to say it: changing his prepared "yes" at the end of his mistaken journey.

They parted, forever. Their incident was forgotten: a misadventure. Their mating encounter was at a false market, jointly decided on by both but apart and in private. What if one had persisted with "yes"—would it have won out over the other's "no?" A dry bone for the academic dogs to growl over, exploring a speculative meat that isn't there. Bury that bone. Forget. Other couples do couple. This one never met.

MARGE ONCE, AND THAT'S ENOUGH

Meeting Marge meant I had to face a problem: should I risk seeing her again? It was risky, since seeing her a second time meant I would lose my heart, and that being the case, was she (objectively considering) a reliable one to lose it to? (Would she ever return it as itself again? Or would it be a withered thing I'd retrieve, flattened and never functionable again?)

The temptation was recklessly to accept the gamble, for illusion painted my prospect the color of hope. I plunged, then failed. I'll not describe the misery. Misery is wordless, and grief takes refuge in dumb horror. I survived to live in the numb memory of it. But Marge had taken her toll of my heart. It's back in place, but so shrunken that no normal love can ever fit in it again. In Marge I failed. I have this tale, but not a heart, or not the whole and proper one that may hold love. Technically, I live my life out, by the course of mechanical years. It's heartless. Marge happened once. Death takes place *the same number of times*. After death, will I *also* live mechanically?

WHAT THE MAN SAID. THEN WHAT THE WOMAN SAID. AND THEIR SAYING SHROUDS THE FUNERAL OF WHAT THEY MIGHT EVER HAVE BEEN

You and I are attracted to each other, an inch away from love's doorstep. One final stride would close off every distance. I'd be within your circle, in your venturing into mine. Yet the verge is what we stall at. And hesitation widens, growing the divisive breach.

Your analysis confirms what our situation is. It defines and terminates what we were. Here's an end, and our possibilities die.

WHAT IS DISSATISFACTION LOOKING FOR? THE OBLIT-
ERATION OF THE POSSESSOR OF IT, THE SELF FEEL-
ING IT. A STRANGELY UNKNOWN CHANGE IS ITS RIPE,
BUT VAGUE, PURSUIT. DISSATISFACTION IS CONSTANT,
WITH TRIVIAL ALTERATIONS: THE ESSENTIAL STATE
REMAINS, WITH INSUFFICIENTLY RADICAL VARIA-
TIONS. OUR CONDITION HAS MULTIPLE FORMS; BUT
IS STILL THE SAME OLD SELF, IN STALE DEGREES OF
MONOTONY. A REVOLUTIONARY VIOLENCE GROWS
OUR DESPERATELY INSANE IMPULSE. WE WOULD BREAK
OUT, STRIKE THROUGH; ANYTHING, WE'D TRY. BUT
WE'RE UNRID OF OUR CONSERVATIVE STERILITY, PRE-
SERVING US JUST AS WE ARE, AND AS SUCH, TO DIE;
UNHEROIC; WITH NO TASTE OF ADVENTURE OR QUIT-
TING OF THIS FAMILIAR MILDNESS. SUCH A NICE, COSY
TRAP. WE'RE SICK.

BUT ISN'T A ROCK BORED, TOO, OF ITS EVER-CLINGING
INERTIA, AND ITS NEVER-VARYING WEIGHT? WE'RE
SUPPOSED TO BE ANIMATE; BUT OUR MOVEMENT
TAKES US NO FARTHER THAN THE ROCK'S STILLNESS,
REMOVES THE ROCK FROM ITS STEADFAST CONDITION.
DIDN'T EVOLUTION ADVANCE US *PAST* THE ROCK? NO?
THEN WHAT SPECIAL GOOD IS IN LIFE? WHAT'S ITS
MYSTIC PROPERTY, THAT CONFERS US A PROUD AD-
VANTAGE OVER THE FEEBLE MINERAL RACE? IN WHAT
IS OUR BOASTING PRIVILEGE? JUST WHERE DO WE LO-
CATE OUR SUPERIORITY? IS LIFE *INTRINSICALLY* WHAT
IT'S SUPPOSED TO BE? OR MUST WE GO TO GREAT
LENGTHS, PURSUING IT? TO REVEAL, AND IDENTIFY,
AND STRIP IT? TO LET IT GLEAM. TO PIERCE THE GOD,
TO PUNCTURE THAT CORE, SO THAT THE BLOOD'S
FLOWING SUBSTANCE CAN BETRAY WHAT HEART IS AT
THE SOURCE. SUPPOSE WE GAIN *THAT*; HOW DO WE
APPLY IT?

Do you ever need to cry?

I do, but my source is dry. For I have nothing tragic to remember, in the course of a bright life. I didn't do enough suffering to earn the material of which tears are made. I should have been gathering, and hoarding up, a providential store of accumulative weeping-stock, acquired by active combat with woe, where pathetic disappointment is all the return for ideals submitted. Instead, I went out and found, for variety, the degrees between joy and serenity, which constituted my "ups and downs," leaving misery out altogether. I'm envied, I suppose. But I miss the normal share of setbacks and aggravations and other reverses so abundantly allotted to endowment of misfortune that other people are bound to receive as a birthright in the midst of acting out the plights and slights and undelights and unsightlinesses that weigh down the somber scales of existence's strife. I have no bruise to show, and no gleam to start a tear from: all went placidly well, with me.

You must have been abnormally sheltered from the usual hard blows that knock most people about. Were you born to protective wealth?

Yes, but kept unspoiled. I dearly knew the value of things, and didn't demand a pampered overindulgence that would inflate pleasure by craving and consuming more than my measure of goods. Very little delighted me. So I grew up, knowing no spite.

Then you have no problem.

I'm not complaining.

Why need to cry?

To exercise my tear-duct. It has layers of dryness. It might be a barrier to sight. It's cluttered with dust. I must clean it out. So I can see through. My inward temper is good, I'd like to see the world as such. Grace it, with my fair vision, beaming on it, generously. Convert it, if necessary, to my happy tone. Give the world the aspect, for all people, that it has for me. Make the world such as I see it, so others can, too.

That's noble. But will the world take on the affirmative demeanor you ascribe to it, for the benefit of other sights shed on it by people susceptible to your warm influence? Isn't your own sight too private for the world to conform to it? Though your intention is admirable, can you enforce your vision of the world, and impose it successfully, as its standard measure for others in seeing it? A farseeing ideal, but too unlikely to become projected. The universal is too subjective. You own the way you see. It's no one else's property.

Couldn't I share it, socialistically?

No. Have you now occasion to cry?

The weeping has started. The locked-up solitude of happiness can wrench *any*one's heart. Now I've dug the geyser of a source, for woe. And can resort to it, in need of tears.

How fortunate: to be happy; and have its weeping consolation, as well.

Already, my spring is deepened. My happiness has sprung its depth. Knowing it goes no farther past me, than even tears may conduct. If only I had an art to vehicle forth the products of pleasure, and the joys of delight. But I *feel*; and that's all.

What a waste, not to reproduce what you feel, into transformed terms of equivalents, for others to understand. You have a lot to give. But it dies inside.

Thanks, I'm contentedly sad, to round out an otherwise barren happiness. A productive balance is struck. And I have raw material, to manufacture tears from. I feel more fruitful; and won't stop, until my happy dirge releases an ocean burial pomp, for tears, and their melancholy benign mercy, to overflow my serenity and fill its life's emptiness. And I'll grow rich and strange, suffering a sea-change. My birth was unleashed in water. May I keep a moist eye, in commemoration; and by way of preparing my launching out, on the opposite side, I'd like a purity of horizons, and my absorbing life drink of all the full seas, reaching past the human stop. Or retiring back, before life's happiness-dripping body moved on to dry soil, to try out the complications of a further luck: leading to all this—which I dismiss, for I have it. Or do I really want misery?, so supreme it leaves me emotionless, and the hard eyes will stare, until the objects of sight stop coming. I'd like to be void of feeling. A rock, with its suitable inertia, would be the likely model, I want to be what I'm not—just to change my state. Even happiness is too much of one kind, through whatever variations. Or do I look for tragedy? A transformation, to lift the self's shell, and permit flow into the All? I'm discontent. I needn't be me; I'm already too much that. What's left? I know too much already, for one condition. Success is a form of death, and sterile happiness is too placid a goal. I'm looking outside, I see through the world. What I want is unseeable, I need a mystery to conquer, I'm growing stale.

You sound dissatisfied. Things as they are are too much yourself? You want a complete plunge?

I want new terms, entirely unfamiliar. I've already survived in *this* state; let me fail in another.

You're looking for death?

Or some equal change, living perhaps. Drastic, radical, revolutionary—and unknown. What I know tires me. A new set of rules, outside my skill, to challenge my utter failure, and make success irrelevant. I long to assume foreign sense, and undergo an unmastered language. My vitality is self-destructive; it feeds on ideals of danger, or horrible destructions, on impossible rebirths under alien metamorphoses. I want no longer to be me. Under the present circumstance, I'm unavoidable to me. I *hate* me, having seen enough.

What do you venture to do?

For all that, nothing. I'll stick still. When I disappear, I'll feel another guise, or else dip under knowledge. Ignorance would keep up mystery's suspense; innocence would be all right. Instead, I know too much; and the dear value has turned worthless. Let me be all things; but not *(Pointing to, or indicating, his outward skin-self:)* *this.*

LOVING CATHERINE EQUALLY AS LOVED BY THE SAME CATHERINE: A PROPOSAL FOR EVOLUTION TO CARRY OUT, EVENTUALLY

(Secondary title, as bonus for finishing story, will reward reader upon story's conclusion.)

I was on a train in a compartment that a stranger sitting opposite me was sharing. The window was going by, I was always looking out. The scenery was going by. So was the world going by. But time wasn't; for we were moving so fast.

The train was going from the eastern end of the continent to the western end, but all in the same country, a famous North American country which had been the birthplace of such splendid poets as Wallace Stevens, Robert Frost, Marianne Moore, and a score of others. But I refuse to divulge the name of the country, for fear of an international spy ring that pries into national secrets.

By now, the train was roaring through the middle of the country, passing scenery so startling that it must have been mountainous, with valleys below, not to mention such canyons, cliffs, and other natural wonders. I was awed, it was beautiful. My book was resting on my lap a long time. It was about poetry, and it quoted some lines of verse to illustrate points. But my mind was in the romantic wilderness that roared outside the window. The splendor inspired lofty thoughts. My compartment-companion was smiling, shaking his head. Through all the journey so far, not one word had been exchanged between us; not even a courteous gesture. But shyness was rubbed away by the wilderness roaring outside. Our spirits felt free: our tongues wagged.

We spoke at length. We introduced our identities. I was poetry professor on my way to attend a poetry professors' convention on the western seaboard. The gentleman opposite me turned out to be a publishers' representative out to attend a sales conference at the same city *I* was going to. Not only were we both going to the same city; but the *train* was going there, too. We had picked a winner.

∞

We compared our marital states. I turned out to be the father of three children, and a devoted husband. My whole family were poetry lovers; thanks to my pedagogical lead. And you, sir? How do *you* fare? Your situation, domestic or otherwise?

"Bachelor," he stated. Ah, he's free, then, to have affairs. I envied such a bohemian. He must have numerous girl friends. Discretely, l inquired as to the state of his heart, in the realm of lust.

By way of reply, he lectured me on love! It was a lengthy oration. It specified a very deep love he cherished in memory, for a certain "Catherine." He led up to it by a direct progress. I remember his every word, while the majestic scenery passed by, outside our fleeting window, which we shared in common, the view of grand wonders, of enormous vistas, of prospects linked to heaven. Our stature was immense. We were floating, not riding.

That's the setting. Here's big speech:

∞

"Love is a special feeling. You feel it for exclusively someone, it applies to only one, at any given time. You might meet her by accident (such is usually the case). I've been in love a number of times, they highlight my memory, they're the memorable moments of my life! I'm moved now to remember in particular a girl (she must be a women now) for whom my love was *extraordinarily* intense. Catherine; sacred to memory, Catherine, as immortal as my soul itself. She was so real, I couldn't imagine it—at that time. Now I never see her, so I can *only* imagine it. But my love for her faded, it doesn't torture me any more. The remnant is her image, it's valuable. And comfortable, for I'm 'over' her: I can bear thinking of her, the pain is gone. My heart quickens; but it's quite bearable, 'Catherine' made magic by love. I'll dwell on her, and reminisce."

∞

The tale moved me. Between that and the incredible lake scenery outside (full of floating islands and decked in the regalia of sails galore, deep and purple blue under the sun's golden supervision, a spectacle too immense for words, being then the *poet's* domain, which I'm not), I was stirred to mystic intensity. Then a tragic shadow swept over me, a sad chill: for I realized that my companion and his adored 'Catherine' no longer made one, but were apart. Why were not they one bound heart?

The view outside the window stupefied me, with rainbow-colored wings. Harmony leapt at me, like flying fish. Perfections and ideals crave love. I was secure with my own dear wife, from whom I would be briefly absent. But I pitied my companion. Where was his Catherine? It wouldn't be ill-mannered of me to inquire. An intimacy had sprung between us, or an openness, due to the astounding scenery that kept splashing at us upon our magical windowpane that unrolled a scroll, of gradated tableaux in such procession that nature's pageantry gave fire to patriotism, in this national country where Walt Whitman and Emily the Maiden Dickinson once quickened to the pulse of the visiting Muse divinely sprinkling home stray meters on them, some random inspired moments.

So I took upon me the poetic license to probe the Catherine mystery by posing it direct to my amiable companion. "Where is she; why didn't you marry her?", I gently prodded. My companion took no offense in surly privacy. He deemed it a kindness that I should ask; was gratified by my compassion; by my simply caring. He'd launch into the tale, once night had fallen, we were treated to sunset. The glory seemed to weep, in joy. What a beautiful land! No wonder Hart Crane and T. S. Eliot were born here! With soundly poetic foreknowledge, they knew to intuit that this country would provide them with themes, enrich their language, spin them into song. And it did. Fair land!

∞

A gradual dusk steeled us off from the losing visibility of things. Night was mechanical, in our train.

No sense looking out *now*. Nothing to see, but our compartment's electric reflection. We draw the shade down. We were sealed in. We moved out to the eating car. We bloated up our appetites with the nourishing food of our land in quantities prodigious though lacking French fanciness. We were richly satisfied, with bulges to prove it, if we coarsely cared to. We returned to our compartment, having become good traveling friends, fellow travelers, on a course west, in our land of mystery, in the lovely youth of its history. We sat back opposite each other, stretched out, in solid comfort. The seats ware plush and soft, the backrest easy to melt into. My companion, gentle soul, was to tell of Catherine. What happened? Why didn't love join them? Was it not sufficiently mutual? I waited for my sad tale. *His* tale. Mine too. My hearing was deeply prepared.

∞

"First *she* loved *me*. We went traveling together: idyllic in bliss. Gradually I grew to love *her*. The more my love for her increased, the less intense fell her love fur me: an inverse ratio, of a sort. Why, I don't know. It seemed that there could only be one given quantity of love allotted between us both; the more on my side, the less on hers; the more on hers, the less on mine. In the beginning, the balance 'favored' me; I was more loved than loving. Gradually this reversed itself: *I* became the lover; she the loved. Then it grew so lopsided, unchecked, out of balance, that she simply had to leave me. I was left with grief. We broke up."

∞

"I'm very sorry," was what I was reduced to, on hearing my companion tell of his gradual loss of Catherine that coincided with his gradually loving her more and more. The descending stop to loss: the ascending slope of increasingly despairing love. It bothered me. Why should hearts operate this way between people? One estranged partner gets loaded with a sack of pain. It's even *tragically* unfair. It just shouldn't be. There ought to be a law against it. God made people wrong, in the love business. I was ready to campaign, to crusade, for a reform policy to stop this atrocity. It's undemocratic, this unevenness! It's *grossly* unfair. Romance and sentiment are *holy*. Between partners, they should be *requited*. Our young ought to be educated, along the lines of achieving reciprocity, *enduring* reciprocity, in affairs of the heart, in the passion of amour. I wanted to reform the whole internal system: to align it more to the *e*ternal, I wanted ideals to *be*. I hate the *potential* of ideals. I'm impatient that they be *actual*. I'll *fight* for this! I'm in a rage of fervor. I'm indignant. I'm a righteous crusader, "*Love*-equality." That's my slogan, and my goal. For mankind's great benefit! To improve the future. To take the danger out of love, ease the risk out and put in a guarantee. Hearts *need* security. Oh mortal frame: please change, by evolution: it's not too late. Let there be "love-equality." We have a right to such happiness. This be the credo I'm committed to. My life's dedication shall be that. All my craze has been for poetry. Let poetry now aid, in this *greater* cause!

∞

My zeal was firm. I confided it to my traveling companion. He felt humble yet proud that *his* woeful tale was to be *my* affirming inspiration in curing human nature (the slow labor possibly of centuries) of its love-inequity, its unbalanced allocations of adoration between consenting couples. Even pairings! An ideal to work for. How, though, to implement it? By what means, to strive thus, in uphill struggle? Let *love* seek out the means. The heart has its reasons: which reason is in the dark about. Nothing so sacred as the heart's affections. Let this be our governing rule. Let equality be *enforced*, in each love-match. *How?*, though: *how?*

∞

Determination is not enough. I pondered "how." No solution occurred. My companion was sleeping, sprawled out on the soft upholstery. Opposite him, here was I, still awake. The train was charging through the dark tunnel of night. The tunnel of blind darkness.

Oh Spirit. Help me, in distress. Rid the world of ill-fated love; as you'd rid us all of any scourge or plague. Disease must go; and also unrequited love. Tear all sadness away. Make all men happy. And women, in equal love. Let there be sacred pairings. Let them all last. Grant them eternity.

∞

I prayed, I vowed; but "how?" "How?", I didn't know yet. The screeching train was in the night. It wailed like a ghost: It diminished. It recedes. It's in the far distance. Beyond that horizon. In it, I'm awake: fiery with my plot. My companion is asleep. Catherine's image is upon him. He dreams, sad man. By that means only, can he possess her. Oh fatal curse of human nature! Be rooted out, please. Right yourself. Stop giving suffering. You've done enough. Ill-starred love, *cease*. Be equal, please!

∞

The train is a ghost. On it is my mind. Awake. And my companion's dream. Of Catherine, ever receding. Of the pale Catherine. Of Catherine, loved. Of Catherine, unhad. The moving country is headed west. The train. is on the rails. The rails are over the horizon, an invisible track. Catherine retreats in dimmer levels of invisibility, on my companion's dream. She won't come back; Gone, and lost. The black dream. On it the emptiness. Where bright Catherine should be.

Oh that train is me. I'm far off. I'm out of sight. My sight is out. And in the place of my sight? The ideal of love. For each Catherine loved, one loving. The kind and receiving heart. Partners as one. The blessing heart, blessed. The symmetry not mathematical, but by the heart's strict law of geometry. Simultaneously, one Catherine hovering: for each Catherine loved. (The *same* Catherine: in all cases.)

Let it be. Be it must. Oh heart, evolve!

(Secondary title: the promised bonus for finishing the story:)

CATHERINE LOVED, BUT NOT LOVING BACK: A HUMAN CURSE, A CRIMINAL MOCKING OF EQUALITY. LOVE

SHOULD BE FAIRLY TWO-SIDED. BALANCE SHOULD BE ENFORCED, HAPPINESS THROUGH REQUITED LOVE. THE MIRACLE OF THE COMMONPLACE RECIPROCAL. MY IDEAL PLAN TO BLOT OUT ALL ILLS, IN THE SPHERE OF PURE ROMANCE, GIVEN AS TAKEN, AND TAKEN GIVEN. TO AND FROM EACH, EQUALLY, THE WELL-BALANCED PAIR. LOVES AS THE GLAD REINFORCER OF MUTUAL HAPPINESS, NOT ITS DISMAL DETRACTOR FOR ONE.

THE VIRGINIA NOT OBTAINED

How much essence does an object give off? It depends. Let's take Virginia. (I'd like to but she won't let me.) There's plenty of essence she gives off. It has her name written all over it. (Virginia.) She's just *stamped* with it. (Her essence, not her name.) It's that something indefinable—a mystery, I call it.

There's only one Virginia. (Though nominally there are hundreds of thousands—but I'm speaking spiritually, not nominally.)

I love her, and so I'm aware she's pretty. If I didn't love her, I'd be *impersonally* or indifferently, or disinterestedly, aware that she's pretty. That's a different quantity or quality of awareness of how pretty she is. Love makes it *important* that she's pretty. (Or else vitally *un*important—vitally.)

Three things that every person has (two by coincidence beginning with the same letter; but is that so wonderful?): Existence; identity; essence. Sometimes those three overlap. They merge into funny combinations, or proportions, of those three ingredients (also called components or elements, just to be fair).

Virginia is no different: She has those three things too. But love heaps a heap of meaning on them, for me.

Her essence—indescribable. It would take a Shakespeare, Rembrandt, Plato, or someone like that, to do it any justice at all. So let's *assume* her essence. We don't know it.

That leaves identity and existence; Virginia is devoid of neither. Love enhances their significance, for me.

She has plenty of both. Plenty!

That leaves only Virginia herself. Who's she?

After polishing off her essence, identity, and existence, only Virginia is left. A mere remnant? No: the total whole!

What goes into Virginia? (*I* don't. She won't let me.) Some great qualities. They all go to make her up.

She also has attributes, properties, characteristics, traits, stuff like that. But when all is said and done, and all is taken into account (essence, identity, existence, all that defines or doesn't, whatever reveals, whatever describes), Virginia takes on meaning because I love her. (I wish she'd take on *me* for the same reason. But she's too mean. That demeans me.)

She's someone so special—oh!

And oh! again.

That's Virginia, all over. (I wish *I* could be all over her. But she keeps me off. I'm denied the mounting of her. Instead, my tension mounts— though not her. I wish prayers could move mountings. That would amount to what I wish. If wishes were beggars, the king would ride.)

So there she is. (But I'm *not* there. I don't occupy her same space. Wish I did, though.)

I wish I could keep her occupied. (I have just the thing. It would enter long and hard, and leave soft and small.) But she says, "No." That rubs out my "yes." It's her will, over mine.

ONE MARYLIN WANTED BY TWO DIFFERENT MEN. FIRST IRA TRIES AND THEN I. WHO GETS HER IF EITHER? READ ON.

My heart was full, making solitude gloomy. I needed to unburden myself. I phoned up people to visit, but everyone was either out or otherwise engaged till I hit on Ira, who just happened to be available, and welcomed me over for a visit.

A girl would have been more ideal for such a bachelor as myself, but I can't complain, having made no prior appointment,

I was in love, but she didn't know it, and was anyway temporarily away.

Ira as well was a bachelor, and he also lived alone. But he had a better job than I, and much more money. For that I envy him. Our friendship must not have been very pure, otherwise my envy would not have occurred. So much for theorizing, anyway.

My heart lifted slightly, as I walked the mile or so that divided his from my apartment. I had been in, working, all day on that Saturday off from work, and a sedentary solemnity had settled on me. The exercise did me good, my physical walk to his house. And the outdoor sights and sounds I found agreeable. On my arrival, I had considerably cheered up.

Ira opened the door to let me in. I looked forward to the drinks he was going to serve me.

He knew my preference was gin-and-tonic, so omitted the formality of asking. I now anticipated, drink in hand and sipping it, the conversation (as afternoon declined and evening grew Its gradual back-door big bruising bulging way back in, in that early and poignant spring season) that was to befall us as surely as the elongated shadows when the sun panics to get home in a hurry.

Not its subject; but just the conversation, was of an inevitability. We didn't have too much to say to each other, but managed to saturate time with volumes of talk. Where did it all go? It vanished into tunnels of memory. To what effect? Unknown.

This time, what would the subject be? I was neutral, had no pet choice. Though in love, I didn't want to touch on it, but rather retreat. This would leave *Ira* to the initiative. But what if *he* had nothing to lead off with? Or was *also* holding something back?

Drinking and company were in *themselves* worth while. Talk is embroidery.

So much of history had happened before us, on so many world areas, that a topic of discussion would plentifully be unlacking, if we cared, from a brilliant range of choices.

Ira would take a stand, and I the opposing one. Conflict would be the fuel, to sustain our talk endlessly.

Ira was making, and had, more money; but conversationally, we were equals: as was only fair.

After all, having more money doesn't in itself make one man's opinions weightier, more decisive, or closer in logic; than the opinions of his poorer neighbor. Money goes only *so* far: in the *intellectual* realm, it runs out of gas, and becomes *beside* the point. Is that why money-loving people hate intellectuals?

But that's a digression of a horse of another color jumping over a different lake altogether, if I'm to be permitted this untransitional shift into a figure of speech.

Ira was talking. His voice came over in waves.

His subject was love. Is love more obsessive to a bachelor? There are no figures given by the census department.

"I'm in love with Marylin," Ira confided, his voice booming into the deeper ranges of anguish, sentiment, pathos, and self-heroic pity. It meant I was going to have to be impressed. So I tried to look sympathetic. I was listening to be looked at.

"She's so beautiful!" added Ira, plaintively. "Ah, if only she could love me back!"

I was really not interested. I had to put up such a pretense! That's a boring waste of time, when I *could* have been delving into something that *mattered* to me. But I had to be polite, I was obliged. It was I who phoned Ira up and had myself invited. I was his guest, now on my third gin-and-tonic. I wasn't even *slightly* tipsy: I wasn't immune to the dullness of this enthusiasm.

He was praising "Marylin, Marylin." I got tired of hearing her name spoken. (Though it rang an inner bell, unconsciously.) I was angry, and would soon rebel.

He kept "going on" about her. I waited for him to stop. But he had himself hypnotized, and the subject grew increasingly fascinating from his personal point of view. The lover was raving. But what was their status?

I asked him. He replied that his adored one had no notion of the passion aroused on Ira's breast.

She was a typist and file clerk at his office, occasionally doubling as a telephone receptionist. His love for her was undeclared, from a distance. This state of affairs, or impasse, had been a few months old.

"Why have you hesitated?" I asked, impatiently. "Why have you kept it from her? Haven't you even 'dated' her?! To ask her out doesn't betray the bashful state of your heart or by itself reveal your hopeless passion. What's prevented your boldness from matching your order, in wooing to win, in daring the luck of the game, the perils of the chase? You're not *ordinarily* timid. That's why you've succeeded in business and earned steady promotions from your corporation masters. So why not pursue Marylin *outright*? Is she too sacred, or sacrosanct?"

"Fright in love is not inconsistent with cold *business* efficiency," he icily replied. "The spheres are unrelated. Love moves me *one* way; and my job invokes other habits altogether. I'm a novice when it comes to Marylin, though I'm an asset to my firm. They just don't compare. Do you want to know *why* I haven't asked Marylin out?"

"Get it over with," I pleaded, "so as to exhaust the topic, terminate it. Your ravings hardly interest me. I have my *own* problems to ponder. I'm in love, as well. But she's out of town on a vacation, and when she returns I'll have to start courting her in earnest: in short, to *take* the advice I've just given *you*."

Ira was angry that I had denied him an uninterrupted flow of continuity in the relating of his *own* romance. I had diverted his frantic tale and brought into play a totally unrelated concern, with a different girl entirely: one, moreover, that was *mine*, not *his*.

But yet, come to think of it—and I *did* come to think of it, with a rather glaring lucidity—*were* the two girls *that* unrelated? A horrible coincidence was arising.

"I beg to inform you; Ira, what I've just been realizing. Not only is the girl *I* love named Marylin as well; (for what's in a name?', quoth the bard); but they *are* the same person."

"What:?" Ira jumped. We were now enemies, that was clear.

We wore rivals-in-distress, adversaries in adversity; I was now on the tail-end of my fifth-gin-and-tonic. Ira had been consuming scotch, meanwhile, at virtually the same rate. We glowered at each other. Marylin's image stood between us. We both loved her, in vain.

This called for an explanation—the coincidence. However improbable, it was now possible; remotely it had been *im*possible.

Yes, she *did* work in Ira's corporation, as a typist, file clerk, and occasional telephone receptionist. Ira, in fact, *was* her immediate supervisor: a point of advantage with him, that called up envy in me. *I* was is bitter contestant.

Yes, she was the one and same person. We compared descriptions, they jibed precisely. Even her last name was the same, and she shared one same skin complexion, hair color, height, build, and personality with her own self. She was away on a forced vacation though in the big business season of early spring, due to an out-of-town family affair that demanded her presence. Would Ira and I fight? What difference would it make? The winner might no more easily get her than the loser would. Perhaps she had a secret beau, and was dating steady, or already engaged. This would drive a bond between Ira and me. Equal victims of her betrayal.

Ira and I by now had consumed even more of our respective beverages and were unhappily drunk. Also, we regarded each other uneasily. We were rivals for a beauty's hand. What was fair, in this contest?

But we were both undeclared to her. We were cowards, in imaginary palaces of hope. Not bold enough to dare advance.

We built a pact between us, the rules of our game. We would cease to be withdrawn, one by one. Marylin would be forced to *choose* between us, if her heart was free and so inclined. We'd wait for her return; then, by turn, Ira first and me last (he had *confessed* first, or confided, and so had earned the opportunity conferred on precedence to take the prior leap), ask for her aloof hand. To the victor, goes Marylin.

"Why did you never ask her out?" I asked.

"I was too shy," came the admission. "Though I would ogle her in the office, very furtively. I could order her around. But I'd lack the courage even to invite her to lunch. But *you* don't work there. How do *you* know her?"

I answered I had met her occasionally in a circle of friends and had enjoyed (suffered?) her casual contact, I had been afraid to force the issue of my heart, fearing that I'd scare her away altogether. Better to see her occasionally slightly, than deeply but never. The staunch philosophy of a coward.

Ira and I were like each other; we had a similar interest in common, and had been equally reticent in pushing out for attainment. Our drinking stopped, we could hold no more. The moment blurred, and time went by. The calendar turned its pages. Marylin was back in town. First Ira, then I, would siege her, successively in showdown. The contest was on.

The result was in, on Ira's campaign: it had failed. He had been turned down, outright.

My turn, next. To present a persuasive suit.

So I did, but got rejected.

Love was over, its present object having spurned us both.

Forever more, I avoided Ira; and he me. We wanted no more reminders, of failure and prophetic cowardice,

Goodbye Ira, and Marylin. I'm in my newest phase of life. You're neither included. I need to forget. For that purpose, the past posts its memory.

THE ABJECT RIDICULE OF UNLOVED LOVING, INFLATED TO THE CRUSADE OF A FOOL'S PUBLIC ROLE

Do you love her?

Yes, in order not to waste her beauty.

Does your loving her *consume* her beauty?

It has, with time's help. She was twenty-four when I *started* loving her, and thirty-two now. Her beauty is slightly fading.

Is that attributable to *time* primarily, or to the wearing effect of your *love*?

To time, for she hasn't *allowed* my love to wear her out.

She spurns use, to be preserved?

No, she submits her use to my *rival's* successful hands, keeps his body in a boil of company, inscribes her artful whims and arduous devices on his bold heart's heaven of high ardor for her. Mirrored in him, her resourceful bloom bulges out into June's primary bough of blossoms that pop the eye open.

Then she's quite occupied with *him*, and has no use for *you*?

She *confides* in me, when things go wrong between them, or excel her capacity to keep quiet about them.

Does that console your romantic frustration with her?

It despairs it into angry defeat. I hate the rival she confides in me about. I advise her to exchange him for me. She requires in me a *disinterested* confidence, and scolds my affection for exceeding those bounds she's drawn for friendship's exchange of limping wisdom and pouting loyalty. "Don't be personal," she drives in, with her sticky refrain of self-love. She toys with my adoration and drains it into anguish. "Let me complain about him," she goes on, while I sigh and pine to compress those lips into a kiss worn and owned by my proprietary lips. Then she tells me, while I must chastely look on and hear with restraint, of the riveting magnet and steel web of entrapment she's snared by, in the conquering arms and heroic cruelty, the snarl and sweat of secret secretion, at the pumping device of her mighty warrior. How he plays with her!, while I must play the harmless brother, the morbid recipient of her coy aftermaths from a dank nest of lust. I'm tempted to utter torment, but must press myself still, and listen like a priest whose balls of youth were a recent charity donation. And my love soars higher, in the flaming fuel of futility.

Must you *submit* to this torturer?

So long as love's grip binds me fast to her.

As the wrinkles creep upon her face, your love will alter.

Jealousy offsets time. I spy upon her lover, and his rival triumph steels my doom in monumental masochism. I belong to them. Let *him* confide in me, too. My role is such misery, I inherit its per-

manence and wear it in fool's livery. Misfortune won't let me go.
I perpetuate its state.

Then as you volunteer, you deserve no pity. Go and rejoice: and
live mocked to your perverse choice. Tragedy is contemptuous,
from its surly height, of your puny willingness to be played on.
Serve the one you love. And lose in repeated exile from dignity's
quiet loss. Be the debased dramatized villain of your created perversity. (*Other blushes in shame. The curtain ends his ignominy, with
its rescuing intrusion. In mercy, it covers his embarrassment from public exposure, and drives it back into the self-ridicule of privacy, where
it may pluck at itself in rage and futility, spared from the sentiment of
sympathy. The audience is relieved of its ordeal as a witness. A lacer-
ated fool creates discomfort in those he compels to contemplate him as a
pathetic spectacle. The audience is released to normal pursuits.*)

REDUCED TO TOTAL DESPAIR,
HOW COULD I EVER REPAIR?
LIFE JUST DOESN'T SEEM VERY FAIR.

If you love somebody,
ask her to requite you,
so you'll be in a better position,
and it won't be an imposition.
But what if she refuses?
For you she has no uses,
explaining: "I don't give a damn
about your so-called love for me.
So why don't you go climb a tree?"
Thus rejected,
I felt dejected
and totally disrespected.
Slowly I walked back home to the tenements,
burdened with my lonely sentiments.

MY SUPERIOR RIVAL

**LOVE IS UNRELIABLE
AND SUBJECT TO A SUPERIOR RIVAL
WHO RENDERS YOU DEPRIVABLE
OF THE WOMAN YOU WANTED
AND ON WHOM YOU COUNTED
AND HOPED TO HAVE MOUNTED.**

Love of course is a gamble.
Its potential is ample
that it gives us one united heart,
with each expected to do our part.
However, regarded as an upstart,
I'm frowned and dismissed
instead of ravagely kissed
by your thrown arms on my shoulder
to inflame me to be bolder.
Why should you suddenly have turned colder?
Love is fickle-hearted, at least,
though it starts off by unleashing the beast.
I must gnaw on a bare bone
rather than join in a voluminous feast.
I'm abandoned, and left on my own
to find my misery newly grown
to the musical background of my moan.
Down on my luck, I'll ask for a loan.

**GETTING REJECTED BY BRIGID
DESPITE MY BODY BECOMING RIGID.
SHE FROZE ME OUT, FRIGID.**

Sitting next to Brigid,
my body soon grew rigid.

I told her, confidentially,
that my cock grew exponentially
as we sat alone together
in a snugly tight tether.
To back up what I'd just said,
I asked her to consider that we wed.
She pondered on this proposal
which I put toward her disposal.
Finally she replied: "No, thanks."
(At that, my optimism sank.)
She went on, saying:
"I'm already engaged
to someone your superior,
by which token you're inferior.
I adore him to the extent
that I must frustrate your attempt."
Thus ended my flirtation with Brigid
who eked cold air, frigid,
and made me feel like a midget,
a stupid and dumb idiot
in miscalculation,
lacking Brigid's invitation
to her life and also body
that frustrated lust came to embody.
I was a lonely study,
not being Brigid's buddy
with permission to be cuddly.

THE "SUPERIOR RIVAL" DIALOGUE.

I was dating a girl, but my Superior Rival took her away.

Did at least you resist him? Or were you a pushover?

I tried to clutch on to that special girl, whom I aspired to marry, but on his arrival my Superior Rival just swept her away. I offered practically no contest, as his superiority just cleared the field of me and left her well within his jurisdiction.

Did he marry her?

He had no intentions to. Finally he abandoned her.

Now she's free for you to reclaim.

I tried, but she pitied me.

Why?

He was such a hard act to follow.

No wonder you call him "my Superior Rival."

At least I know my place in relation to him.

Now I have no respect for you.

(Ironically:) That's it: Hit me while I'm down. You're a true friend.

Former friend.

MY SUPERIOR RIVAL
STOLE MY WOMEN UPON ARRIVAL.

My Superior Rival stares me down
and I wilt in front of him
who wears a superior frown.
Whenever I fancy a new woman,
he sniffs it out and out-wins her,
leaving me in the dusty lurch,
so I have to take consolation in Church,
where I sit in a long row and weep,
inwardly calling my Superior Rival a "creep."
How does he step along a line of women so steep
who all crave him, and I get none?

He's a masculine man whose physique can stun.
When women look at him, they sigh: "Number One!"
and dream of hugging that big lug.
The image of him bites them like a bug
and creates unusual commotion
by plunging his loins into mechanical motion.
Perhaps he partakes of some superior lotion
that stirs women into more feminine emotion?
They amply display their curves
that play upon his groin-deep nerves.

MY SUPERIOR RIVAL ROBS ME BLIND.

Couldn't I enjoy my women in peace? Why does my Superior
Rival compulsively have to wrest them away from me?

Because he values your taste in women, which he wants to cash in
on.

But at my deprivation!

Well, if you want to make an omelette, you have to crack an egg
or two.

Why do I always turn up losing, as he adds up his women conquests at my expense?

Because he's a successful predatory exploiter, valuing your initial
good taste for his own rapid acquisitions of delectable women.

Isn't he a parasite?

Sure. Give him credit.

But it's immoral, if I suffer. I'm like a pimp.

I'm sure he's grateful. You produce.

Not willingly.

If he steals women, go acquire more.

It takes time and effort for my wooing them.

With him, he just grabs. No sweat.

This is a free market economy. There's no equality among consumers.

They flock to him.

I'm envious *and* jealous.

Pick one. Don't be a hog.

THE EVIL THEFTS OF MY SUPERIOR RIVAL.

I didn't dare desire any special woman, for fear that my Superior Rival would hear about it and then step in to deny me of her favors and grab them for himself.

You feared his intervention, in his huge sexual greed, finding his prey by learning that you coveted her and then simply stealing her from under you.

The bully! He used me as a scout for discovering the most desirable women to go after, at my sudden loss.

Could you resort to the law and sue him?

No, it's a free market for success to triumph at failure's expense.

So you were the fall guy, and he beefed up on your finds. You were his unwilling scout.

The exploiter!

You served him, ironically.

Is there any justice in this world?

Yes, for predators like him. He rules.

Am I a permanent underdog? Have I any recourse?

Yes. Conceal your women from his opportunistic discovery and raid.

I'll hide them in an underground shelter.

Yes, like a subway station after midnight. Good luck. He'll come up from the screeching tracks and bite you.

A subway rat! Make room for nightmare time! Free nightmares, all night.

Well, the morning rush hour will afford relief.

Only if I wake up, to nurse my bites amid the gawking crowd, with police nestling in.

MY SUPERIOR RIVAL,
DOOMING MY COMPETITIVE SURVIVAL
TO NIL, ON HIS VICTORIOUS ARRIVAL.

My successful rival took away my woman,
by charisma I couldn't match.
If she's so easily go-awayable,
why would I anyway continue to want her?
So "good riddance," I climactically concluded,
and blessed my Superior Rival for relieving me
of someone, by his snatching her, of reduced value.
Without his intervention, would she have remained true?
Why should I resume puzzling that?
She's gone, he got her, and that's that.
Do I need challenging him to wrestle on a mat
to see if my slim chances could have been fat?
She's gone, he has her, so goodbye.
Now I'll seek a new woman to hide from him,
who if he found her, he'd steal her on a whim,
allowing jealousy and envy to eat me grim,
as my romantic eyes close wet-fully dim.

Oh my superior rival!
He ruined me by his arrival.

MY SUPERIOR RIVAL
DEMOLISHED ME UPON ARRIVAL,
DEPRIVING ME OF SURVIVAL
IN SEXUAL ROMANCE—
A BITTER GAME OF CHANCE.

Anne was my favorite dame.
But I was put to shame
when my Superior Rival—along he came
to intervene and take Anne away
to screw her right and left,
centralized by her cleft.
Anne now was no longer mine.
My Superior Rival is doing fine,
having stolen her from me
like an ape who clambers up a tree
with Anne wriggling by his side
like looted booty:
my pilfered beauty.
Anne belongs to my Superior Rival,
who readied to snatch her upon arrival
for his promiscuous sexual survival,
compared to me:—I'm down in the dumps,
left to take my battered lumps,
contemplating suicidal jumps
for lack of female rumps.

HOW I LOST NANCY
IN THE FRUSTRATION OF MY FANCY
TO LIGHT UP HER WHOLE PANTSY.

I had my sexual eye on Nancy,
whose assets were more than fancy,
so I asked her for a date
with the prospect later we may mate.
But Nancy alas refused.
Was my ego bruised!
Angry, I was not amused.
Her excuse given to me
was: She just wasn't free,
because my Superior Rival
had dated her upon arrival,
spelling doom for my survival
in the longed-for Nancy stakes.
I was damn defeated, for heaven's sakes.
So Nancy was out of the question,
and my lust had to quest on.
My prospects for Nancy were gone
to quell my fire, good and done.
Sadly, Nancy is not the candidate
with whom to make a successful date
with the promised prize that we may mate.
Will frustration blame "Fate"
That's the usual scapegoat
for when my eager boat
stays at the dock and refuses to float.
Don't you dare snicker or gloat,
or I'll kick you under the castle's moat.

SUPERIOR RIVAL STEALS MARY.

My strenuous love for Mary
was treated most contrary.
She shocked me with rejection
that marred my perfection
as a perfect marriage candidate.
We'd already made the date,
which she annulled right away
when she was the victim of a play
of seduction by my successful Rival
who spotted her just on arrival
to the scene and took her from my grasp
as I watched in horror, all aghast,
when Mary submitted to that obvious thief
of love, costing me endless grief.
I punched him in the nose for relief,
but he sued me and won Mary,
whom then he proceeded to carry
into their far away honeymoon
serenaded by Mary's panting swoon.
There I was, a defeated man
thanks to my successful Rival
who militated against my survival
as Mary's intended husband.
I was polished off and sent to the dustbin,
since my Superior Rival had to win,
and drove me to booze, mainly gin.
Mary meanwhile enjoyed a lecherous grin
at my severe loss, thanks to my Rival's spin.
My outlook never recovered from being grim.
She had to choose between me and him,
knowing my chances were exceedingly slim

when he pounced and won her on a whim,
even though Mary wasn't his type,
causing me a further gripe.
I swallowed my windmill through my pipe.

THE BROKEN MARRIAGE,
INCLUDING THE LONGED-FOR BABY CARRIAGE
AND ITS DEEPLY MISSED BABY
WHOM WE WOULD HAVE LOVED, MAYBE.

Are you sure that love is the best thing,
considering what assets it will bring
to the sheer togetherness of life
between adoring husband and requiting wife?
Yes, and therefore we agreed to marry.
When love is obvious, then why tarry?
Securely we sealed our love with a kiss,
and opened wide the gate to mutual bliss.
So how could anything come amiss?
Suddenly my "wife" had remained a "miss."
A horribly handsome rival came into the mix.
She preferred him, so her attitude to me turned to "nix."
So my sure marriage came suddenly off the books,
thanks to my improvised rival, one of the worst crooks.
He stole her already promised heart
with such betrayal, I stopped feeling smart.
What could I do with my broken love?
There were no gods to appeal to above.
So I was stuck with my mystery,
a discordant note to romantic history.

SO MANY THAT FAILED
TILL I PERMANENTLY AILED.

I lost my girlfriend to another foe,
who won her love and gave me woe.
So sadly I gave her up.
Which new woman will fill my old cup?
So I went on a series of dates
to feel out possible necessary mates.
Finally I was passionately chosen
by a warm woman who thawed when frozen.
We married soon with the maximum haste,
so none of our lust will go to waste.
However, soon she betrayed me
with another she loved better.
So again I failed as a go-getter.
By now, I was too old to try again.
(I was not so lusty as back then.)
So Death smelled a new candidate
for his next dark, ghostly date.
He became my temporary mate.
As a match, neither of us could wait
to seize the opportunity and make it inflate.
It dignified our new, unearthly state.
We married, and it was first-rate.
However, he was so promiscuous,
our silly marriage seemed mischievous.
His other spouses were all suspicious
that perhaps it wasn't so delicious.
Did I mix up the genders?
Now I must wear suspenders.

TENDERNESS APPLYING ELSEWHERE

"Toward you I have such tenderness!" he said. "I don't toward you." she replied. So his tenderness changed into bitter anger; finally into indifference. So he forgot her. He never bothered to try to see her again. He kept his tenderness, took it with him where he went, and applied it to new things, new people. It had once been "intended" for her: it had had a "tendency" toward her. With her "no," it went elsewhere—where it was more welcome, and could lavish itself the more for being welcome, like the free spirit of a fountain enamoured by the neighboring cool air that drinks in its melodious spray and clamours, "More!"

With a twinge of regret, years later, the tenderness shook its sad head: "Too bad. She would have been great, for me."

REVERSAL AND ITS EFFECT

All my energy was funnelled into overwhelming passionate concentration on this one girl I met and was talking to. The dose was overpowering, I trained my batteries of attention on her to such an imposing pitch of intensity that threatened to explode and shatter us both. It was unfair to subject her nerves to this. She would loathe me at this rate, in my obnoxious invasion, my immoderately premature romantic assault.

Therefore I desisted. I went limp, with total indifference. The shock made me essential to her. She's pursued me ever since.

LOVE

(Dialogue with explanatory title:)

**FIRST LUSTING FOR, THEN LOVING, A LADY IN A PAINT-
ING, BY A MUSEUM SPECTATOR LOOKING AT AN OLD
MASTER. DIFFERENCES BETWEEN ART AND LIFE, AS
WELL AS SIMILARITIES, COME OUT IN THIS MUSEUM
SCENE, TAKING THE FORM OF A SPOKEN DIALOGUE
BETWEEN THE LUSTER-LOVER AND HIS MORE SENSI-
BLE COMPANION WHO SERVES AS HIS FOIL. THE THIRD
CHARACTER IS THE WOMAN IN THE PAINTING; BUT
SHE'S SUCH A SIGHT, SHE'S GIVEN AN UNSPOKEN PART
(SHE'S FOREIGN ANYWAY, AND NEVER KNEW ENGLISH).
THE SCENE IS SET. IT WOULD *UP*SET, SHOULD IT BE
*OB*SCENE. END OF TITLE. SPEAK, ACTORS.**

My cock is beginning to get long and hard while I contemplate
that lady's breasts and her hips, God I'm so stiff now.

But we're in a museum and "that lady" you're referring to is a
series of painted daubs on a painted canvas framed as a painting
and painted centuries ago, now a valuable old master worthy of its
prominent wall space in this fine old public museum maintained
at the taxpayer's expense. You're a fool, your reaction was out of
place.

You mean this museum was the wrong place for my sexual arouse-
ment? Or you mean the crotch of my pants trousers was the wrong
place for my phallic inflammation? Use wards precisely. They're
for conveying meaning.

I mean that your reaction should not come at the hands of a *painting*.

The *hands* didn't arouse me—the breasts and hips are what did it.

You exasperate me. I mean to say, if you'll only let me, that you're
a living and real person and the lady in the picture is not and

shouldn't be regarded as such and you take her too literally when you give her a sexual response, which is like Don Quixote thinking that the windmill is a real dragon and so charging at it to get sliced up and his lance batted away, his horse knocked down too, and bodily bruises through his plate armor.

That's not what that painted lady did to *me*.

She didn't have to; the point is, Don Quixote and you were equally the victims of erroneous supposition, foolish to act upon your delusions.

If I really *did* act, there would be a hole perforated in that canvas where the lady is, and guess where the hole would be?

It would be reckless vandalism, public insanity, indecent morality.

Are those criminal charges?

They *would* have been, had your lust gotten out of hand.

I didn't have my hand on it in the *first* place.

No, but you made your point.

Oh.

(Pause. Then last speaker resumes:)

Listen, what's art? Why is that painted lady art despite her being made centuries ago, and me not art though I'm real and living? It just doesn't seem fair. Why should *she* have all the advantage? Just because she posed as a model for the master and the painting turned out great so this museum dipped into taxpayers' fund to buy it from a foreign country to be so hung here that my cock stuck out at the sight of her though she's not living, and though she still looks young she's now probably a skeleton in a graveyard of the same country where the artist painted her? What is art, and why doesn't it include me?

I don't know aesthetics enough to define art. But you *could* become art if a great painter put you in his picture—in *paint*, of course, not as you *are*.

What's the difference? It's the same *me*. I want to be immortal.

Why? Are you tired of living?

I'm tired of being only me as me. It seems so short-term, trivial, local, and not far-reaching enough. I wish to endure. I can't *create*; so then let me *be* created—as *lasting*, not as clay.

Then get a job as an artist's model and pray he does well enough for critics to recommend his painting of you to posterity and their heirs forever.

How should I pose? In the nude?

I'm no artist; it's up to *him*.

Who's "him?"

The artist who would immortalize you.

Oh. How much will it cost me?

Fool! *You'll* be paid. The artist will pay *you*!

But it's *my* privilege to get immortalized. I should be paying *him*.

Money and immortality don't mix.

Oh.

(Pause. Last speaker resumes:)

Why are we still looking at the naked-lady picture?' We've looked at it so long now it must seem like we *own* it.

Looking *confers* ownership.

You mean "I'm master of all I survey?"

To that effect, yes.

Then let's wrap that painting up and I'll take it home with me. Maybe the museum guard will help us. He stands idle all day like a dummy in a uniform. Let's inform him. The painting is ours—or *mine*. My intention is to *marry* that lady. I've lusted for her so long, I'd rather marry than burn. At least my *intentions* are honorable.

But how can you, who are real and living, marry with a painted *image*? That's legally perverse. That's sin versus art. You're crazy just to *contemplate* it; you're *worse* crazy if you *do* it.

But I'm a man of action. *(As though quoting:)* Man cannot live by thought alone. By *deeds*, are we known. And *bold* deeds bespeak the bold man: more than the mere speech of words can.

It *sounds* impressive. But the law says that no living man can take a dead woman for wife.

Dead! Why, *look* at her. She looks younger than me! Almost *too* young, in fact.

Looks, looks; but not *is*.

But she's *alive*; can't you see it? Her skin glows. She's burning with inside fire, her form is the bristling seat of spirit. She lives. The artist *intended* her to; he succeeded, he endowed her with immortal life. Otherwise, why would this venerable institution, this taxpayer's drainpipe, this so-called museum, have paid hard cash to a foreign country for this picture I covet? Isn't that sensible?

Your logic skips few heart murmurs or pulse beats in its vital reasoning. Otherwise, you're dead right.

Well, I *want* her *(Pointing:)*—that woman; Do I need her parents' consent?

They're dead too. The *artist's* consent would do—*he's* her parent, for her life came from the vivid brushwork of his fine loins. But *he's* dead too.

All those foreigners are dead; I'm glad I live in *this* country.

Stop your petty patriotism. It's out of place before this great work of art. For art is *universal*.

What does "universal" mean?

It transcends country and age—it's for all times, and anywhere.

Then it's good for *me* in *my* home. I wish to marry the lady. The artist is too dead to grant his permission. Shall I make the request of the museum curator, then?

If you do, he'll arrest you, or have you "put away."

As certifiably insane?

That's the official term: And he'd be acting in his official capacity.

But I *love* that lady in the picture.

Love? Oh, that puts a different complexion on it.

You mean the lady blushes at the word? *(Admiring her, fondling her from a distance, possessively:)* The innocent dear! Can she hear me?

No, what I meant is that love is sacred. With mere lust to recommend your carrying her away, you'd have no ghost of a chance. But *love*—is a different story. The law makes exceptions, where love is concerned. For "all the world loves a lover."

Ah, so love entitles me to her. Thank God for love. It slips around, any legal loophole. Let's ask that museum guard for wrapping paper. My bride-to-be, my intended, my betrothed, must be carted home *in style*. I won't just *drag* her away—that would be rough caveman technique. I'm civilized. I love art.

HOW, UPON REFLECTION, TO BE AMOROUS

(A Mirror's Eye View of a Girl Narcissist Stripped to the Quick of the Nude With a Self-Devoured Image)

(Characters: The male interrogator, and the gleaming, reminiscing, though flat-chested, mirror: who lives off Nancy, who's reflected indirectly in this play.)

Are you a thinker?

Yes. I reflect a lot.

What are your reflections?

It depends on who stands in front of me.

Then you're a—

—Yes, a mirror. Isn't that mercurial of me!

Quicksilverish. You're sure on the beam.

I give off rays too.

That's to be expected, considering what you are.

Let's not make a scene.

You can; I can't.

Are you jealous of my powers?

Yes, for their psychic penetration.

Quest me, and I'll reveal.

I will. Do you detect vanity?

In those who peer into me, yes.

The naked girls ever peer into you?

Yes. What an eyeful I get!

But don't you want to screw them then?

How can I? I'm only a mirror.

Oh yes: I forget.

I can't. It's *easy* to remember I'm a mirror.

What's your formula?

When people look into me privately, I *know* I'm a mirror!

Full length, no less?

You bet! Otherwise, how can I pursue my lechery to the bottom, in the case of unclad girls?

Did you fall in love with a pretty one?

Yes, and she *requited* me! She's in love with me, too.

How can that be?

She's narcissistic, that's why. She falls in love with what she sees in me. And what an immense deal she can project!

But are you confident in being equal to it?

Must I draw a picture for you? I'm quite faithful, in regards to her. Is that clear?

Illuminating, in fact. You paint a very bright picture.

Nancy deserves it—that delightful creature! How radiant she is! *(Aside:)* (I see to that, in fact. She and I see eye to eye. We make a perfect pair. -The ideal couple: a girl and a girl.)

But are you the mere passive recipient of her glorious being?

What more splendid occupation could I want? That lovely bundle of limbs, in full magnetic color!

But can you call yourself a man, if you haven't *consummated* your love?

Don't get me wrong. I *do* consummate our love; in my own way.

How?

Platonically. For my strength, you see, is in reflection.

I see, Quite a nice voyeur's spectacle, you have, open in front of you. Plenty revealing, I bet.

If there's any revealing to do, I do it. Nancy is plenty satisfied with me. I do her justice.

I'm sure you do. Is there any doubting you?

I'm too *straight* to be doubted. I'm fair.

Impartial to all comers?

Especially with Nancy—whose treatment gets special preference, with favors thrown in; and deservedly so.

Do you get a *complete* view?—unobstructed? All her ample charms open to you, with positive clarity?

I take no chances that I might miss anything. To *assist* my sharp vision I wear a pair of contact lenses. (Concealed in my frame, of course.)

But why do you require such an aid? Aren't you *already* a glass?

You've captured the very split image of me. Bright of you to detect that! I *like* being seen for what I am.

Yet isn't there a vicarious side to your nature, undeniably?

Oh, I exist for other people. I'm not the selfish type.

You *are* nice. Nancy's the name of this voyeur's paradise you're passionately involved with?

Yes. We're deep in love.

She gazes arduously at you? With a sigh of visible longing? Panting with the refined perfection of desire, in its highest sublimated state?

I'm lucky in love. But I return it. I return every inch of the love she pours into me by way of a safe investment with the maximum return. At the highest interest. My reputation is at stake. I'm a broker you can trust in. My methods are appallingly direct!

You reflect it all back?

Instantly, not the slightest delay.

What a beauteous narcissist she must be! That arousing little piece! What signals there must be, fleshed back and forth between you!

Love invents games, yes. And what private parts she has! I'm their intimate at all corresponding levels. I instantly devour her luscious everything.

You must hate to relinquish them, once they're so amorously flashed. You must long to hold on to them, not have to give them back;

It's my job to send them back, alas. *(Chants, philosophically:)* What do we own? What is ours? All is borrowed. In all the hours.

Are you reflecting poetically?

Yes, but I prefer reflecting Nancy: whose body is a flow of poetry, needing no rhyme.

Whisper me a secret.

Yes?

Can you reflect on her kissing?

I can, But *first she* kisses *me*. I'm shy, you see,

Can't Nancy *cure* your shyness? That bold thing!

Her boldness *needs* my modest shyness, as its suitable counterpart, and its flatter-fawning foil. *I* can't presume. But she can. And I back her up every time. To fail her would crack my game, completely.

How faithful you are!

How easy it is, being faithful to her! A fundamental task in aesthetics, purely considered.

But you lack initiative. She must make the advances.

But they're returned, in kind. I'm never disappointing. Her self-love is all I crave. I fill in the rest. And do my job. And bask, in her image.

Is *she* the radiant one? Or are you? Or do you just have the negative role, like a supporting actor who brings out the *prima donna* fully while himself relegated to background? I'm not insulting you: but *is* your role the negative one?

It's *positive* where *she*'s concerned. *Glow*ingly so. I'm content. *she* certainly is. May her youth be kept, And I'll keep up. And on and on, we'll go.

Then your love is permanent?

As eternal as she is. And that's the end I serve: infinite.

Are you idealizing her?

No. My speciality is in detailed realism. But *she* can take it. And comes back for more. And she gets it. And likes it. While I adore.

She's loving?

Reflecting her loveliness. In matching measure. And to the essence of symmetry.

May God behold. For *I* do.

LOVE'S ROMANTIC SOAR ON WINGS UNCRITICALLY VAGUE

How I love romance!

Why?

Because romance leads love into itself until it surrounds itself through and through!

Romance does all that?

Yes, that's what romance does to love.

Then love is easily led.

By *romance* it is; but by what else? It will not indiscriminately be duped, or else it's done for. Love will be cajoled by the blandishments of *romance*'s syrupy ooze; and on sentiment's soft clouds the wonder-wings of delusion loft love to an illusionary grandeur. I sigh and pine for a girl my eye has in mind. But when the mind retracts its endorsement, the bare eye loses its grip and the girl drops out. Love must be dream-blent, and image-diffused.

Oh. What girl is your mind seeing now?

Love's girl, nameless by sight, but held in solemn testimonial by my dream's arresting power to delay from flight, Love perches as its willing captive.

What does love purchase?

No, it *perches*. My trapped girl is *mine*, in a mental swoon.

Does that girl have a counterpart in the world of *existence*?

Yes, the *true* version of her is owned alive by herself in a matter of physical being.

Have you notified *that* aspect of her?

I wouldn't tamper with her oblivion, nor molest the ignorance she bestows on me. Her innocence legitimizes my love, by preserving

it from the harsher test of her cooperation, suspicion, unrequital,
A dream sustains the affirmative. Love wouldn't escape the wakeful jolt of day. Love takes refuge in a smoking screen of secrecy.

What a lack of daring you have!

I don't *scorn* my lack, but *bless* it. Love *must* be scared. It lives a coward, but dies too brave.

You'll not *declare* your love?

Not to the girl for destroying it. But to my soul for conservation.

Love's economy is by *withholding*?

For evading *death*'s magic truth, yes. Why wake up mourning, and endure grief's bite, bitten by your bitter bit? No, better by far is what the *dream* disguises, to impose what's supposed and drown the unruly fact.

What's her hair's color, and her eyes'?

Love is colorless. Love is featureless. Love is not afraid to generalize. Love would die by encountering its bold particular, in *accuracy*'s military seizure. A single girl will frighten love and frost its nipping bud. Let love fall into place. Then incidental girls will match up.

Love first, and supreme?

And girls secondary: mere figments of a dream.

And phantomed by the dream, love is heaven-kissed?

Sweetened by bars and beams force-fed by the moon, that puffy matron of all romance.

I won't look askance, but blot the sun by day.

Strip it out. Why should a *girl* interfere, in love's sacred temple whose initiates pray a blind praise and place devout vows on idols carved so holy that what we venerate is not identified but in the blurred image to amaze that's hazy lights up love's blaze, to show the blessing of diffusion, beauty's groped-for ideal in the ecstasy of notion. And love's mute sound, edgeless, tunes an indefinite echo. Guided by these vibrations, why should we specify? Love tolls all tinkles at once. A radiance countlessly muffled. On love's rainbow fog, kiss the anonymous girl unsharpened by singularity. What universal meat her bulge will be, to fingers dully sensitized: To be blunt, pour lust in. *Then* who will she be?

A CONFESSION

"Everything I say goes *through* you, such is the gossip you are. I want to be able to confide in you, it would relieve me to divulge things of a serious nature if only it were in the strictest of confidence in your receiving it. But no, it goes right through you, and I find myself violated, or betrayed, by your slack respect for the exclusive privacy of what I need to get off my chest. This is such a disappointment! I do resent your taking it so lightly. I won't tell you another thing again—except what I've just said. It infuriates me, how you just thoughtlessly repeat what's so *sacred* to me that it should only be between me and you. You make light of it. It's your frivolous nature too. Well, out you go from my life as a friend. I've had enough; you sure shirked your assigned function. You've abused me, with extreme disloyalty. So you'll not be told a thing again, unless in anger I care to scold you like this again, to remind you of your offense, since your ease will probably forget it, while in me it keeps rankling, like some curse that's never had enough revenge."

Thus she scolded; on and on. I let her. Once she was done, I touched her, and we had sex. Afterward, she moaned low murmurings, which I remembered in order to repeat, such is thy passion I have for gossip, welcoming to be told only what can most fascinatingly be revealed. It's a mania with me. I can't stop it.

I left the bed, got dressed, and abused her privacy to all I could get a hold of, by phone and in person. Her secrets became open, and shared, through me, by strangers and malicious people. It was her weakness to keep confiding in me; and mine, to relish, even to the point of betrayal, the retelling of her confidences—almost by design to the moat inappropriate people. But she couldn't get rid of me, or leave me, because we were intimately bound. But how cruel could I be, in her case. She, only, tempted me. I wasn't cruel to others, but this one.—well, I can't explain it. She sort of provoked me. I was riled, I had to do it. Poor Sandra, did she really deserve it? Still, she came back for more. It was *her* doing, as well.

A MAN AND WOMAN ARE TOGETHER AS EACH OTHER'S INVENTIONS

(Man and woman; Man's first to speak.)

If I hadn't met you, I would have invented you.

But would I have been the same me, if I were your invention?

Hard to tell. I would have wanted to invent you along the specification lines of the you I've known; but how would I have known what they were, if I hadn't known you? And if I *had* known you, I wouldn't have had to invent you—there would have been no necessity. Maybe, after all (or before all), meeting you *was*, in effect, the inventing of you.

I *was* invented by you when you met me, for meeting you made me a different me. Our meeting was the invention of me, as confirmed by our later knowing and knowing each other deeply. I like being your invention. Let's keep together, so I remain so.

I have to stand by my invention. It's being reinvented as itself, by our continued being together. Inventions, left alone, lose their force. Renewal is sustenance, preservation, maintenance, and furtherance. Let's always have each other. I'm me by virtue of your invention of me as such. I apply for renewed license. In this vein, let me be.

TWO OCCUPANTS IN A ONE-ROOM APARTMENT. MORN-ING.

(Woman and man. She begins:)

It's morning. You're lying in bed. But you're no longer asleep. This is not a bedroom, but a one-room apartment, including kitchen, study-room, dining room, etc., all in one large room-space, except for the of-course segregated bathroom, which has its own independent door for locking. I have things to do now, here, up and active. But the window slats and shutters and blinds are closed. You, if you wish, can go on with your lying in bed. But do you mind if I go ahead and let the light in?

I wouldn't mind. But wouldn't the world outside *need* that light?

It has enough, out there, on such a bright day. It's no loss to the *world*, if a little of its precious light would stray in *here*. It has heaps of abundance, with enough to spare.

Enough to go all around? Unlike the food problem?

If only food were as cheap, and plentiful, as light! No one would then go hungry, on all the sides and surfaces of our world. But food is dear, while light and air roam free for all eyes and noses.

So as I lie here, pull up the blinds, and let the light pour in. Let it flood our little apartment, here. Then with clear eyes, do your visual work.

I will, for *time* is plentiful, too.

Is it? Then lend me some.

You don't need it. You're only lying there. Don't you have enough of your own?

Lying here requires as much quantity of time as all your useful activity going about.

Well, use your *own* time, for lying down. I need *mine*, for what *I*'m doing.

I'd return it, if you loaned me some—even with interest. .

Time is just simply not transferable, from one individual to another. Any more than our noses are. (Barring surgery, of course, which could graft them interchangeably. But equally silly an idea.)

All right, but let's keep time together.

We are. Aren't we lovers, living together? We each give freely to the other of what we have—time included. It's all part of our open, trustful sharing, the generous marriage of our lives. Light, love, time, all intertwined, in a one-room apartment. As well as *outside*, of course. Where the *world* will soak us in. We melt into its history. It's shaped to include us. Our energies lend nicely in. The human team, not just us.

Good. When the light pours in here, as I lie down, I feel a fine blending. With you and all. Light, time, love, and all that the world can afford. Our one ride, in lonely space.

TWO MEN TALK, THEN ONE REMAINS TO TALK WITH A WOMAN WHO APPEARS LATER

(Scene: In the street, ogling women.)

That plain-looking girl is trying to look pretty.

Oh, And *that* plain-looking girl *(Pointing in another direction.)* has given up; she's *resigned* to looking plain.

Tragic, that God mismatched her features.

But her mother and father were *equally* mismatched.

How?

Their sexes were totally dissimilar.

Oh. Now it's plain to see why that girl's plain.

Yeah. She should have come from a *homosexual* marriage. That would have given her features a more equal symmetry.

Blend them into a harmony, therefore a beauty?

So it appears, or seems.

But her problem *does* seem to he the matter—or manner—of appearance.

But if her problem is *real* to her, how can it be one of *appearance*?

It's *plainly* real; therefore her appearance is plain.

Real in the plain sense?

Not, alas, in the pretty sense.

I see. You make it pretty plain.

I'm only making sense.

And she's not making love?

Plainly, no.

She's given up. But what about the first girl—the one who's also plain, but who tries not to be?

For her, there's hope.

Through what means?

Me. I'll seduce her.

How will that improve her appearance?

By the lights being dim or totally out in the bedroom. Darkness can do wonders—especially for her complexion, if she has one. Darkness will rub out her ugliness, you bet.

But I'm in the dark how it can *permanently* deprive her of ugliness.

It can't. Seduction and good looks are only temporary.

They're good for a while?

For a while, they go very well together. A fine team, however illusory.

What about love?

That's ideal.

And sex?

That's even older than love.

Oh. Then sex is showing her age?

Yes. She's *very* dated, by now.

Then she's a wonder, how she keeps herself going.

She's helped.

Who by?

Younger men and younger women, the recent ones. They prop her up, like an aging goddess.

Does she show signs of flagging?

No. New life is pumped into her, by her various practitioners of both pronounced genders.

How are they pronounced?

In the English language.

No other tongue?

All others,

All? That's a lot of words.

A medley, even.

But how will you seduce the girl who's trying not to be plain?

By chasing her. She walked away, but I can still see her. I'm running now. Goodbye.

Goodbye. Speak plain, and you'll make out pretty well.

She'll appear like a beauty, when I'm humping her.

Why?

She'll *feel* beautiful.

Is feeling necessarily appearing?

The one who's feeling appears to herself the way she's feeling.

I feel you're right.

It would appear so.

Then you'll feel her?

Yes. I won't spare her feelings.

How will you approach her?

By asking, "How do you feel?" And she'll answer, "Feel me, and see."

That's a pretty picture.

It's only plain common sense.

Do it. Hurry.

Goodbye. *(Runs off.)*

(Watching:) In the distance, he's just accosted her. How pretty she must feel! Love does wonders, for the human sense-apparatus. We plainly go by what we feel. But feeling is an appearance. And appearance is what's real. What's real? That's plain, to the knower. What's real is what's known. The known is felt. By us, who feel. *(Pause.)* They're walking off together. Now they're vanished, from my sight. I'm left to remember. *They're* left, to feel. *(Pause.)* What

are they feeling? They're off stage, to me. To each other, they're in a vivid scene. The scene appears, to themselves, who view in participation. They're creating it. It's come alive, for them. *(Pause.)* For me, I only ponder. Being alone, is less fun, I'll find myself a woman. How will she look? Appear? Feel? Be? I'll contribute. She'll change, through me. *(Pause.)* Here's one. Hello, *(Woman walks by.)* I was ignored by her. My existence wasn't accepted, for her to act out on. I want my existence to count. I'll find someone, to whom it matters. *(Pause.)* There's a woman. Hello! Ah, she's stopping. *(Woman stops.)* There you are.

(Woman:) Who?

You.

Is *that* how I appear? To *you* I do. But to *me*, I *am*. That's how *I* feel.

Our points of view necessarily differ.

Do I look plain to you?

No. Unplain.

Explain.

You won't complain?

No. But talk on my plane.

I'll cross over, for that.

But you'll merge with me. Can't we be apart?

Yes: we'll be *a part* of *one pair*.

Us?

Us is the you-me compound.

Will it last?

Let's see.

How?

By time's test.

How stern! Will we pass?

Time will pass. That's its test for us. To pass that test, takes time.

Whose?

Ours.

When?

Now.

How *much* now?

As much as we need.

But where will the now go?

To the same now, only later.

Is now all we have?

Right now, it is.

And the next now?

That's our *latest* now. It's changed, to become *this*.

Then it's never *not* now?

Even what's remembered is remembered now. Even what we dread or anticipate or wish for or keenly await, is felt right now. Now is all we are.

Only now?

All of now.

How wide is now?

A building or street is wide; now has no width.

Then what is now?

It's what we are.

But what *are* we?

People whose lives converge, at this latest now.

And the earlier now?

That's included, in this one. All moments felt, are in attendance. The session is on. In the court of Now.

(Preamble-type title:)

A SCIENTIFIC REPORT. (WITH ME AS THE SUBJECT OF THE TEST.) A TENTATIVE "CONCLUSION" OR "RESULT" IS HERE REPORTED, IN THE TEST'S VARIOUS STAGES, AND IN MINE TOO, BEING ITS SUBJECT UNDER STRICT SCIENTIFIC SURVEILLANCE, NAMELY BY ME, THOUGH AT NO SACRIFICE TO THAT SCIENTIFIC IMPERATIVE, OBJECTIVITY. IT HAS TO DO WITH LOVE, AND YET BEING ONE WHOLE PERSON. SUBMITTED TO ALL SCIENTISTS IN THE SUBJECT WHO RISK TESTING THEMSELVES FOR THE SAKE OF PURE SCIENCE AND THE COLD ADVANCEMENT OF KNOWLEDGE. THEY BECOME OVERHEATED, IN THE PROCESS; LATER COOL DOWN. CAN THEY REMAIN WHOLE? YES, THOUGH ALTERED. NOW, TO SCIENTIFICALLY SETTLE DOWN, END THIS ELABORATE TITLE, AND PROCEED TO THE BODY OF MY TEXT, WHICH THIS TITLE THREATENS NEARLY TO DWARF SHOULD IT NOT END AT APPROXIMATELY THIS POINT, SIGNALED OFF BY THE FOLLOWING PERIOD BY WAY OF FORMAL LEAVE-TAKING PUNCTUATION—

The experiment of love. I developed myself privately (and with others socially) as a whole human being unto myself. I became a complete person with the help of years, and was establishing identity even. But it was, still, only me.

So I experimented with love. I depended on another person for love. I was no longer so self-sufficient as before.

For a while I thought I was destroyed by this love experiment. But gradually I recouped my forces, and became even stronger. I survived, helped by time.

I'm experimenting again. I'm more self-protective, this time, less vulnerable in exposure to the hazards and risks of depending for love on another.

I'm me, yet. Still me, in a different way. The love is working, I'm together with her. And I'm no less me, for it.

MY GIRL'S PRESENCE BLOCKS THE REVERIE OF HER ABSENCE AND OBSCURES HER IMAGINED SELF FROM MY DEEP DREAM'S INVERSION, HER REAL CORPOREAL NOW OPPOSES MY INDWELLING LOOK.

The last time I saw my girl was when I forgot to look; the eyes of imagery made her absence visible, But the *real* girl, jealous of her past counterpart current to my memory's loyalty, stepped "between my blind heart and its mused object, to break up that small platonic romance. She accompanied her physical violation of fantasy's faint metaphysics with this vocal defense of her envy-founded interference: "I'm here, outside you: you can't find me unless you reverse the dream-drowned direction of your inverted gaze. Go chase me, and make me concrete to form a firm perception. Realize I'm real, and find me out here."

So I really looked; but image had blocked the view.

ABSENCE'S DISTANCE, GIVING US A WORLDLY POLIT-ICAL SEPARATION WITH PUBLIC SPACE FLOWING BE-TWEEN, TERMINATED BY A TIGHT PRIVATE REUNION THAT CLOSES OUT SPACE ENTIRELY AND DRIVES THE WORLD OUT OF SIGHT

One day, even in imagination, my girl happened to be absent. She was caged in another city's time. Under those stern regulations, I began to have her forgotten. As soon as memory issued her image, the customs inspector would mark "Cancelled" from a red stamp-pad. So steep was the tariff, that a virtual embargo was making her an undesirable alien whom my quota system held off with a foreign quarantine so prohibitive, relations ceased between her national ambassador and mine: both were notified of immediate recall. This commercial blockade of affections did little to increase mutual understanding. Geopolitically, wider and wider oceans kept splashing us apart, featuring a wilderness of fish far from the coastal net of the wily fisherman. Insulated by the isolation of increasing domestic preoccupations, I decreased my interest abroad to turn inward on a policy of rapt internal affairs. In short, I was all government, and outside the worldly sphere.

Having receded from my fiscal expenditure of memory, my girl was remotely active pursuing the mechanical motions of existence not sanctioned by my official acknowledgement in any capacity. Was she feeding herself? My concern was not in session at the time. Our estrangement was dignified by a rigid code respected by international procedure. It was then that her existence was proposed to come under legislative doubt, judicially upheld, and executively ministered to by constitutional oblivion at the federal level of my self-democratic republic. In diplomatic circles, it became whispered into a rumor that I was roundly ignoring my girl. This leaked to the press, resulting in unfavorable publicity an my expense. (She was the sentimental favorite, the darling of the rabble, which my aristocratic disdain could not check.)

Pressured by public discontent, and faced by the mob ordeal of unpopularity, I effected a reversal of policy, readmitting that distant girl to so contrite a welcome as to abolish my former attitude from any admissible record. Her return made entry into my arms, and passion commemorated so dramatic a turn of event. Love took note of her present sensationalism, so unbreakable was our embrace. Lapsing out of control, I paused between pants to ask, "You're here again?" Her "Yes" was sealed inside the cavity of our four lips, and leapt from one bounding breath to mine at a merger, cave-enclosed by the air-tight fortress in the dark depths of our kiss. "We're reconciled," I analyzed, in a private aside to my mounting joy. My only duty was to yield, for sweetness was strutting her stuff. As thought was being annihilated, I could barely see it remark, "I'm swollen with wonder, my girl's the swellest thing alive." She recognized my sentiment, and deliberately enlarged those durable sparks of pleasure that were bending me to her will. "Let's *remain* this time," she required, in her confident presumption of the throne. I was too weak to make overt my entire consent, but all her pulses understood, in our flow of goodly commerce.

LOVE ENDURES, IN IMAGINARY FLIGHTS; THE GIRLS IT WAS BASED ON DISAPPEAR TO RECLAIM THEM-SELVES. LOVE KEEPS GOING. IT MOUNTS ACCUMU-LATING IN VICTORY FOR ALL THAT EACH PARTICU-LAR LOVED ONE DENIES IT. LOVE ADDS THEM ALL UP, IN A SWEEPING GAIN OVERALL, ON A MOUND OF GIRLS SUCCESSIVELY LOST. THOSE GIRLS WERE REAL IN WAYS EVER OUTSIDE LOVE'S INSISTENT IDEAL. LOVE WAS ALL EMBRACING: AND ALL IS ANOTHER NOUN FOR NONE. THE MIND OWNS, FICTIVELY. THE FACTS ESCAPE. GIRLS RETREATED, TO GET THEMSELVES BACK. LOVE ADVANCED, SWEEPING. ALL BEFORE IT. ITS RELENT-LESS LOSSES ARE A TOTAL WINNING. IDEALS ENDURE, THOUGH THEIR PLANS DON'T PAN OUT. LOVE IS THE DOOMED IDEAL, FINELY PRESERVED IN FAILURE.

I idealized a girl so strenuously, that in sheer self-defense in a state of survival-emergency, and just to keep herself intact, she retreated out of existence. My grief lasted as long as her absence. When she continued to be lost, I stopped idealizing her. At that point, it was safe (the "all-clear" sounded) for her to return. She seemed perfectly ordinary. Free of my mental assault, she resumed being what she always was. She expanded elastically, in any direction. The fear of my confining her within love's compulsory fence was all over. Rid of it gratefully, she had my permission (with the bonds of tyranny dissolved) to just *be*. Not strait-laced in the prison jacket of my loving ideal.

Had she gained or had I lost? Or was all back to the way it was before?—before I lost my head and she was forced to oblige by stepping out of existence until the coast was clear for all she would re-assume. Romance endangers liberty, when enforced upon the adored one to dictate terms of identity on an ideal plateau. Backed up against the abyss on that ideal plateau, she had a falling; till such a time that I shouldn't raise her too high in estimation. The liberty to *be* was very bracing for her: based on her ceasing to be my loved object. She danced the joyous dance of the unloved. Eased of the girdle of a smothering interest that squeezed her into deformity— she danced into any shapelessness. And landed on the feet of her real self.

My term as a jailer had ended. On whom new would I inflict— to molest—to elevate—to denature—to fabricate? Whom to victimize next?—to enslave another girl to my abject servility. To prostrate myself before her, and enshrine her out of sight on the stilts of my impossible-making pedestal—erected not in her honor, but in the destruction of the self of her natural mold. In my cruelty, to play it into her cruelty, over me. Then I relent; and she tumbles down from the ethereal, to frolic along the ground and soak up clay's moisture on the brown but comfortable earth. She flies so much easier, without the wings I pinned to her. To be is so much better then to be trapped into idealization by another's amorous invasion. I would have to learn to leave alone those whom I would romantically exalt. For their gain, or my loss? The bubble burst. Day's ordinary light. The dream dematerialized. Love suppressed. So that they all fly away unloved, below that ecstatic ceiling I would raise to them. Love is lowered underground: to roam and romp, as a girlishly liberated ghost. They have fun, unloved. They need "live up" to nothing. With all the room for their unconfinings, hidden far below the star-gazing astronomy of love that falsifies invented planets into giddy orbits of the unnatural. Just to *be*—not to he loved.

But they all *try* to be loved; *then* they run away—upon too failing a success: that restricts their lonely flight.

"Leave me alone," they plead. "Unloved is just the thing to be, if being is to be oneself. I don't need the glorified self you presume to confine me with; I'll trade that in, to breathe in unloved abundance—and fill myself with that untroubled air. Love is in the heart of being unloved—who needs yours, when I can win back the whole Void's love?: that loves me for *myself*—plastic, unshaped, to be. All possibilities open, when identity spins undefined. So stop loving me, put your love away. Else you force me to disappear. Your false image must go, it makes me false. Truth moves in all directions along the void. So stop impeding it. Love me not. For I need All Love."

Yes, and I stand away. They're not had. I own no one. They pass me by—resisting my impositions. Where can I apply my love—so that it doesn't distort? Love *is* distortive.

Not captivating, love is captivated by those elusive spirits. How can I stop loving? And loving, how can I not pursue? All my life, these vain conquests; I vanquish—but lose those whom I vanquish: for they were other than the ones I thought I loved.

I'm compelled to continue; all these setbacks, though discouraging, can't rid me of my habit: a losing one, that sets love in motion and keeps it there, but never persuades. An ineffectual process, love is faced with itself for a reward, having lost all the women. It loves its abstract self. Its concrete female objects won't relent. And I can't learn. I try. I persist, ever expecting failure. Love is self-subsisting. Feeding on itself, but perfectly undevoured. It looks about. It remakes new girls continuously. It chases them out of sight. And falls back on its own motion.

I can't turn it off. It's the very breathing spirit of me. It becomes life itself: victoriously hopeless, overcoming hope's successful opposition, mechanically inverting its goal that vanishes. Finally, love is left with me. It has served me faithfully. The ones it wanted had no existence. But *its* existence has been continuous—on fickle fancying ever. Love remains. The objects are dispersed. Love takes on the reality they never had, in all their aggregate, the collective desirable female. The interchangeable women. The difficulty in "landing" the object puts total weight on the "subject," which is love. So my subjective love, the all-losing love, gains perpetual consolation. It emerges the winner. By its own sentimental verdict.

Love is life is one. All together, we're complete.

IS LOVE STILL IDEAL WHEN ATTAINED?

Love is for kissing. It breeds romance. Oh, let's go to bed. I crave you, in your essential body. Why is in the act, and dies there. Love gives happiness a boost, and projects hope all over the place. If it torments us, then so much the bad. Love is like God: a praying gamble. Some achieve its luck, others are mercied over by grief. Love binds, and two genders connect. But the variations are exhaustible, unless the heart rules. Love is a two-way ticket, on a one-way journey. Thus, a side is punched; but the other part is defunct. Can't allegiances coincide? How about being simultaneous? What a worked-out solution, if both parties agree! It hurts if only one does it. Two can be awfully complete, in harmonious accord, or double concord. Love, both going and coming, a flow of continuous completion. Touch a dream, press life awake, set magic free to be but real again. If love becomes actual, has it surrendered existence, converted from an enchanted possibility to the punctured debasement of commonplace? Thus, is success failure? Love, proclaim your purity. Your rarity measures our suspicion, your fame gives aspiration its standard. Be what you are, if only you can be. Preserve the absolute purity of your essence from our cynical heartbreaks. What are you but a thought. You keep our acts low, in the common consent of their failure. Ah, you shed disappointment. As a thing to be desired, you evade total attainment. Thus, your fascination endures, and men die for you. You cheapen life by withholding yourself, and expose its dearness by being availed of. Love, by serving you we seek to tame you: and your tyranny deepens.

TWO IDEALS

THE RARE IDEAL'S NECESSARILY DOUBLE PROOF

The ideal is that the *us* violates neither the *you* or the *me*. (In so many cases it does—it violates *one* of the pair, at least.)

In my case the *me* gets increased by the *us*, confirmed, affirmed, bolstered, fortified, enhanced, justified, vindicated, extended, made even purer.

That's an ideal state, for *me*. But what does the *us* do to and for *you*? No less, I suspect. Thus the ideal is now mutual, shared, as a proven state. Of necessity it's had to undergo *double* proof.

This doubly maintained ideal, when it actually exists, is a rare state. Look at all the examples to the contrary. Not just in the lives of others, but in the past of one's own life.

THE FORTIFIED IDEAL

Not forty oceans of mud
nor the choking factory of night
nor the garbage of the world
that every household vomits,
could in the grouping of their power
or singly, molest
one hair of love's white head:
where all ideals converge
like sighs with privacy endowed,
courageously primed to outblow
the wiser and sadder winds
that tear at perfection's root.

A PAIR OF SOULS AND THE PAIR OF US

The creeping of our souls toward each other when our bodies are miles apart is being done however unaware we are of it.

It's a stealthy sort of converging and it's outside our control—or too far *in*side for our control.

Our souls have made an appointment and they're wending their ways slowly toward it. Shouldn't we be invited too? Just as chaperones, or for the free ride if there's no excuse?

Our souls are joining, are uniting. Let's *us* along too. Why shouldn't we? They're *ours*, our souls, we possess the, they belong to us.

It's like my pet male cat and your pet girl cat have a tryst or assignation in the secret dark of night, due to love. Well, let's join along. Why should *they* have all the fun? *We* deserve some too.

But maybe I'm wrong to assume that our souls are *ours*. Maybe *we're theirs*. They own us? Could be. In that case, they can meet *without* our permission: and even forbid us to interfere with their sacred union by being bodily present.

Yes. I'm convinced *they* own us. Yours owns you, mine me. But yours own me, too. But *you* own me, too. So I have two masters: you and your soul. And a *third* master, *my* soul. I'm all confused, now. Who should I obey if there are conflicting orders?

I *love* you, *that's* for sure. But I also respect and love your soul. And *my* soul, I know, is magically drawn toward yours, almost like sex appeal.

Why not make a quartet?—just the four of us, like a double date.

It would be fun—and rewarding, too. Plenty of variety, if there's no clash between four different things. Let's all blend together, that's what *I* would like. Body and soul, all in one. Let's *join* our souls. I've just received a message from my soul that it's already with yours and they're "mating" in soul ways. That's our cue, for us. Let's simply imitate them with the faculties and capacities that *we* own. The souls are sublime to emulate. Let's translate what *they*'re doing, in *our* terms.

You agree? Good. I'm happy, soul and body—two excellent sources. It calls for a celebration. It calls for everything we have— so let's *give* everything. And not stop giving. For only while giving are we getting. And we're giving to generosity's source itself.

Love *is* the best thing on earth. Or, for that matter, in heaven, too. In heaven our souls mate while our bodies live and mate here. So heaven and earth are made one. Who made them thus? *We* did. We, thanks to our souls. Our souls helped. I can't thank their co-operation enough. They made all possible for us. Let's give them the grand tribute. Let's mate.

TWO VERSIONS OF THE SAME PLAN OF EXCHANGING OUR SIMULTANEOUS LIKING OF EACH OTHER, FOR THE *ALTERNATING* OF OUR LIKING OF EACH OTHER. AND *WHY*, OF COURSE.

I

We're both constantly liking each other when we're with each other, and this can be too exhausting and wear us both out in no time.

What expenditure of affection, unremitting, no let-up, the incessant pour! It could wither us, and leave us all sear and dried.

So I have a solution, allowing us to conserve our energy. Here it is. Let's *alternate* liking each other. So you can take a rest for the half hour I like you; and then, you can relieve me from my post, and take up the burden, in *your* turn, while in *my* turn I have the next half hour to rest.

That will restore me and replenish my energy, so that when my turn resumes and your half-hour of giving is up and it's your turn to *take* affection, then I'll have plenty to give, to pour out and concentrate in the half-hour allotted to me.

II

A conservation-of-energy plan about our liking each other:

So far we like each other simultaneously (which can be so taxing because so incessant) when with each other. My plan is to alternate liking each other, taking turns: you like me for a half hour, then the next half hour I like you, and so on, turn and turn about. The liker will be so refreshed in doing his job!

But the disadvantage of this plan is in the relinquishing of simultaneity. Well, there's always *some* loss accompanying a new gain. "Give a little, take a little," is what I say. The price you pay. Can't have your cake and eat it, after all. Nothing, in this life, is perfect. Not even in two people liking each other. On well. Can't have *everything*, you know.

PREREALISM

LOVE IN THREE MOVEMENTS

Stripped down to the last memory,
I fondly cancel all the others
so that clean vacancy shields you
from the image-shattering world.

Wine and gaiety lure you
to rub out the picture of the moon
whose painted patrol on our window
kept us in too careful love.

Umbrella the sun away,
our skin is too rare to burn.

The quiet fires of a kiss
freeze summer, and warm winter.

THE MISUSE OF LOVE

An impermanent as tomorrow's weather
whose brief history shall rain or shine,
love masquerades its false hour,
and lips are pained habits of a kiss,
shaped by a numb ritual,
as though the pagan interlude of a Sunday
craved a sensual display of heart,
to cure the drowsy passage
from gluttony to tranquil sleep
with the nude entertainment of that sport.

LOVE DESPITE ITSELF

Love and all love's by-products:
the heart permanently lamed
that no surgery can attend
nor recent kisses restore
to the former prided of innocence;
the memory soaked regret
whose sorrow remains young;
or the marriage embittered
by the too complete discovery
of the bare sunlight's common day
whose habit removes romance
from each partner's normal pigment
whose local color crowns the eye;
and love reluctantly must fade,
its illusion yielded up
while death's advantage turns closer

to surrendering age:

Is love pimp to all remorse,
and folly's pampered shriek
trailed with moaning echoes?
Yet what better is there,
in the brevity of our condition,
than this wise monster, Love?
All joyful things are cruel,
a kiss is danger's deep red pit
where the sensual dream is tossed.

PRAISING TRUTH, BEING, NATURE, ESSENCE, THE MIND, THE IMAGINATION, AND LOVE. (WITH NO IMPLIED *DIS*PRAISE OF ANY POSITIVE ELSE OF A MENTAL AND FEELING THING.)

Everyone can be the truth, what anyone says *is* the truth, what he *does* is the truth, the truth pours out of him all over. The truth is dancing in him, or locked sullen in him. His least utterance is "true," however vain and deceitful a boast it is or a "covering up" for a fancied inadequacy. The truth pounces out of him. The truth oozes from his appearances, like a liquid through the net however tightly knit the stitches.

The truth is dancing out of the sky, like white parcels dangling from parachutes full-stretched upon a swoon of cloud.

Or the truth rumbles up out of the ground, like a mole from his hiding place, or a plant from the dark.

The truth invades us from all sides, batters in on us, with gentle insistence. We can only do one thing: accept it.

I give my heart to the truth, and the marriage gives me a wild imagination. Truth is a riot of fancy, when it's let go like a formerly pet bird to untame its soaring nature up. It leaps out of sight; it's true.

Imagination confines truth like a zoo that doesn't violate its inmates' natures. What's natural in essence and being finds intensification in the imagination: realization, fulfillment, completeness. The imagination does wonders. It parades the truth, in gorgeous raiment.

Pageantry in carnival zest. So explodes the imagination, into truth components. Each one has its role, and the whole ensemble is a brave feast for the eye.

Love comes pouring out. Love is the imagination rampant, in stately triumph, majestic, conquering.

Later the hurt, the rejection. But the truth was during Love, not later.

Love is the fitting climax. I end my eulogy of the mind, my recommendation of truth as essence, my extolling of the imagination which needs no extolling for it does it itself,—with a hymn to Love. which needs no hymn, for it *is* the hymn.

And all the hymn needs is the her.

Then all is Love, and One. Then the mind can sing. And then songs spring.

ANTICIPATION

(Full Title will follow *text, in that order; if it's on* top *here, it wouldn't be understood. The text prepares the reader to understand the title's meaning; hence, the inverted positioning here, of text and title. You'll see what I mean. Now, it's text ahead; with the title at the rear. You'll appreciate that fine order, in time.)*

I like the pleasure of anticipating a desirable event happening, which I'm sure is about to happen, and I'm confident and certain of it, and sure, it *does* happen. I like the whole process, of pleasurable anticipation of the way something will be, and then seeing it be that way; and it turns out pleasurably, even though it turns out the way you thought it might be. Yet, it's still wonderful, while it happens, and certainly doesn't destroy the process or cycle or phases of overall pleasure, broken down into the first phase, anticipation, and the culminating one, its fruition. You feel in *control*, by first anticipating and then seeing it all "come true," marvelously. Confidence, rewarded.

And the confidence was pleasing, and so was its reward. Anticipating, that nice state; succeeded by the event anticipated, *also* a nice state, though different. Put them together, fit them in order; it's a good sequence, practically a magic one: the pleasure of wishing (pleasure owing to certitude, or "a good chance"); and the pleasure of the wish "coming true"—but coming true *somewhat unlike* the way it was wished. Still, close enough, for the cycle to have "magic": the magic of your "controlling" an effect. You want; and you get it. The wanting itself was a fine state—often its duration is longer than the getting it. The waiting for the consummation is fun, sometimes even more fun than the consummation. But the consummation *should not disappoint*: it should not be a "let-down," or anticlimax. It must be worthy, of that pure, serene expectation; or of that frantic, yearning (but incurably optimistic) expectation. A nice sequence. Like two nice notes by Mozart, in their right order.

(Post-text title, as earlier justified:)

A LITTLE PLEASURE PACKAGE, CONTAINING TWO STATES OF TIME-BEING, WELL CONNECTED, IN FINE SEQUENCE, VERY FINE, AND *YOU* FEEL IN CONTROL. YOU'RE FORTUNATE, MAKE IT HAPPEN AGAIN: BUT NOT *TOO* OFTEN; OTHERWISE, THE "MAGIC" MAY ABANDON YOU, DISPLEASED AT THE GREED OF YOUR INVOKING IT TO AN OVERWORK. PRAY, AND BE LUCKY.

FESTIVAL POEMS

(Poems read at the New York Shakespeare Festival)

SUN AND DUST

It's a day of conspicuous sun,
being overbright,
giving strength to the unseen
in crevices and blind corners
from which the moles benefit.
The very dust in unused room
has a walking life,
though all the shutters are drawn
and the lock bolts doubly the door.
The sun's itinerary
violates, it would seem,
shadows ninety years old
that, in an undisturbed cellar,
lived metaphysically dark
in the neighborhood of an obese rat.
Granules of light
prod Hades awake,
and dapple Othello's dead soul
into white patches,
kind illuminations
scars of mercy,
love's tardy dust
that jealousy wasted.

SCIENTIFIC NATURE

Shall we heed our earth's round law,
shall the weight of all human life
join gravity's pull
until the flat safety of our walk
encircles the planet?
Has love a magnetic skill
whereby the genders merge
and unborn babes
receive life's signal?
Does death's foul insistence
attend both egg and seed
at their first strange meeting?
The sun's moderate distance
neither burns nor freezes.
When summer's hilarity deepens
and brilliant autumn begins,
my nature turns immortal,
and the freest bird's most elastic wings
are my own soaring property.

PERSISTENCE

Where does time vanish?
Is it visible,
like the life of an autumn tree,
which the wind removes
from green prominence?

I kissed you on your onetime lips,
and the kiss has never dried,
although you are since vanished
from love's stubborn sight.

WHAT THE WAITING CAME TO

Waiting was part of living
when happiness had its hopes in.
Loving was happy waiting.
Loving outlasted waiting
and melted the hope's petals out
in flowering worth waiting for.
A more barren waiting waits for me.
Hopes have fizzled out their outcomes
earning fewer happy incomes
from loving's slackening store.
Living must live off its past.
Loving's become an absolute idea
when waiting's young objects have passed by.

THE TRAGEDY OF MOTION

Let's say that the target moves,
giving the archer trouble.
The arrow's flight is unsure.
So, against a changing woman
my love strays from the mark,
and, hitting aside the painful air,
strikes her in the phantom past,
having lost her permanently today.

THE TELEPHONE

The telephone has a mobile touch,
its task is a time away,
past a hurried army of trees
into your voice.

TIME VERSUS HUMANITY

One vast motion ticks us all.
Are minutes children of an hour?
Is time's circular face
given to regularity,
like a fastidious clock
that hates uneven rhythm?
Or is time hearty and natural,
like some gigantic moon
who puppets a whole ocean?
Does time intervene
at autumn's burial
and winter's white beginning
to set up barriers
between the year's alien parts?
Or are all divisions glued,
made swift and gradual,—
the blossom and the fruit
neighbors on a single bough?

The heart has four seasons
and is yearly spent
in hot and cold pursuit
and alternate chase
of bitter love and joyful hate;
and survives weather
to gain doubtful wisdom.
The brevity of death
mocks love's prayer to time.

LOVE IN TROUBLE

The person with whom I'm in love
approximates, but only so,
the image of the personal love.
Sometimes they're amazingly one.
Most times, they're at foreign poles
hopelessly reconciled.
I make do, I must.
I've got to love; and who?

HOW TO HAVE EVERYTHING, AND STILL LIVE MODERATELY

Cultivate a little garden plot
and thereby possess the whole world.
Perfect your play on an instrument;
possess thereby the whole world.
Be firmly involved with someone in particular:
and you possess the whole world.

SEX

SOME THOUGHTS WHILE . . .

While he was having sex, he thought: "How dare I be reflecting now! I should be totally engrossed in what I'm doing with my partner. Instead, I'm contemplating, lonely, in isolation,

"I bet no other animal but man is capable of this audacity—thinking while doing.

"What *is* man, anyway? Or *who* is he?

"Some commentators liken man to a machine, others to an animal, and others to God. Yes, but what *really* is man? The answer will always elude me. That's because I *am* one, a man, and nothing can ever know itself while being itself. The act of *being* precludes self-knowledge.

"That's because 'being' is all-engrossing. How can you be on the outside of yourself, looking in?

"But *doing* is another thing. Here I am, *doing* sex; and yet the reflection part of me hovers somewhere far outside of this act I'm sharing with my partner: and my reflection is all for myself, un-shared by her. Is reflection selfish? Yes, because it must be private, to be reflection, It's a very solitary act. It sets one far apart. My *body* is being interlinked with that of my partner; but my mind is free, outside, mine, Would it offend her to know that? But she *herself* has an individually autonomous circle of thought, at this very minute: so she has no right to blame me. We're two separate beings—linked on a momentary basis. A brief merging of separate autonomies.

"I'm feeling an awful lot of pleasure right now; it's getting unbearable, I'll pause in my reflections and blot out extraneous thoughts so as to get the full brunt of this exquisite pleasure. Ah! My thought is being cut off. I'm all feeling. God, what feeling!"

So he stopped thinking, for a while. He later resumed his thinking when the sex was done: but with new trains of thought, for he was in a different place.

DASHING COLD WATER ON LOVE'S SENTIMENTALITY

Love is often sentimentalized, in plays, operas, poetry, fiction, films, television drama.

It captures the public's heart.

And why not? Love opens the door to sex, which is an irresistibly universal fascination, even obsession, as an exploitable topic, even for selling cars.

Humans have a weakness for that which helps to reproduce themselves.

Yet, frankly, they can be reproduced *without* love's valuable assistance.

How?

Through lust alone, irrespective of love.

You mean out of wedlock? Illegitimate bastards?

Sorry to spoil your sentimentality with brass-knuckle tactics of ugly reality.

Oh, that's all right. Mistakes happen.

BRIEF ENCOUNTERS

HOW DISAPPOINTINGLY DRY

I poked my thing in, but at the other end was an oasisless sandy Sahara Desert teeming with such barren dryness that "aridity" wouldn't do as a mere word to describe it. Rather than pitch a "what-the-hell" tent in such infertile wastes, I pulled out and rode my camel elsewhere.

"I wasn't in the mood," came her apology (subsequently translated) on the rasping wind as I was trotting away leaving tracks but as I couldn't understand a word of Arabic, the verbal futility blent in nicely in post-harmony with the more familiar futility of our traceless bodies; she was a speck I left behind, veiled and robed of dry-goods fabric. Would the open pores of her carnal thirst be ever quenched from within?: no chance from outside.

PROVOKING. THEN HOLDING BACK
SO HE DOESN'T UNLEASH HIS PACK.

The one who touches my penis
admits it's she whom my queen is.
There's such a lot of nerve centers there,
she must take fright and stare
how lengthy the penis has become.
But she holds back: it's too soon to "come."

WRONG PLACE, BUT MAKING THE MOST OF IT

I couldn't find the right hole—I stuck it into her navel by mistake. (It was dark, so I couldn't see.)

Wasn't it too tight in her navel?

An excruciatingly tight fit. While there, I gently whispered into her ear (punning on the word navel), "I'm in your navel, dear: we're both in the same boat."

Did that hold water?

Yes, we drowned.

THE PHASES OF RESOLIDIFYING

When I enter my girl I'm hard, but when I withdraw it's another matter. What on earth happened, to make my end different from the beginning?

To blame nature in general for the particular change in one part of me, would be a lazy way of taking the truth out. Why was

I hard before I went, and soft after I came? From *my* point of view, the difference was appreciable; the *girl*, however, found it hard to appreciate the softness on my part. Both she and I were contemplating a diminished aspect of myself: since contemplation was all we could do, as activity was no longer erected on a firm basis. But at length, time will resume its strength: the proof will conclusively be felt, for I believe in putting everything to the *test-icle*. Then knowledge hardens, in its permanent mold.

IN A BEATEN PATH

My girl is so busy fending for her virtue and protecting the im-pregnated fortress of her long-disappeared virginity, she has no time or strength left over, or even the moral inclination, to sum-mon the most pretended modesty of rudimentary resistance, that's why entering her is like the last lap of an endless rat-race. The notion that I've been preceded is reinforced by the debris and me-mentos I encounter, there, piled up like archeological strata from the preserved disorder of innumerable entries. "I'm late," it oc-curs to me; then an afterthought; "and not the first, either." *My* girl has stopped counting. In her case, arithmetic is futile; nor can compiled addition subtract from the multiplied indivisibility of her natural aversion to self-conscious scruples. Though the expe-rience of being inside her is the least exclusive in the world, and comes close to the democratic ideal of popular majority, that's no reason for me to be fussy and desist from one of the free joys of life. She's my instructress in a non-credit course on advanced real-ism; making love to her has broadened into a human cliché. Thus, she stifles my originality.

TEETH VERSUS PLEASURE

When my girl smiles, her teeth get in the way of her softer texture behind. Thus I can't wedge in between to kiss her.

When she grins *broadly*, the teeth are even a breast-protector, and clamp down on my exploratory hands.

When she *laughs*, those same upward teeth grow so prolonged a range that they serve to chastity-belt her crucial hip region. What's there left for me to do to her?

When her mouth is closed, her teeth can be transferred to other parts of her same over-all person, so integrated is it. Her teeth not being used by her mouth, they were borrowed by a spot where they lay in ambush for me. No sooner did I enter her, when I got badly bitten, and have had to wear a bandage on my poor sore tool that had the effrontery to wage warfare where her teeth were waiting. It wasn't funny, but my surgeon kept it in stitches.

For post-operative treatment, the nurse tended to it. Following doctor's orders, she kept it hard.

I KISSED A GIRL BUT MY CONSCIENCE, LIKE A CONTRACEPTIVE, PREVENTED TRUE CONTACT

"I'm a dog with a muzzle," I thought, and went around the corner to drop into the psychology store. "What can I do for you," the clerk said, looking at me very intently. Before I could reply, he added, "That will be ten dollars, please." I paid him and walked straight out, with a great burden off my chest, a load of conflict off my mind, and a genuine catharsis in my wallet. I tried kissing the same girl. That night, she conceived three kittens.

LIFE WITH BETTY.
UNDERNEATH HER IS HEAVY.
ON TOP IS ALSO GOOD,
IN THE SAME NEIGHBORHOOD.

When I'm in bed with Betty,
the temperature gets sweaty.
She's rather slightly heavy,
but that's better than being a wisp
with a too narrow hips,
as long as the beneath action is crisp.

∞

My estimation of Betty
makes me always eagerly ready.
She writhes, but I hold on steady.

∞

Being with Betty in bed:
What would I rather do instead?
Isn't that why we wed?
No, we also talk,
and eat with knife and fork
a little fish, a little pork.

AN AMOROUS DIFFERENCE IN HEIGHT

There's not only a *sex* difference between them, but a *height* difference.

The man being the taller?

Yes, by far, and the girl shorter.

How can *she* be shorter, if *he's* taller?

It's part of the sex war.

Does their comparison include them both?

But not in equal degrees.

Why?

For there's more of him to compare with less of her.

Does she feel left out?

Partly.

What compensation is offered her?

He temporarily occupies her with part of him. She pretends it's permanent.

And when he must withdraw?

Then there's the same gap between them. Only, accentuated.

In whose favor?

His, of course.

Still at the same ratio? Undeviating?

Until such time as again, by extending himself his utmost, he fills her with the more of the difference, and they're at one; with she having confiscated a goodly part of him, to lessen their height inequality, especially as they're lying down and pile into the same horizon, with him stoopingly on top, by the slightest margin, and height doesn't matter. Their extremities aren't involved, so much as their middles: which neutralize the outer inconsequentialities. And they both triumph. Neither is greater, and neither less. For they found the way *together*.

LIFE'S SWOLLEN ANTHEM OF SEX AND SIN

The sacred cult of nature, taking a bull by the horns and driving him through a cow, produces reproduction aplenty. Everyone is afflicted, if not affected. Including, to be practical, plants. While animals merely fornicate, humans derive the satisfaction of sin from the unholy evil of their couplings. Nature practices religion, and crowns man king of guilt. Woman, his consort, is an accomplice in this crime, the queen and empress over the kingdom of the openly secret forbidden pleasure from which the dirty mind of man gains a mass multiplication, sweeping his impure thought across the tolerant face of immortality which his seed upholds into the bargain, maintaining a pace upon survival. How fit it all is, and the earth throbs. *(The bed shakes.)* Nature is too hot to quit, and now a really rich glory is truly here, all the passion in her unkempt creature craving in madness the finality of joy and pain, harsh ecstasy and a dearly-purchased peace, the hellish race into paradise, How sweet.

HOW TO ANSWER AN INVITATION TO THE ORGY

If you attend an orgy performatively, the chances of acquiring venereal disease are higher than if you turned down the hostess' invitation with a rude apology.

Turning it down would add to the safeguarding of your health, under the "safety first" policy which doctors recommend.

But what a load of excitement you'd miss!

All those writhing bodies in obscene fornicatory positions might, if you jump in to the scrimmage, squeeze your genitals to orgasm.

Sounds like fun.

But at high risk.

Oh well. Life is short.

Opportunity taken advantage of will yield either good or bad dividends.

At those odds, how will you decide?

Either one way or the other.

Isn't that a metaphor for life?

Life is so super-charged, does it really need a metaphor?

For literary escapism.

GIRL TROUBLE: THE MORE I SUFFER, THE MORE SHE'S WORTH.

My girl is one of these demanding creatures. Even when she gets, she demands. She's especially demanding when her demands haven't been answered with prompt satisfaction. Then, woe, and behold her fury.

One day, she demanded a kiss I had an adequate supply on hand (left over from unused ones in previous years), so I gave her one of my jalopies. When the frontal collision had been investigated by a parking inspector, some of her most obvious front teeth were reported missing from the fray. My foremost casualty was my tongue, which had been used to vary English speech in American vernacular. Thus, let it be said that we kissed not well, but too violently.

From that date on, she ceased demanding. She's delegated her greed to me, on her terms. Thus I'm hers, in the most possessive case. All she has to do is want something, and *I'm* the one to feel the lack. I take pains to supply the want, but all the fulfillment credit goes to her; she reaps satisfaction, from my provided labors. This is enslavement, an anachronism considering this late hour of history's cyclical clock.

"Get food," she specifies. And I raid the grocery to trudge home, a round brown bag bulging from my flattened limbs. She drains the bag empty, consuming everything but a wrapper, a pit, a shell, a box, a bottle, and a can. These she hands over, and includes a well-chewed bone, plus the drip and slop from an erstwhile solid.

"*Your* turn now," she beckons, transferring her former hunger to my starved husk that used to function as a belly. It's understood that I'm to eat; so I wait for two currents of air to get caught in the same pocket of space, their transparent bulk so fortified by their overlapping zeal that their compound resembles the approximate solid, instead of soupy thinness. So I drink down the thick substance: my lungs prosper, but my stomach weighs even less. To confirm my relative deficiency of intake, my girl belches up her recent nourishment; smelling it is already half a meal, so I inhale that compact stench.

"My greedy pig!" she squeals, as my skeleton disrobes from its skin. Fat is just dripping off her, in many pouches, in layers and tiers, like a well-crowded baseball stadium.

"When I've eaten, you may pick your teeth," she relented, and stuck a pin in my gum. No bloody geyser came through, since a parched dryness had ceased circulation altogether. The pin had a germ in it, which I quickly absorbed: now, it lodges in me, to multiply. Thus, I'm steadily getting back my well-diseased stick of health. But there's no glue in my loins, for patching together the links of my race.

Lust inspires my girl. She taps the area, but I've got no sap to grow a stripling, even a weak twig. (No virility branches, where the root drains a meager soil.) My girl's barking up a leafless tree, in the winter of my evergray. Then she inquires after my manhood, while I, abandoned by it, say that it's orphaned me. "Often? Yes, very frequently," she echoes, searching the while for a mere wholesome man. A candidate offered himself. "Are you whole-

some?" she asked. "If you're holesome," he replied, glancing between her hips with rather forceful intent. "Then I submit," she
guessed; and in front of me they supplied an envious exhibition of
the atomic power of combining parts. For comic relief between
bouts of meaty pressure, it afforded them amusement to call me a
eunuch, thus condemning me to a masculine limbo, for lack of the
robust limb. Then, they ground out new fun, while I, by contrast,
remain the single observer.

"Have I been unfaithful?" asked my contrite girl, when her
lover had vanished. "Yes," I reported, supporting my analysis with
the tedium of a begrudging honesty.

"I'll always have a warm place here for you," my girl suggested,
pointing not to her heart but to the forked bridge where her legs
started their descending journey of separation. "I'm not a suitable
lodger," I offered, putting in a plug for my self-pity. Flatly stating
"That's your loss," my girl walked away, tossing her hips provoca-
tively.

My loss consumed me. "I'm dirt," I estimated. My clay started
to flake off, being but half-baked. Never would I how inferior I
am, were it not for my girl, whose standard of inadequacy is easily
within my expert qualifications She, alone, is my guardian against
too fond a self-appraisal within the shade of vanity's delusion. It's
thanks to her that reality is an unpleasant chore, in which I drudge
without gain, earning fatigue for the day's wages. Why do I submit? I suppose it's for love that I find a balm in humiliation Recog-
nizing that motive, my girl retraces her wandering ways to grant
me her warm solace. "Can you kiss?" she queried; I did so, but
her face had been removed in advancer leaving a phantom to re-
place her in proxy, inserted by the image of her stead. Cheated in
the presence of her absence, my alternative companion was loneliness, ghosted her shape by an act of vacant desire. My love has
scant powers of discrimination; is it herself that my habit adores,

or the pain of wanting her in vain? Either way, I'm quite the loser, and win at this game repeatedly. Suffering is my soul's way of representing my girl, who stirs my quickness to be slowly bereft with foretold patience, since it's my lot to be doomed to be in the lack of her. Where's a more drastic apology to condone my steadfast state of sadness? Ah, while I wither, where goes my girl?

AN OTHERWISE MORAL PROPOSAL

Sex has corrupted our youth. Either one or the other will have to go. Some educators say that both should go. But then our policemen, guardians of the law, would be the victims of such idleness, that their own employment might be at stake.

Perhaps the problem is best to be solved by shutting down the movies. That way, sex should have lost its chief propaganda vehicle, and youth, no longer wise, would have to seek its amusement in its own innocence, and so develop the virtue, at an early age, of self-reliance. That way youth will survive, leading gradually to maturity, while sex, like an actor without a publicity agent, will play a reduced role in our public affairs.

A LATE-IN-LIFE POSSIBLE TREAT:
SOMETHING THAT CAN'T QUITE BE BEAT.

I'm only a helpless human male
whose sex is old and frail.
So I need a lot of help
for me ever to cry "Yelp!"
She's got to be packed in the groin,
where centralized is her "coin,"
with two heavy thighs beneath
to hoist it as a treat.
Then she'll sway her voluminous hips

as an invitation for us to come to grips,
and even take a detour at her lips.
So though I'm old and frail,
I'm still designated as a male.
I may respond slow as a snail,
but she could make me quiver and quail.
What a package! Can it be sent by mail?
Will the Post Office require a stamp?
In impatience, my feet I'll stamp
before extinguishing the bleak lamp
and feel along, to see if she's damp.
Groping thus with my fingers,
we'll see how long my lust lingers.

THE METAPHOR.
WHAT WAS IT EVER FOR?

When I think of my loved one, my heart rises,
but not my prick—I'm too old,
lacking the energy to be bold
in the old-fashioned sexual way
when youth enjoyed its sensual play.
So I apologize to my dear love,
who rises over my qualm—haughtily above.
Without the capacity to "make" love,
at least we still declare it—high above,
like a twittering bird on a tree
in love with a cloud—which then burst free
of the bird and abandoned the sky,
on which the bird could still flutteringly fly.
What is this metaphor for?
That my dear love I could still adore,
if she doesn't suddenly consider me a bore
or some old fool on whom to wage a petty war.

FROM: EPITAPHS BY POETS ON THEMSELVES (1965)

Marvin's doomed no more: he's dead for true.
His cock's phallickly useless; in short, he can't woo.
His numerous girl friends feel all commonly blue
mourning a tool that fed on them and deeply grew.
Their grief fertilizes Marvin, in a dirge of wept dew.
Virility's honoured: a fame accorded to few.
Around their bull's carcass, cows shed their living moo.

MARRIAGE

ARNIE, THE FAILED PAINTER AND BERTHA, HIS NON-MISTRESS. MEDIOCRITY, IN SLOW DECLINE.

Arnie was painting for fifteen years, if he had been painting a day. But he had nothing to show for it, except a studio littered with all uneven-sized canvases in all degrades of styles, schools, and genres. He was a Sunday painter who proclaimed *all* days Sundays, and so he was a dabbling dilettante who painted in earnest, keeping professional hours but with persistently amateur results. He attained a level of consistency in one class alone: mediocrity.

Arnie had a private trust fund-from dead wealthy parents, so no salaried employment stood in the way of his giftless devotion to his dreadful brand of so-called art.

Traditionally, artists had mistresses, at least in Paris. Arnie hoped that living up to the artist "image" would generate inspired work. So he asked a girl, Bertha, "Please be my mistress. I'll support you, and you needn't work."

She was tired of office routine and dull business files, so she consented yes.

He set her up in a modest but comfortable flat. All would be well, except for the unfortunate discovery they concurrently made of his sexual impotence. "Well, let's *pretend* you're my mistress," he decided. "You can have a boyfriend, but only slyly on the side, unpublicly divulged. Still, you must preside as ceremonial hostess at my parties, dinner and otherwise. Let it be *our* secret, but keep up appearances. My career is at stake, in reputation to the artist's life. I'm going to invite all the art dealers in this city to my studio, and thence to dine. One of them, if he likes my style of art and life, is bound to offer me a one-man show during prime season in his art gallery, even if I have to guarantee him a higher percentage fee for gallery rental than he'd charge the better-known artists. I *must* have an exhibition. Stand by me, Bertha. Can you even love me a little bit, despite my sexual incapacity? I'd show my gratitude in ways you couldn't resist, if you do."

She wanted the easy life, so she said yes. But his plan didn't work of obtaining an exhibition. The dealers visited his studio, were his dinner guests, but all refused to offer him show space, fer fear that their galleries would lose their good name of esteem were *Arnie* to show there—a man laughed at, in every art circle everywhere.

Bertha lived through all this. Arnie "kept" her, not in luxury but in comfort. She had a lover, even two sometimes, but was loyal to her word to keep up appearances for Arnie. She presided as hostess at his dinner parties, cocktail parties, or after-dinner parties. But *she* earned a laughable name, too, for allying herself so closely to a lost cause. In time, she left him, to marry a well-known painter. Arnie was abandoned. He was a failure: in love, in work, socially, in every way. People attended his parties, but mocked him privately. He was exploited. He was a fool.

In time, he got too old to paint, his fingers were always trembling. He flung away his brushes, and realized he had no friends. No true romance had brightened his life. Only unearned wealth, had he had.

Bertha had divorced the well-known painter, but without alimony, and childless. She had affairs with other men, but had to earn a living, with a series of dull jobs. She decided, being now old, that to live off Arnie again would be the easier way to end her life's days. She phoned him. He was lonely, so he couldn't resist.

But he slept in the same bed with Bertha. He wasn't alone, nor was she. Each had *someone*: undistinguished, but preferable to no-one at all.

Their days decline. But they have each other. Art is out. But companionship is there. Not love as a passionate state. But at least they had consolation: each other's living presence, puttering about. The minimum communication. The most trifling dialogues. But they weren't alone. Death was their dual prospect. They faced it, with cheer. They were darlings, for each other. Forget about youth. Plans. Ambitions. Sex, or non-sex. They had basic security. They wove daily grooves into a well-worn familiarity. Without hostility. With no "feeling." They were reduced. They were just animal presences. At that stage, such would suffice. Arnie who failed. Bertha, unremarkable. Living two old lives out. Cosy, comfortable. Helped by a servant or two. Leaving life, soon. Who first?

It didn't matter, "who first." For now, they were one.

MARRIED ART

A man painter and a woman painter married. When the nuptials were over, they painted a conjugal picture. He did one stroke, then she another, with the same brush.

But the romantic honeymoon set, so they went back to painting separate pictures. In different rooms, yet.

Then, marital discord set in. Hate replaced love, in easy stages of argument. They felt bitter.

Destructive vengeance moved each to ruin the canvas of the other. He tore hers apart with a palette knife; while she squeezed oil tubes on his surface, and spread primary color to thickly obscure his precious doodling. The resultant abstractions transgressed the sanity of art itself, and achieved feats of incredible modernity.

The man painter and the woman painter divorced. Now their approach to art is exceedingly individualistic.

TWO OPPOSING VARIATIONS ON THE THEME OF MARRYING YOUR WIDOW'S SISTER

1. A CLASSIC CASE TO ILLUSTRATE THE PHRASE "IT'S TOO LATE"

I was in love with my wife's sister. That replaced my love for my wife, whom now, by loving her sister, I no longer herself loved.

My wife's sister said it would be immoral for me to abandon my wife and marry my wife's sister. As long as my wife and I were both still alive, I couldn't marry my wife's sister, for the latter prohibited a divorce from my wife as the means of becoming free to marry her.

Nor could I kill my wife either. Her health would outlast mine. It did, so that at last I was able to marry the sister—of my widow.

Not much good in that. Or bad, either.

2. MAKING THE DIFFICULT EASY, AND THE IMPOSSIBLE INEVITABLE

Among the many difficult feats is to marry your widow's sister. Try it, but at your own risk.

Not even a *brave* man would accept such a challenge; nor would a *boastful* one gamble on it. Yet, to the mind, all things are possible.

Not only possible—they *exist*. All things do exist: but in the mind.

In not *any*one's mind: but in the *one mind* that *everyone* has.

That's the *big* mind, that painters paint to, and poets intend their poems for. It's the one mind we have, in the biggest sense.

So marrying your widow's sister is being done now, as these words are written, in your very comprehension. Proof: Try to undo it—you'll fail, forever.

WHAT ERIC OVERCAME

Eric had to admit, out of all fairness, to Sheila soon after their first meeting in world history ever: "Because of an Oedipus Complex toward my mother who's a Jewess, I'm sexually impotent with any Jewish girl, and you're one, so I'd fail you if we ever went to bed."

"Thanks for the warning," she said, and walked out on him, left him astray, and their lives would be kept apart forever.

However, there was an obstacle to their plan of permanent separation, which would prevent them from never coming together again as their intention was. By coincidence, they were in love with each other. So they arranged an emergency meeting.

Eric explained his painful history with girls; Sheila promised to be understanding.

"My mother was a dominating, overbearing, emasculating, insufferable tyrant," he began gently, "and so I became prejudiced against any girl Jewish, in whom I would see the replica image of my fright of a mother who had demoralized my confidence and spoilt my assertion or natural behavior in the company of any girl Jewish."

Sheila murmured, "And so it's to your fiendish mother I owe my being deprived the favors of your embrace which in our modernity-ridden times is a prerequisite-bar-none of a prelude toward actual marriage, which ought to be our lawful wedded state if only your mother had not tampered with that branch of your masculinity that concerns itself vitally with girls Jewish. But am I given to understand that your pathological inhibition is waived in the case of the Christian girls of the world, who outnumber their Jewish sisters? If so, I'm racially jealous of those advocates of the doctrine of the Lord Jesus.

"Would it help if I converted to the Christian faith?"

"It wouldn't help. I'd still be conscious that you were conscious of so conscious a volition as conversion to a new sect. To become a member of the opposite sect might save you from damnation and redeem your God-forsaken soul, but it wouldn't convince me at the seat of my instinct (at which crucial joint my inhibition is pitifully located) to treat you as a real girl Christian, which would mean ardently and manfully to rip and roar, carry my act of love back and forth through you, into you, with you, at you. No, it wouldn't do, you remind me too much of my mother Jewish. Whether religious or psychiatric, our predicament affords no hope. Our sole consolation is romantic melancholy."

They both wept. They were in love and chastity, a hopeless combination in paralyzing passion from its normal goals. Their love deepened, by their enforced abstinence. Their physical continence only fed a further fuel of furnace to their incontinent emotional flaming, whose heat soared white-hot for its below-the-belt deprivation.

If only Eric had not had a Jewish mother! (It was too late now to change, that; it was in fact *always* too late.) Or, if only Sheila had never become a girl Jewish through the faith of her parentage. (Too late now to change *that*, as well.) Fate had conspired against the young lovers from the normal expectation of a conjugal consummation. To ask God whether that was fair, would not have availed. God has been indisposed from granting petitions since the Age of Faith had waned.

The suffering young couple were the innocent victims of circumstance. Curses on Eric's mother. Curses on Sheila having been forever a girl Jewish.

So they parted for a long time. Eric used to have Christian girl friends, now he hadn't the heart for any, he only moped in the lassitude of despair. His vigor vanished altogether, in the waning of the whole sexual appetite, even for girls Christian. Would he turn to boys? He would probably be potent with boys Jewish, since his Oedipal Complex had no *paternal* orientation. But society frowned on homosexual activity as being shameful. In addition, he's he'd lose Sheila's respect if she found him coupling with a man, a man of whatever religious persuasion or denomination by faith. So he abandoned *that* idea, and concentrated on the Sheila problem. Could it be solved by his killing his mother? No, guilt would *further* inhibit him. A solution less harsh might yield more positive dividends.

Those Platonic lovers had a sentimental reunion by candle light, and kissed each other's tears dry. What could they do? They wept some more, in default of a more practical solution to this physical, moral, or whatever this dilemma might be, which made their mutual affection poignant and cast a shade of tragedy on their intense impasse.

When an obstacle can't be budged, and frustration mounts higher, what's the obvious recourse to take? Eric didn't know, nor Sheila either.

They bent their brows and thought in unison. They were in a stalemate, as stale mates. They were beaten by the insolubility of the whole thing. Futility suggested itself. They'd renounce finding a way out, and practice resignation.

But what kind of a solution is resignation? Semantically, none at all. Would *philosophy* afford refuge? Or self-flagellation? Not one bit. They had to face the reality. Reality was unflinchable: it outfaced *them.*

They tried an experiment. Eric got drunk. But no, it didn't work. Even while drunk, he knew what Sheila was: a girl Jewish.

Then Eric thought of something rash. Why not seduce, rape, or do *something* erotically, with his very mother, the demon cause of the problem? He'd grapple with the *roots*, and tackle the core, in a bold stroke of daring. He'd return, like all criminals do, to the obscene of the crime. It might *work*, too! The source—there's no substitute for the source. *That's* where he should be saucy.

Fifteen or twenty years ago, his mother might have been attractive. Now, she was just an old hag. He lost his appetite thinking about it. Truth is, the appetite had been false all along. It didn't turn his saliva on. It was all in his head.

Sheila, meanwhile, was being courted by a new man, and was tempted to accept his proposal of marriage. Eric, whom she still loved, had become a lost cause. She would have to renounce him, for her youth was almost fading and while in the peak of her prime she must secure her woman's-destiny by becoming a wife and a mother *somehow*: even through marriage to someone other then Eric, however distasteful the whole idea of a second choice was.

She had been granted an opportunity. It was a very eligible man who had proposed. His financial situation and business prospects were superior to Eric's. And he had no sexual doubts about a girl Jewish, though he himself was also of the same persuasion. The reason being, that in *his* case, his mother had been mild and timid, thus leaving him air and space to develop and expand his assertive self-confidence and masterful initiative, even where it concerned girls Jewish. He loved Sheila, and begged for her hand, pressing his suit (though not literally, for he wasn't a tailor committing an act of laundry) with ardor, brio, insistence, pertinacity, and a flattering single-mindedness of stubborn perseverance in spite of Sheila's trying to put him off.

"Give me time," she asked. "I'll decide, once and for all, Monday at ten o'clock sharp, following dinner you're to give me. There will be no announcement till then. It's now Friday. I want the weekend to think it over, and consult Eric. Relent, then, till Monday, in the pressing of your suit. That's only fair, after all. Despite his sexual problems, Eric *did* come first, and won my heart to this very moment. Before making the crucial decision to *shift* my heart from his to yours, I must deliberate fully, and give the matter the most thorough probing from all angles, so as not to leave a stone untouched. I promise that once I've decided, it will be permanent: either in your favor, or to abjure you forever. You're a sweet man, kind and loving. Take your weekend full of patience, and courage in case of my adverse decision. Commune with your soul. Be devout, pray for my guidance. In *my* book, marriage is irrevocable, once undertaken. I'm not a divorce-believer, like so many of my modern sisters are. I'm a girl old-fashioned, spun out in the Jewish tradition. That contributed no end, alas, to the problem. Too bad Eric has to be impotent with girls Jewish. His Jewish mother monster caused it, and spoilt his life for me, and mine for him. Otherwise, we would have made an ideally suited couple, well matched: our height differential is just fine, our skin complexions tend to blend, and we share often the same interests. It was a rare marriage, made in heaven. But his mother Jewish, from hell, just ruined it. How I hate her! He does too. He carries his hatred, alas, in his genitals. It inhibits him with forbidden, illicit guilt, smarting at his erection, causing a complicated complex, which Freud named after Oedipus, the Rex of Greece. That was in classical antiquity, of course. I'm 'behind' in my literature. I'm 'behind' in *many* respects. Eric *admires* my 'behind', and wishes he could only climb it, to mount it, and be a stalwart male.

"But as I'm a girl Jewish, he can't. With *you*, it's no problem. You and I already tried it, dozens of times, and you did it with ease, which pleased me immensely, though I did feel a disloyal betrayal for poor Eric, from whom I've kept it a secret. He'd die if he knew. I'll keep it from him, in mercy and consideration for not wounding the delicate male pride of his feeling; and in guiltiness toward myself. You'd make a nice, handsome husband, be a good provider, and be robust in bed and give me a child. But my heart's love goes to *Eric*. So I'll thrash it out this weekend, leave me in peace. Good night, gentle Sir. My future husband-to-be, possibly, and I'll let you know Monday night. Brood and pray over it, meanwhile. Lover, good-night."

Thus Sheila took her leave from her prospective groom. One last chance, she'd grant to Eric. He'd have the weekend to solve the problem. That would be final. One sole *weekend*, that's all. Would he still have a *weak end*? It would be a cruel penalty for Sheila to pay for her innocent crime of having been born a girl Jewish. Unjust, unfair, by any scale. But she wasn't without recourse, now. She had the resource of an ardent wooer, an eligible man, a most attractive husband-to-be, should she so select him as one. This put the pressure right on Eric. He'd have to produce the goods, this weekend, and prove his vital manhood. She'd waited too long, it was his last chance. Soon her youth would be over. She wanted to become a Jewish mother.

"Eric, extricate yourself from that bitter bond that wraps up your genitals in gelded placid eunuch's tape, curled softly in its pathology of apathy when it should be stirred to a virile tip. *Despite* your mother, try being a man. Even with—yes, *especially* with—me, a typical girl Jewish. I'm almost engaged to a tenacious fiancé, and must let him know Monday night whether I've succumbed to his 'fate'. Try something desperate, Eric! Else, it's goodbye forever! Till heaven, when carnality doesn't count.

"Yes, Eric, I've been proposed to. Of course I wouldn't let him kiss me, I'm a proper prude. But, unless you can prove your manhood in my particular case Jewish before the deadline of Monday night, I've vowed to accept his hand. It's come down, between us, on time's mounting ultimatum, to now or never. Try hard, get an erection. Pretend I'm *not* a girl Jewish. *Know* I'm not your mother, of course. I only *seem* to be like her. The resemblance is only a *Jewish* identity. That's where the comparison stops. I'm younger than her, and not even related to you. I'm from an outside family. Between us, there's no danger of incest. That's a crucial point I'm making, can't it sink in? Get over that absurd identification of me with her. Rid yourself of that most ruinous confusion. It insults me directly! I won't tolerate it. I'm a stranger, not a relative. I *can* be your relative—your wife. But only if you seduce me. Show me the goods.

"Look at my soft and supple hips, as I lift my dress; aren't they succulent, those softly firm, opulently-fleshed thighs? Look how they grow wider as they go higher. See how they converge, toward my groin itself? Aren't you lust-provoked? What an intimate spectacle, I'm putting on, to edify, liberate, emancipate, and excite your fiery steed of manhood.

"Look how my buttocks curve out, and the Venus mound, and my slim but soft waist. It ought to stimulate you out of your mind! Isn't your groin hardening up yet? I'm going to sit on your lap and touch it. I'm *determined* to get it stiff.

"Pretend that you're all-powerful, muscular, brutal; while me, I'm so slight, so helpless, in your power. Assert yourself, you can crush me down. I'm just feminine, slight, soft, your just-barely-resisting slave. I'm at your disposal. I plead for mercy. I beg you to spare me, my virtue, my honor. But no, you're ruthless. You take advantage of a helpless female, Your passion conquers us both, pins us together, combines our wild bodies into one. I surrender. You've won.

"Look, I'm all naked. See my throbbing breasts? I bet *you* don't have them! I defy you to touch them! I defy you to enter me—"

Eric by now *was* roused, and hard. He took off his *own* clothes, so as not to clash with her nudity. They tumbled on the bed, in foreplay. They caressed, kissed, in flirtatious hugs, coyly to embrace, in exciting poses of tease.

His erection subsided. He had thought of his mother!

Untimely image, cruelly visiting him! It put an absolute stop to all festivities.

Sheila was upset. She sobbed herself to sleep, in the bed in his apartment. It was only Friday night—or dawn Saturday. They had until Monday yet. Could the tide be reversed, that would sweep them apart? They had enough time to explore, to try. But they had had time before, and always to the same pitiful result: a flop, a dud. Their bodies couldn't be bridged, through supple penetration. Fiasco after fiasco. They were doomed. His mother was always present, the omnipresent chaperone, claiming and guarding her son, in an iron band of jealousy, the field barred to any competitor. From her womb, Eric had emerged. It was doomed to be the only Jewish womb he'd ever know. He was possessed of her as a demon and muse, so bewitched by her infernal presence, he couldn't perform the normal sex act within the vessel proper of a girl Jewish. Thus the mother resided within Eric.

A male virgin was Eric, in the upper bracket, under his mother's protection. In the *lower* bracket, let him slum and have his fun, with the girls Christian—who consume his scum. Eric belonged to his mother from the very first. She jinxed and hexed him, like a gremlin, to thwart his machinery as a male factor when juxtaposed to the box Jewish. His faculties couldn't operate, he was deficient, and let Sheila suffer—that usurper if she could: Eric *couldn't* be hers: except by the pathos of a sterile and sobbing sentiment. His virility was blocked up. *That's* where the chains fit, to do their job. Paralysis—perfect.

Saturday morning, in his apartment. Their last frustrating weekend together, on earth. Monday night would estrange them. The grief was for the tasting, in advance.

"Well, another failure," Eric had to admit. They were lying in bed, apart, bodies not touching, sharing one blanket. "Should we give up, since every attempt is bungled, and the results dismally uniform?," he mournfully asked. It was lugubrious, there was death in the air. Death of romance. Love's death. Love's resting place.

"I want to stay with you all weekend," she insisted. "We'll go down fighting —or rather, not fighting. The captain stays with his sinking ship. If we'll have to part; let's bind ourselves fast to the end. Let love go down in a blaze of—ingloriousness, I'm afraid. You're a futile weakling eunuch. You bear a cursed body. It's crippled the wholeness of our love. I'll be renouncing you Monday night; and after a swift engagement, a whirlwind marriage (You're not invited to the wedding—but I'll invite your *mother*, for she was responsible for it.), I'll leave on my honeymoon, and bear Jewish children. My sons will be unlike you. With God's help, may it be so. May my sons grow up to be *men*. To be a *man*—is that a foreign concept? How *could* you understand? I taunt you, like a bitch. *That*'s understandable, too."

Her bitterness was constant. Tenderness was now venomous. She became vile, like an ugly Fury, a vindictive Harpy. For Eric, it was miserable. His suffering was acute. For all his needs, his impotence enlarged, and took over. It reigned, relentlessly. It ruled him, under its thumb.

They were chaste, like brother and sister. Sheila didn't try to entice him again. She wore her least revealing clothes, to keep her charms smothered up. Neither wanted to start what couldn't be finished. The cycle being incomplete was excruciatingly frustrating last night: to repeat it would be so dually sadistic, that they blanched under the aversion of so absurd a trauma. Enough. No more attempts, please. The lesson had come home: desist.

But they did decide something. Hand in hand, they'd visit Eric's mother. For a futile showdown. For a feeble truce. For a confrontation, on terms of surrender.

They would admit defeat. To give up. To wince as she gloats. To declare her the winner. To be battered over, by her.

They took a bus, then made a transfer to another bus. Eric had phoned her saying he'd be coming, but hadn't mentioned that Sheila would come too.

They arrived, he pressed the doorbell, Eric's mother opened the door. "Oh, I didn't know you would bring company," she exclaimed, delightedly, behaving immediately to Sheila as to a prospective and hoped-for daughter-in-law. She tugged the young lovebirds in, and stuffed them, on the sofa. Eric's father was all gallant courtesy: "So you've brought a girl home!" he winked: "What an occasion!"

The four were seated in the living room. Eric's mother said, "I never had a daughter. I always wanted one, I've been *waiting* for you to get engaged, Eric. This is a blesséd event, we'll all celebrate. We'll celebrate with milk and cake. You're my only child, Eric, I so badly wanted a daughter as well. But never succeeded. Till now—*now* I succeed. Sheila is your name, you way? Here, shake hands. I've been worried about my son being a bachelor too long. I was desperately waiting for him to take a bride—for years I've been waiting. Now my waiting is ended. I'm so happy I'll weep. My life never had such joy."

The mother was crying, the father was crying. Eric and Sheila were embarrassed: what could they tell his parents? In the circumstances, the truth would be too cruel. Let the parents assume what they wished. It would break their hearts to break an illusion, like this. Oh, what a horror life is! It's not to be managed. The dead are better off, spared all this. On and on the parents wept, they were in joy. They were weeping for celebration.

Abruptly the mother started up from her tears, for suddenly a doubt had crossed her mine. She looked straight at Sheila, with terror. "Tell me, please, young lady, reassure me, pardon to be so personal, but it's a life-or-death matter, no less than that, my heart hangs on your answer: Are you Jewish?"

"Of course," Sheila replied. Inwardly she kept to herself a sad "unfortunately." She wouldn't want to hurt this nice woman, whose son she adored. *Why* did Eric have to be impotent, with a co-religionist of his mother? It was too gross, it was unfair business practices, but where could it get corrected? This being Saturday night, only forty-eight hours remained till her suitor would be answered Monday night. What drastic thing could be done, meanwhile? A radical departure. To unEric Eric of what he was.

It was cosy, lots of food was served. The milk and cake would come last. Eric's mother wanted to stuff her son and new daughter. The best wasn't good enough for them. Thank God Sheila turned out to be Jewish. The mother's joy knew no bounds. She poured out generosity, with mad delight, in staggering abundance. She heaped the Saturday night table with wonderful goodies in such profusion that all appetites were raped. Chicken, meat, eggs, vegetables, soup, fruit—everything. Later would come sweets, dessert, milk. It was so lovingly tendered. From loving tenderness. Eric's father agreed. He *always* agreed with his wife.

"We love you," Eric's mother said to Sheila. "You'll make a lovely bride for our son. And that will make him more ambitious too. He has only a fair decent job. He should get ahead more. We're middle-class parents, and we want him to be like us. Make him ambitious! Give him incentive. You'll have *power* over him, as his wife. A Jewish wife *always* has influence. It's in the contract.

"Oh, my husband and I love you, Sheila. You're just the very daughter we always dreamt of. How much money do your parents have, what's your father's business? I'm not being too personal, I'm only being curious. Will you bring a dowry into the marriage? Could your father set Eric up in his business if he owns one and make Eric manager? Oh, my wildest dream. comes true, then! Answer, lovely child."

"I must put a stop to this," Sheila replied sharply. The mother pulled up snort. She was in a state of shock. Then she fainted.

Her husband revived her. "Why did you shock her?" he asked Sheila. Sheila was about to bare the truth. She'd tell on Eric, of his impotence with girls cursed Jewish. This would be the crowning jolt: would his parents ever recover?

Eric's mother was sitting semi-sprawled, on the rug. Her husband was kneeling alongside her. Sheila and Eric were sitting on the couch. The table was laden with food, with plates prodigiously emptied but with more lavish heaps left over as though an army had been expected beyond an ordinarily hungry son and the bride he'd brought home. But the bride had just "floored" them, by the tone of her remark. They begged for an explanation, those exemplary, too-well-meaning parents, to their son's saviour-heroine. Sheila rose, and curtly delivered this:

"Your son is sexually impotent with any girl Jewish—that being what I am; since a girl Jewish reminds him of his mother— yes, *you!*— who's Jewish also. Though I love him, how can I be his wife? It's the same as my being barren, his being incompetent as a husband in bed. I want to have *children* Jewish. He wouldn't be able to give me any . . . Please, you're blushing too loudly, Mrs Eric's Mother. You think it not nice of me to talk like this? But it's the fatal truth.

"Our generation is different from yours—there's a big gap between them. I say this because I anticipate your argument. Your argument is a nice Jewish girl wouldn't know about sex till she's married; right? So to test Eric's potency pre-maritally is an unfair test and therefore invalid, since it's morally disgraceful, it's not right, he *should* abstain until the wedding proper. You'd maintain he's' to be *congratulated* for his chastity, forbearance, restraint. Well, that's what *your* generation thinks. *Ours* sees it a different way.

"Birth-control methods have grown more airtight, as morals have loosened up. A son of today who's obedient to your old-fashioned prohibitions earns only contempt from the girls he dates. They want him to plunge and poke— and penetrate.

"That's the crucial friction. We've reached the critical point. Penetrate?! Find Eric doing it to me! He can't! The crud!

"Yes, I fling scorn on him. He's a Mama's little baby. I remind him too much of *you*, Madam, so he's courteously unable—due to psychological repressions—to be a man with a girl Jewish.

"You wanted me to be his wife: Well, let me puncture your dream now. I *won't* be his wife. I'll marry another, though loving Eric.

"Sorry, Mrs Eric's Mother. This is disappointing you no end. But that's only fair: Eric was always disappointing *me*—'no end'.

"So I leave Eric to you, Mrs Eric's Mother. And to you also, Sir: Mrs Eric's Mother's Husband. *You* obey her, Sir, and so does your son. But the line is drawn with me: I *don't* obey.

"I'm storming out. I've just made a scene. It was a stormy one. It'll wake all you Victorian Jews up from your nice middle-class hypocrisies full of delicate and earnest little morals.

"I've been shocking, haven't I? I'm paying you all back for being sexually frustrated at the hands—or at the something else—of your dear son. Take him back, I don't want him: he's yours."

She ran out of the room and out of the house, slamming the door. Eric gave chase, while his mother subsided in a scream and his father stood dazed, immobile.

Eric caught a glimpse of Sheila, She was dashing to the subway station. Eric ran to overtake her. He would, too. But what good would that do? Would he then rape her? Things stood as they had before. Their impasse would only continue. She had delivered a severe denunciation, to clear the air, in an exceedingly unfriendly scene that was an ordeal of terror for his parents. But words didn't change anything. They had stated the truth, they were *her* words. He would remain being what he was,

The time was now pre-dawn Sunday. Monday night was the deadline. There was still time, but for what? He'd stick by Sheila, spend it with her. First she must be located. Surely she'd be heading for her own apartment, at this hour of the night, She wouldn't be seeing her "fiancé" till Monday night. Eric reached the subway station, but a train had come and left, bearing away Sheila. Eric would follow in the next train, and call on her. For what good, he didn't know.

There was a long delay before the next train arrived. He got off at Sheila's stop; ran to her building, and rang the bell. No answer. But she had given him a key once: he had it on him. He let himself in. The place was dark. He switched on every light, but Sheila was in no room. He then remembered—*she* had the key to *his* apartment. So he ran to the bus stop and after quite a delay in the late dawn of an early Sunday, a bus pulled up and took him. He clamored at the door impatiently, and was let off at his stop. He ran to his own apartment and looked everywhere in there, but not a sign of Sheila. Had she called on her fiancé? Yes, that must be it—she had broken her agreement not to see him till Monday night; But Eric didn't know the name, let alone address, of his rival.

But Sheila had a close friend and confidante, Betty, who would most likely know. Eric phoned her up. She was angry to be wakened. He demanded his rival's phone number and address. "What for" came Betty's annoyed voice. "To track down Sheila." "Now?" "Yes, now." "She's here, she's with me." "Then I'm coming over." Eric was in joy. Sheila wasn't lost yet. He managed to find a cab and took it to Betty's apartment building. He was let in after buzzing. When the door was opened, by Betty, Sheila was readily seen. Overcome, Eric leapt at her. They wrestled on the floor. Their love had come ecstatic, demonic, in frenzy.

Cool and glad, Betty made a generous offer:

"Sheila's been sleeping on the couch, Eric. But now *I*'m taking over the couch. You two can take my bed, it's much bigger. Careful not to wake me. See you much later: preferably afternoon. I leave you to each other: that's good hands. At least you're capable of kissing, if not of copulating. Do some of that, but not loudly, please."

Eric and Sheila profusely thanked this true friend for such a loyal gesture. They were quickly nude and hugging under Betty's blankets. These innocent exertions soon tired them. Their ardor "spent," in innocence, they were soon sleeping the benign sleep of the innocent. This doomed couple, in love.

They woke up Sunday afternoon, clutching each other for dear life. They were really latching on, tightly attached all along their bodily alignment. They were gripping in, they were kissing. There was desperation to this. They cleaved, for the severance to be.

"Couldn't we be a sexless married couple, is that possible, Sheila? Just to remain together. And your reward might be, for your sacrifice, that one day as a married pair my virility might suddenly start working. Out of the blue, just like that. A miraculous mutation in me, to transform me into what I ought to be. Your love will change a toad into a handsome prince—or, *release* the prince from his toad's captivity. Perhaps you're being tested. Let's look at it that way."

"Eric, that's too unlikely. Being realistic is the only way to keep love in safekeeping. 'Held' by dreams, our love would fall apart. I'm still stymied, and a solution seems far away."

"Only the remainder of this day remains, then all of tomorrow, till ten o'clock when your decision will be announced to this rival I've never met. But what if he's like me, and unable to perform?"

"I've tested him, and he's not."

"But you swore to me you were a proper prude with him. You had lied. So I'm deceived, am I?"

"Eric, I'm only human. I had to allay my doubts. I doubted my own femininity, thanks to you. I took the blame for your failure of manhood, despite my bitching against you. So I needed reassurance: and your rival was the man."

"I'd like to kill him."

"He loves me. He's not *deliberately* harming you, since he never met you. I won't let you resort to him for a scapegoat. Be man enough to look *within*, and take the blame."

"I can't face it in there. So I seek a displacement."

"Well, you're too aware to get away with it. Let's get dressed now, I think Betty is awake. Sunday afternoon is already fading. Our prospects diminish, our hopes surely dim, for our love's future. It looks bleak. Sorry."

"Suicide has crossed my mind."

"Let it not cross your body. Dismiss it, it's too self-destructive."

"But if I lose you—what will I have?"

"Sorrow, I'm afraid. But go on living."

"Our dwindling hours make me morbid. I wish I could control this body, and keep my erection durable for penetration of you. But it has its own say, and goes its own way; that is, away: on me."

"No, not in me. For the lack of a bridge between us, there can't be any further commerce between our banks."

"I'm worried about my mother and father—my mother especially, since my father doesn't get so easily affected. Your speech might have killed her, I must revisit them."

"Do so, but let's meet tonight: our final night it might ever be. Visit me, and I'll give you a little dinner, What a lonely date, it looks like being. The fate has booked our separation for tomorrow night. We're given up on a solution. We're now dramatizing our departing memory, and building up toward it. Our love crawls to its end: limp, like your—"

"—Don't *dig* it in. I can do without your mocking. Our sentiments incline to sentiment. Don't betray love mentally as I do physically. Lovingly tender it your respect. A fading is coming on us. Till the bitter end, let's cling."

"Go now to see that your mother is all right. Then report back to *me*, tonight. For our last time in bed the night through with as usual nothing happening. Sentiment alone doesn't suffice—nor man nor woman can live on its disembodied essence and only that. Not in *my* prime of age, anyway. I'm dying to have a child Jewish. A boy, to be what you're not when his manhood rises. I'll be sure not to name him after you. It would be a living dampener to curse his virility out. Sorry, there I go, again. Slap me, I deserve it."

"I won't slap you; My *palm* is impotent, too."

"It's spreading, then, to all your limbs?—an indiscriminate impotence to take its toil all throughout you?"

"Through*in* me. My body *looks* well. But not so well does it *do*. That's a truth to end love: as well it will."

They gave a light-tapping kiss goodbye, and Eric was off to see how his mother was. Betty tried to console Sheila with big-hearted compassion. But Sheila was weak and used the remaining light of day on Sunday to weep by, so as to contain the path her tears took in orderly channels down her tragic cheeks by the help of a lugubrious mirror; the grooves and ruts for her tears were so well-worn, for Eric's sake! More so than her *vaginal* walls, that were in no rut at all.

There ought to be a formula. She'd consult Betty.

Betty had on her personal library shelf some modern sex manuals on technique of performance and the curing of difficulties between any oddly combined partners. The two friends pored through the manuals to find any key, to hit on whatever hadn't been taken notice of before. "Male Impotence" chapters were combed for every letter in every word; for a clue overlooked. Sheila had continuously to wipe away her tears. She was distraught. Without an intervening miracle or a momentous discovery to do a great trick, Eric would become finally lost. The one major love of her life: its numbered hours trailed, in their injured jeopardy, limping, to the end.

"What will be have discovered with his mother? That might influence tonight's performance. Better get going, to cook him his meal. Have lots of wine. Some beer, too. Darling, have a good night. That's my feeble wish. I can't help you. Take your care to the Gods. Invoke Venus, possibly. No, he loves you already. What God confers potency? I forgot my Greek mythology. Enough babbling. Be brave. Go."

Sheila was at home preparing. Eric was due soon. What would he report?

"Hello," he came in. "What's to eat?"

Suspiciously his voice had a cheerful note. He seemed like a changed man. Something had turned around. "What's up?" Sheila asked guardedly.

"My mother's in a major coma, she can't recover. She's in the terminal critical ward at the hospital, her imminent death is expected soon.

"She collapsed by your speech. All her values, assaulted by your words, cried 'Too much!' My mother couldn't take it. She's near to dead. The world's Jewish population will go one less."

"What does that mean for *us*?"

"I feel dashing and confident. Object to being seduced, honey?"

"Before dinner? Never!"

"Well, turn the stove low. It's enough that *I'm* burning for you. But let the *food* keep and not burn. Food can wait. I invoke priority."

"Something, takes precedence? What is it?"

"Guess."

"I won't. But let's do it."

Neither had a drink. They repaired straight to the bedroom. They did it, they made it! It was done!

Eric was calmly elated. "Wait here, dear, don't get up. I still need some therapeutic reassurance, so I'll come back and prove I can do it again on a short time interval. First I want to phone the hospital."

Yes, his mother was dead, the official nurse answered. Eric was half of an orphan Jewish: the *major* half.

"She's dead," he said, as he climbed in again. He performed very well. Sheila was lightly amazed. Such virility! It exceeded Eric's "rival's" by a long shot, by a considerable dose.

"Have we solved our trouble?" Sheila rhetorically bade.

"I've been waiting all these years," Eric said, gaining will; "so let me try a third straight time, of consecutive successes. If pulled off, what an amazing feat!"

It was done!. She was Jewish. But so what?

"You remind me of my dead mother." he said. "Care to take her place?"

"No, I have an aversion to incest."

"Would my being your husband mean incest, if we're not otherwise related?"

"No, it's quite proper for us to be wed. There are no complications."

"But shouldn't I have a mourning period for my mother?"

"You mourned her *before* death. Now, celebrate."

They got up from bed and dressed, They ate her cooking; it was good, They planned to have children. Boys would be best.

Lots of little bouncing Erics. The proper mates for future brides Jewish yet unknown. The Jewish race is not dead. Not while good couples Jewish like Sheila and Eric survive in adult love. And to time's ceremony add the children Add those future Erics. With good mothers Jewish. With easy lust and grace.

Eric's pathology arrested him. He's free now. Sheila has become pregnant. It's their wedded future already. That Monday never came, that was to be a deadline. Calendars skipped it. There's the dynasty Jewish Eric. Borne bountifully, in the belly Sheila.

REPLY TO A SUGGESTION THAT I MARRY OUTSIDE MY OWN KIND AS A RELIEF FOR BEING TO LONELY AMONG MY OWN KIND

I don't want to marry out of my own species. That would be unseemly. A female beaver, cow, even a female seashell—my desperation makes me indiscriminate. But I must stick to my own kind. I should marry within the human race—though that kind of inbred incest might produce progeny with weak chins and other deformities by which degeneracy announces itself. Besides, there's the matter of loyalty. I *belong* to mankind, I'm even *one* of them. So I should keep it all "within the family." None of it should leak out, to betray secrets to perhaps a spying enemy. It would even be ungrateful not to be clannish. I might be accused of parochialism, provincialism—but that shouldn't deter me from contributing to my blood community, the collective fraternity I'm issued from. I'm *stamped* with humanity—to deviate would go against my grain; to defect would be to disown my birthright. Let's face it, I'm a man. So either I should marry a human, or never marry at all. I'm a runner or sprinter in one race—the human race. Let me keep to that track.

CHARLES' COURTSHIP, ENGAGEMENT, AND MARRIAGE, WITH IRENE HIS HAPPY BRIDE

I

Charles equated being confused (which he always was) with being complex, hence deep. Girls, philosophical problems, social procedure, political strife, conformity to the rigors of environment adjustment to the unexpected—all these withheld their labyrinthine mysteries from the simple art of solution: causing him to esteem the rich, entangled complexity of his mind, perplexed by the slightest intrusion on its consciousness.

Confounded, molested, befuddled were his thoughts, like a turbulent storm at sea, when confronted by reality's symbol of torment: Irene. To say "I love you" was perilously simple: an approach he was terrified to dare. His busy head used its full employment force, in a prolonged campaign to become unconfused.

Irene vanished in a crowd. Charles plunged into the crowd. He was equally lost, but in raging solitude. He sought vainly for her, but not she for him: she didn't know he existed; she worked in the floor above him, and discreet research had revealed his discovery of her name. They had never spoken; but to flame romance, they occasionally shared the same elevator, or the same cafeteria. Charles' timidity had barred further intercourse.

II

Their firm occupied floors five to fifteen in an eighteen-floor building, so it had a controlling share of elevators, lavatories, heat regulators, air conditioners, janitation supplies, incinerator shafts, and other maintenance equipment essential for personnel service in a modern building dedicated to the art of commerce. Irene had been working there a year. Charlie was no novice, either.

He would trail her after work. (To a subway entrance, or to a date appointment with a boyfriend.) But would not inflict his presence on her mythical awareness: he hid in the shadows of anonymity, keeping well within those public boundaries known as "the background."

Why doesn't she love me in return?" he pondered. Irony cast its sheltering ambiguity on this fatal question.

III

Weekends, he was resigned to not glimpsing her. They were both free from work. Their city was too vast for an accidental convergence of their paths.

Like pear juice distilled from the blossom of an apple tree, an inspired solution at once clarified Charles' love life: "The trick is to *marry* her: his strategy crystallized. Here was initiative, allied to determination, married to a resultant satisfactory merger. But Irene lived in her own circle; Charles had never yet been admitted to her consciousness.

To provide her with a dowry that she could give him, he put aside almost all of his weekly salary, trusting to the compound interest of a regular savings bank. The economic basis of married bliss was now gilded with a material foundation.

Charles was a model future husband. He hoped that Irene would be an equally excellent wife.

Since *he* had chosen her, she undoubtedly *would* be.

Conflict being eliminated, the bridegroom-to-be's brow surfaced a deep stronghold of serenity.

But his parents, and his parents-in-law, had so far not been notified. He would set about to correct this deplorable omission.

His and Irene's firm, expansively imperialistic, bought out the bottom four floors, and the top three ones, and so obtained a monopoly hold on a total eighteen-floor building. Charles was promoted to the floor *above* Irene. Nominally, his job remained the same.

Irene typed away. She became engaged to one of the smart junior executives. This delighted her sense of institutional conventionality, which she possessed to an extraordinarily average degree.

Charles hadn't informed his bride-to-be, or her or his parents, of his impending proposal to his ideal serene Irene. Why ruin a delightful prospect with unruly haste? Let nature brood its maturing plan.

IV

"Charles," said his office neighbor, "that girl on the floor below got married. The very pretty one, Irene." This way, Charles found out that patience could not unlock all doors in wisdom's house. Disappointment swiftly became his mood.

"She did that without consulting me!" he reflected, with furious indignation. Her infidelity stormed his impulse loose, so that he miscalculated an office form, bungled up his figures, ruined some statistical column, botched an original copy's carbon duplicate, and cluttered the files with irrelevant clerical errors. His supervisor was at a meeting, so these incorrectitudes were not arrested in ascending levels of processing from the mechanical inaccuracies at their lower origin. In time to be, that entire firm would be put back months in their contabulations, in the multiple spiraling to appalling magnitude, from those slight minor atrocities in Charles' recording of facts sprung awry. He was not detected, but his anger's riled wrath had been purged by a superlative outlet, notably commercial anarchy, a company's fall from disciplined precision to an unaccountable catastrophe that hundreds of accountants would labor to put straight. Irene was lost; and revenge was misplaced; but Charles' feat of destruction sweetly soothed his restored sanity. Irene *had* been a good wife, after all.

TO DECIDE TO STOP LOVING HARRIET

I really loved Harriet. God she was pretty!

Trouble is, she didn't love me back. And the way I felt made that a *big* trouble, bothersome, gnawing, just chewing me up. What to do? Study my goal, and on that build a few calculations.

The goal was Harriet, her attainment. Right off, there was bad luck: she was engaged, and desperately in love with her fiancé. Hardly a promising beginning.

Yes, but there's a catch. If she was engaged, meaning she was due to get him and the bond would be knotted, then why was her love for him *desperate*?

Desperate is when you fear not being able to get what you want. But Harriet was securely guaranteed of having it—him, her loved one. I had to study this further.

Her fiancé didn't love her! That's why her love for him was not secure but desperate. Then why did he consent to wed her? I could study and find hope. But to love someone who loves another is humiliating, and would debase me should I pursue it further. If Harriet wasn't loved by the fiancé she loved, that still didn't make *me* loved by her. My position was ignominious. It held forth no promise.

Harriet's fiancé is marrying her for *convenience*. It stands to improve his worldly prospects, due to the business eminence of her father,

Harriet *knows* he doesn't love her. She's joyous she's to get him in marriage, but in despair that he wants her not for herself but for ulterior benefits and advantages by connection. She'll marry him anyhow, hoping that the wedded habit between them will create his post-marriage love for her, however unromantically belated. She'll stake her all on that, however pride-suffering it is on the onset. So she'll go through with it.

It's useless my loving her. Now she's just married him. I stand by. I'm just another wedding guest. He's an opportunist; *using* her love. *I* felt so pure. *I* would have done her justice!.

I give up on Harriet. She's now officially pregnant. I'll withdraw my love, and cast it somewhere else, with more promising results in the offing, for this purity I have, of bestowal. On *whom* to bestow? On Harriet no longer. She's her husband's victim. Whose victim am *I* to be?

GETTING MARRIED, AND THE TIMELY HAZARD OF LOVE LEAVING OR BEING LEFT BY THE UGLY SPECTACLE OF AN AGING, AND THEN, GULP!, DEATH BITES OFF ONE TO LET THE OTHER GO.

I met what to me was a beautiful twenty-one-year-old girl. I would have liked to marry her: she would be mine then. Ideally, I wanted to take possession of her.

To my surprise, I proposed. To my incredibility, she accepted. I couldn't believe it. She was to be my bride.

I was a lifelong bachelor of over forty. Did I dare to hardly deserve her? Yet she would soon be mine. I was dreaming: It was *still* real.

We were now engaged. I went out with her, and she seemed older. I said nothing of it.

The *next* time I went out with her, she seemed older *yet*. But I could still recognize her, to identify with: it was *her*, all right.

I went out with her *again*, three weeks after we had first ever met. And she was *still* older: or *looked* it.

I got *very* suspicious. What was going on? It was confusing, I was depressed.

But I was in love, so what could I do? I was trapped. I had to go through with it. I wanted her.

She was aging so swiftly, I couldn't slow it down. I would hurry up, marry her quick.

I went down the aisle to greet my bride who was at the altar. She looked ancient! It was hideous.

It was really bad luck.

I loved her, and went through with it. The minister pronounced us man and wife. I was now a husband, but to a crone.

Eagerly I took her home, I madly wanted sex, we hadn't had any till now, due to our civilization's puritan custom of traditional chastity till the wedding day.

I undressed her, in our "bridal suite." She was loathsome, she was withered.

I lost my lusty appetite. Now I would have to wait for her to fade, to die. Then, if I had the heart, I'd try all over again. Curses! Aging, so unexpected. Damn it! I left her a "virgin." I wouldn't tamper. It wasn't consummated. Only *legally* were we man and wife, but not by actuality. She repelled me. Ugh!

She died, at last. Good. Now I have another chance. I won't fall for someone so *young* next time. I'm wary, it was so deceptive, as the proof turned out. I'm leery. A *slow* one I want: who'll stay the course.

I want staying power. I want a *steady* bride. Not one running down in a horrendous downhill torrent to decay. What I loved went old by magic. Out of control, life went tragic.

I was now sober, and wise. I was still in the same year of being after forty, having met her and seen her to her grave. I looked cautiously about. I went marketing. I wanted a *slow* one. Even let her be lethargic. Better than mercurial, better than slipping away.

Having is one thing. *Holding*: that's the *next* phase. And *keep on* holding. That's crucial. Love is not the flower of a day. It's supposed to be eternal. That's what the idealists say. We like to avoid grief. We want to *keep*.

Love will win against time. I'm taking my time about it.

I browse about the market. There's the likely one. She's stunning, I propose. Coolly, I expect to be accepted. Surely, I am. Good. We get married soon.

She's arrested from decay. *I'*m the one that's aging. The end of my life nears. She's so young, but far away.

She's only twenty-two, this one. Till my end, I'll *always* know her as that. For my end is nigh. My demise is at hand.

I tried it a second time—it turned out *worse*!

The first time I was left. Now, I'm making my *bride* be left.

At speed, at speed! I *did* have sex with this one. Already, death has cut off my balls. It's marred me as a husband. I leave the one I love. May she take another.

TWO WAYS OF LOVING CLAIRE

I don't know what life is; maybe because I'm living it, so that I have an interest in it, that is, a personal interestedness, to advance and maintain myself, too selfishly active to know it. So life I don't know, too busy being or living it. Love? I know what love is when I'm not in love. But now I'm *in* love. Something is at stake, I want something. I want my love to be requited by the one I love. It isn't yet, but I have hope. The object of my love is called Claire. That's purely an accident, determined only by what her parents chose to name her. If she were called "Ruth," I would love her just as well. By any other name, she'd still be she, and my love would go to her. I've kept my love a secret, held back its evidence. I hope she doesn't suspect it. I'd love her to love me. In her presence, I'm freshly bathed, hair combed, shaved, wearing clothes calculated to make a good appearance. I *care* about how I impress Claire. I want her to love me; I behave accordingly; as yet she doesn't love me, but hope is not dead. It may take time for her to love me. Her love for me would increase the power of my own love to gain its way. What does my love want? It wants to be with her often, in the closest approximate intimacy that two people are capable of. It wants to lie with her in bed, in very close contact. It wants to be *glued* to her, body and soul. It wants *her* to love *me*. My love makes these demands. It's acutely sensitive to Claire. It attends to her every act or word, hangs on it, fearing, wishing. Love is an obsessive state. It focused on Claire. It bears pressure on her; but not obviously; it's learned to wait. It waits for Claire's response to increase to the point where *I*'m loved. Till then, it can't relax. It's tense; it's on edge. It studies Claire, waits for a sign. It sighs, while waiting. It's in a state of desire, it's dependent; it's Claire-concentrative. Has she a de-Claire-ation? Her feeling toward me—I'm eager to have it a certain way, I mustn't push, I must remain passive. Let her own heart conclude; I can't force it.

∞

The preceding paragraph in accurate, and that's all right. But one thing went wrong. It was accurate for too long. What it described remained unchanged and that state referred to is *still* true. My loyal and constant heart kept waiting and hoping, cautiously, not betraying itself, tending "casually" on Claire with the most studied negligence. My love never advanced or became encouraged, its "progress" was kept in a hush of expectation—never realized: no breakthrough. Now I'm wrinkled, and am no closer to my object. Claire has settled down into three successive marriages, while I "waited." I must conclude, irascibly: my patience never paid off. I'm less romantic with all the wrinkles time has given me while I cleverly concealed my love. It's obvious I'm bitter: what else is left?

I hate having aged. My virility waned, my body slowed up. I'm not fit to be loved any more. Hope has died. This is the first radical departure from the first paragraph, which had been tense with sustained hope. Here in the third paragraph, I've gotten to the point where it's true no longer about my hope, thanks to the enormous time interval elapsed, which abstractly I term "years." I've progressed to the death of hope. Life *does* change.

∞

"Claire, we've know each other for half a century. Is there any significance in that for you?"

"Of course, Bruce. You're an old, tried, and true friend. You've seen me through thick and thin. I appreciate it. My children have all grown up, I was married three times since I first knew you. You're one of my few constant stables all through my life, which otherwise has confused me with all the changing. I hope to know you even as I'm dying. It will be a fitting unity to end my life."

"Without me your life would have lacked consistency?"

"Oh Bruce, I'm tired of these abstractions, always analyzing. That's what *your* mind goes for. Mine is tired with all the living I've done. Thank God my current husband I'll never divorce, the harmony lacked in my first two marriages. I like to end up peacefully. I'm glad I know you."

"Claire, it's time I made a slight confession. I've kept it from you for fifty years."

"You mean that you've always loved me? I kept my *knowing* it from you, so we're even."

"You knew it from the start!? I thought I was being so subtle. What slip revealed it?"

"My instinctive woman's intuition knew it all along. It's as simple as magic, and just as natural. Well, now it's out in the open. We're neither deceiving each other by feigning ignorance. It's about time, too."

"Is it too late far me to be angry at you?"

"I have no regret in not informing you, my dear friend, that I knew you loved me. No guilt or remorse, since it was up to you to conquer shyness and declare your passion manfully. You were untrue to us both, with your closed-in secret. The first step had to be yours. You never too it."

"If I *had* been so bold, with enough courage to declare my love in the agony of its sincerity . . . would you . . . were you . . . ?"

"No. I would have rejected you. I never felt for you as a *man*, just as a friend. Does that soothe you?"

"Ambivalently. Were you in love with another when I first conceived love for you?"

"Yes, I was engaged in an affair, but it turned out bad, he didn't care, then for a rebound I met the man who turned to be my first husband; and all subsequent developments you've been following since. Now the history is brought up to date, clear, by inserting the belated missing piece of the beginning. You're not offended, Bruce?"

"I never stopped loving you. Half a century of love in vain. Isn't that a record?"

"The heart's records aren't public. I'm grateful. Have I hurt you?"

"For fifty years, yes."

"I apologize. But I can't atone. I'm not guilty at fault. You were too scared, cautious, and secret. Now you pay the coward's penalty."

"I've been paying it all this time. I won't *stop* paying it. The grave will be a further installment."

"You poor man. No *wonder* you never married. Being in love with me all this time! A lifelong sacrifice, and a broken heart."

"This is senile sentimentality. We're both old."

"I've had a fuller life with my opposing gender than you've had with yours. How sorry I am for you!"

"Why didn't you snap my spell, break my fruitless enchantment, by informing me while there was still time for me to recover and find another woman?"

"I know you had physical consolations with other women."

"But I never gave myself totally, for I was still enchained to you, tyrannized over by hope. Hope kept me fast and true to you. If it had been snapped early enough for my liberation, I could have had a fulfilling love *with* another woman: instead of these barren years wasted in a love *for* you."

"Are you recriminating me? Accusing me of ruining your life?"

"Precisely that."

"I'm not to blame. Your cowardly half-a-century of silence is to blame. *You*'re responsible, it's *your* fate. Sure I wanted to hold on to your love. Yes, I *was* being selfish. But you were the fool, weren't you?"

"That's starkly evident now."

"Is our friendship ruined?"

"It's come to that."

"It's late in life for me to end our relationship." Think of all the tradition we're tossing away on a peeve of vanity and a grievance of silence. We've come so far, and only now have undeceived each other. Let's hold on. The grave is close."

"Lonely for me. My unrequited grave."

"I love you as a *friend*. But I'm in love with my *husband*."

"Yes. All my rivals were always successful. To a man, they always won, to keep me forlorn."

"Stop whining with your self-pity. Be a man for once! Take it on the chin."

"My chin is infirm. I'm tottering."

"Old people should stick together. Loyalty brought us so far."

"Loyalty kept my life barren of love's happiness every man has a right to. I've loved you loyally, and in vain."

"That's the way it turned out. We can't undo it."

"We're both responsible, Claire."

"If you want a conclusion, I don't have any. What moral do *you* find"

"It's too sad for morals. I lived my life to length, but fooled myself in being too prudent in love, afraid of rejection, stalling off the truth till fifty years too late. I could have adjusted and had a better life, once reconciled with the blow of losing you. I held on to the canker, hope. I held on till it rankles that it never fall off. Hope enslaved me. I nursed it too closely, I didn't test it. I didn't dare. I didn't want to find out."

"So you admit it's *your* fault?"

"*You*"re no angel in this. What you knew stole your innocence."

"Wisdom has come. Do your life over again, and use it,"

"Are you mocking me?"

"I'm protecting myself. Don't accuse me."

"I still love you, Claire."

"And for the first-time without hope: You're getting versatile. You loved *with* hope, and now *without*."

"It's about time my love's monotony played on a different key. All this living, and I still learn."

"Let's laugh it off. And keep our friendship."

"Unequal though it is. Yes."

THERESA BEING DISCUSSED

(Two men sitting in a gradually darkening room, facing each other from a moderate distance.)

Her beauty staggers credulity.

I don't believe it!

Her curves lengthen as she stands, and broaden when she squats.

This descriptive flattery—does it do her justice?

When the shadows lengthen and twilight pierces the room, her face so stealthily darkens that the process of dusk will steal across it. Her beauty turns dark like the internal glow of an owl. How nocturnally is she become!, capped by the crow's fiddle in the moon.

Yeah, but what happens when you switch on the light? Is her illusion spoiled blankly white again?

The light does *not* get switched on! The romantic must cast its spell. A moody darkness throbbles a silent song.

All mere twaddle! Merely dressed-up nonsense, to strum on the idle keys of reverie. What's the name of this beauty, so-called, of yours?

Your skepticism has a mockery in it. Why should I betray my heart's tone, where sacred affections are at play, to your gross and unsympathetic insinuations? My lip seals its shrine, closed tight on its devotion.

Your hilarious sentimentality rings untrue! What do you feel, and for whom? Are you in *love* with this alleged creature? I must seriously doubt even her *reality*, unless you breathe her name forth, to mingle with the world's assortment of names, from that precious and insular secrecy you clad her in artificiality, as though fearing exposure. Brave the true light of day, or night's sharp electric shock! Call out her name, at once!

And desecrate it, for you sacrilegiously to despoil? Your ear has a ruthless interpretation, so I won't feed it. Seeing Destruction gleam forth its malice in your eyes, why should I make a sacrificial presentation of her to them? You're barred from seeing her, or hearing her name.

(Baiting) Her?! Who is *that*, "*her*?"

Stop your toying! Can't you respect another's dearness? I must sterilize what you approach!

My words are not mocking vials of poison or the germs sprayed in dark malignancy on the virginal flower of your wound! They just *question*, to sound out your sincerity—to what hollow caverns of depth, or assumed depths in hollowness?

I won't submit to *testing*. You're a defiling agent. Do you claim clinical exemption for your cynical serpent's hiss? Your bitterness spews out. It seeks to storm, by violation, the tower life erects on its heart's fond base.

You inflate emptiness itself! By hell, who *is* she?!

Not for *your* knowing, foul seeker!

Has she sexual equipment somewhere?

My limit is intolerably passed! Go smell out baseness elsewhere! your nose is the greatest instrument perjury can devise.

For the sniffing out of *phoniness*! My doubt breeds its own righteousness. How sincere is your passion for this dame?!

It passes sincerity itself!

Then by that much does it overdo itself.

Overdo? Your *repentance* is overdue! My nameless lady's sorely tried honor must vindicate your abusive threat! Repent your vile tactics of persecution. Your unfounded suspicion detected unreal realities. Retract your smirching, and unsmear by apology's oath.

It's not your *honor* I've offended, but your ability to conceal a lie!

Her honor is my protest! Mine is entwined in hers.

Have I diabolically intruded?

Yes. Her name is withheld.

Have you veiled her anonymously?

For you, she's unseen.

Unseen, unnamed—unknown.

And preserved. Injure her no more.

How can I violate what's immaculate? You've stripped me of harm, in her gallant defense.

Good. Lay down your arms.

I respect her right to be unknown.

Has curiosity abandoned you entirely?

Yes, and cleaned the slate for the emergence of indifference.

Are you cold to her beauty?

Her beauty's unbelievable. *That* I can believe.

Then you deny it?

What?

Her beauty. Her assumed beauty that I advertise.

No. I'm gullible. Do teach me,

Shall I name her, first?

Yes; that's a likely start.

Theresa.

Ah. Is she lovely?

Unaccountably so.

So you find her?

And *know* her, that way.

How much of truth is in her beauty?

Her beauty *is* truth. It is what it is.

What an enchanting creature.

Yes, admirable, in every respect.

Has doubt crept across your voice? Does reservation cast its scruple?

There's no compunction. I'm adamant.

Oh. You stick by your guns?

She's *real*: I *made* her so!

Yes, you fibber! Have you created her?

As she is, she stands created. Therefore, she is.

You disclaim authorship in the matter.

Never mind. As I find her, so I take her.

Then you treat her casually. Is your regard infirm?

I highly esteem her.

Who? Theresa?

Theresa, yes. And she's beautiful.

I know: you have the right to make her so.

How?

What we concoct, is fancifully endowed. Art confers privilege on its subject. Can Theresa breathe?

Yes: you should see her chest!

Then you're not above a little lust for her!

Don't I deserve it, for all that I spent in making her?

Yes. Then *do* marry Theresa.

We *are* married.

Then, though delayed, my congratulations are in order.

I accept them. Theresa will be charmed.

Is she above a little adultery?

Don't try it! My warning is severe.

I don't impose a threat. I'm merely curious.

Temper such rough interest. Theresa is delicate.

Ah! A *frail* girl excites me! I feel aroused!

But she's *my wife*!

Theresa?

Yes: who else?

Oh. Some men have a harem's worth of imagination.

I'm faithful to Theresa.

The she's *singularly* blessed!

Her beauty *inspires singlemindedness*.

It sure does! You've been on the subject all afternoon! Draw the blinds, pull shades down, night has invaded us. We're in darkness. Where's the light switch?

(Warning:) Switch on that light, and Theresa goes off.

A good bargain.

WIVES

HOW MY WIFE AND I MADE AMENDS
AS NOT TO FOLLOW TWO DIVERSE TRENDS,
SO ARRIVE SAFELY AT MUTUAL ENDS.

If you and your wife are at a loss
as to which one of you two is boss
(a dispute possibly leading to divorce),
calm down and pursue a safe course.
Why can't you both be at the helm,
so neither one can overwhelm?
What about applying democracy,
rather than dictatorship's autocracy,
that distorts any fairness of policy?
Thus politically you're both correct,
yet neither proves him- or herself perfect.
My wife believes that life is hell,
an opinion that could at times ring a bell.
Very few can dispute her point
that life has a capacity to disappoint.
Thus we share some beliefs on this round joint
of earth that make us both profound
that the starting of agreement has been found.
Thus she and I shall remain married,
because sheer rational logic has carried
into both our heads, my wife's and mine,
so what kept us apart has now made us twine
to pure similarity that we're both in align
and follow the directionality of the same line.

WITH MY WIFE I ASK FOR HARMONY, BECAUSE THERE'S NO HARM IN ME.

When a married couple
is in disrupple
due to basic disagreements,
the search is on for sweet-heart-ism.
Both believe in meritocracy.
Both oppose dictatorship
with its wielding of the whip,
and also strict autocracy,
the enemy of democracy.
Both believe in fair play
from early morn to end of day.
Both oppose inhumanity,
but don't mind a little profanity.
So what are we in opposition to?
To the squelching of what's true
and the affirmation of the false.
Both believe in Strauss's waltz
due to its melody of tune.
So why aren't we more in attune?
Which way is the most opportune?
Perhaps we should kiss and make up
while wife cooks us delicious sup
with a generous supply of wine
to stop her nasty negative whine.
Thus we achieve a superior mood
to exterminate all tendency to brood,
nor on each other to fling complaint
because neither has been proven a saint,
which both regard as a blamable taint.
Under such high standards, we both faint,

collapsing so in common.
Tolerant leniency we should summon.

HOW MY WIFE AND I GET ALONG:
I PRAISE HER IN MY LYRICS FOR HER SONG.

My wife is wonderfully kind to me,
and doesn't scold me too harshly
when foolishly I disobey
her stern commands and orders,
that far exceed logical borders.
My attitude toward my wife is meek.
It's peace and quiet I seek,
and get it when I don't protest too much
when my wife's treatment of me is much too tough.
Although my wife treats me slightly rough,
I still love her and make her know it
by praising her highly in my role as poet.
With a ripped shirt, I dare not ask her to sew it.
Even a needle is her weapon
if she condescends to threaten.

IF MY WIFE DIED,
HOW I WILL HAVE CRIED!

If my wife died, I'd cry my eyes out
till no visual instrument was left,
leaving me optically bereft.
I'd miss her so much,
but most of all her tactical touch.
Her absence would be too much.
Years later, my weeping would stop,
and the tears gradually dry up.
Then I'd get my sight back,

including the extra bonus of *insight*,
which uses the eyes, but has an additional bite.
Then I'll be all-seeing like a sage,
who deeply knows the guarded secrets of every age.
It's like getting a degree in history,
which automatically solves every mystery.
Thus I'd become slightly hysterical,
so my new subject would become mathematical,
including the geometric.
Altogether, it's so scholarly hectic
that I'd have to invent a new metric.
That would lead to the electric,
so I'd have to fly supersonic.
After that, I should drink a tonic
and consider that life is so ironic.

THE UNSUNK SHIP.

My marriage slipped away on wings of discord.
Love's waste was more than we could afford,
so again we resumed partnership,
so as not to drown our good marriage ship.
So here it is, sailing along,
making the ocean sing along
on frisky waves of song,
all with a nautical air
to drown out despair.
All the money we saved
stopped our marriage from sinking in deprave.
We were real sailors, true and brave,
not marriage bailers like a joint knave.
We needn't now to each other goodbye wave.
Thus, our marriage is observing thrift,
so we keep benefitting from our good ocean gift.

We once were tempted to dive for a dip,
but that was too dangerous for a trip.
Love is also aboard our ship
like a stow-away, avoiding the captain's whip.
We don't dare risk an uneasy slip,
otherwise our adventure would be a gyp.

WHAT IF?

If your wife dies, how can you stop weeping?
It moistens your eyes when you're sleeping.
Thus, loving her doesn't need her alive.
Even when she's dead, loving her can survive.
Memory keeps her going.
The lost hours are bestowing
her continued company on you,
accompanied by an imaginary view.
Her face appears before your eyes
as a mirage or a dream.
Your love for her remains supreme.

CONFUSING BORDERS
AT SUCH SMALL QUARTERS.

If you have a nasty cold,
quell it before it gets so bold
as to wake up your sleeping wife
to introduce marital strife
that threatens your husbandry life.
Don't allow a cough to emerge,
so make your nightly discipline a purge
of the slightest disruptive urge.
From panic your wife already suffers,
guaranteed to make you weep

with being so unforgiven.
Don't forget your lives are a live-in,
so if she argues, you have to give in,
since controversy's aim is for her to win.
Then finally your wife and you
set a pact that's fair and true.
A bed is such a small quarter
as to make confusing the ambiguous border,
to determine as you will an arbitrary order.

SOON INTERRUPTED,
SLEEP DISRUPTED
AFTER YOUR RESTLESS NIGHT
LEADS TO A MARRIAGE BLIGHT.

Married lives resume
in your silent bedroom
after interrupted sleep
by your wife's sore-throat cough.
Her cold is just a little bit off.
Your mercy on offer
forgives that guilty cougher.
Soon she's back asleep,
at which you wakefully peep,
resentfully accusing
her of ruining your rest, unamusing,
for which she's put under blame
for crippling your morning lame,
which is surely her fault
for putting daylight hours under assault.
Retarded mercy is too creepy,
as you mix anger with feeling sleepy.

AT THE CORNELIA STREET CAFE

On May 2nd 2018, Marvin Cohen gave a reading at the Cornelia Street Cafe, Greenwich Village, NYC, which was partly recorded by Williams Cole. All but one of the poems in the video are included in Sadness Corrected *(Sagging Meniscus Press, 2019). Here is the untitled exception:*

If two people really love each other
then being parted constitutes a tragedy.
If their love is contaminated
then being parted can even be a blessing.
So what am I confessing?
That luckily the first scenario applies to me
minus the tragic parting.
We feel like we're just starting.
Such good fortune in a romantic vein
is infinitely preferable to loving in vain.
Happiness in this matter
is what I can barely restrain
with no loss yet to modify my gain.
So let me rejoice to the top of my voice
as if I was given a choice.

MARRIED TO THE FUTURE

I have a wife, Suzanne. But she doesn't know it yet. I only have her as a future wife, and haven't even told her. She has no idea. I'm waiting for her to feel fond, tender, romantic, towards me, culminating in that powerful passion, love. *Then*, I can safely ask her to marry me; but I have to wait till then, and let her feelings cruise through their gradual courses in an as yet unconscious process in all due course leading to love. In her own ripe time. I have her in the future. The future will burst open, like the spring flower. I own her now, however. I keep her safely in the mind: a safe place. That will preserve her, till—

SEPARATION

(The title, normally at the head, is at the tail of the text. Don't cheat. Read the text first.)

How to get yourself cuckolded:

One: Have a wife.

Two: Sexually non-satisfy her.

Three: Introduce her to a lecherous and handsome and lonely man, and leave them alone for hours in a non-interruptibly seductive, continually temptatious, situation of hermetic, attraction-convergent, tensely relaxing intimacy with increasing heatedness of warmth.

Four: wait.

Five: it's over. You're cuckolded. You've been successful. *Now* what?

(But success *is rewarding, though success at* what *should be considered, not just the mere success itself. Of what* value *is the success? Or is success, for its own sake, the sole value? The mere mechanism of the success* process, *its ruthless, goal-oriented efficiency? In some cases,* failure *may turn out better. Failure to get something bad is a negative form of success. Success in getting something bad is a negative form—or positive?—of failure. Consult the end result, and see.)*

(Title:)

SUCCEEDING AT SOMETHING UNDESIRABLE

A VERY COMMON TALE

The unpleasant feeling of loneliness led him to search for and find a wife. At first there were pleasant, wonderful feelings with her. But they were together so much, living in the same place like all married couples, that gradually he got more and more unpleasant feelings being with her; till finally he couldn't take any more. He left home, they separated, divorced. He got his freedom from her, he's alone. He's alone, but now he's feeling unpleasant loneliness. He would even like her back again, his memory seems to harp on their *better* times together. But it's too late, she's found someone else. It's unbearably unpleasant, he can't put up with it, this loneliness, loneliness. He frantically searches for a new woman. But he's older and less attractive than he used to be. He's desperate, but his standards are for young and pretty women —or were. Since that type of woman rejects him, he's had to reduce his standards and settle for middle-aged, less attractive women—his loneliness begs for assuagement. He's compromising. Loneliness aches, The less romantically older woman will *have* to do. Ah, what of his old dreams, ideals, realities? They're in his head only. They'll have to satisfy him there only. The present conditions won't permit them any more.

UNION'S WAR AGAINST A PAST APART

I

From being a boy, Henry kept on till he was twenty-five. That year, Sue was twenty-three. That's how old each was, when they converged from separate paths of time, met, and shared their time with compound unity thereafter. (Or no it was their ideal to hope.)

They were engaged at once. But this immediacy wouldn't console them. Sue mourned those twenty-five years of her Henry's life in none of which she had even remotely participated; they had been out of her hands, and it was too late to intervene in them; the *belated* Henry, formed by factors outside of her scope of influence, was all she possessed: and not the years before.

Henry felt it likewise. Sue had lived for twenty-three years; where was he, in her independent undergoing of them? He grieved their absolute loss; his life was poor, having made an incomplete start. He couldn't make up for them now; their product, only, was his.

Driven frantic by their tardy, overdue, over-ripely most mature twinning from separate branches of fate, each dove desperately into the other's previous years, clutching at temporal intangibles of experience in the ferocious possessiveness of greed. Why had those years been allowed to happen? They were not real, if not really shared.

For twenty-five years, Henry had been living. He had even been in love before. Those twenty-five years were a secret Sue clutched at, in torment. They had eluded her mark, her brand, her stamp. To Henry alone had they belonged. She joined the corporation late; she would force Henry, for her sake, to be reborn at twenty-six, cancelling to null and void what those previous blasted years had abortively wrought; this would square things between them, for she vowed to have her first twenty-three years discounted, wiped off the register of an unfounded existence. Her birth would begin at twenty-four, endorsed by the authenticity of Henry's commemorative presence. This justice was the only fair poetic retribution in the sanctity of their love's service; in gratitude, love would confer a magical benediction on them; an enchantment air-tight, fool-proof against the banalities of chance.

Sue nurtured a grudge against Henry's *selfish* former life. She had *also* been selfish, but unwittingly. Sue resented Henry's not having had the foresight to arrange for their meeting to be prepared to occur much infinitely earlier than it already did; that bum wouldn't be forgiven for that stupidly complacent privacy he had indulged in before his true life began. The old Henry was hated; starting from scratch, the *new* one had impressive credentials: her overseeing of his overdue reformation.

At first, Henry didn't even know *whom* to be jealous of, in that illicit intrigue, the concealed mystique, of Sue's earlier maidenhood. What precocious romance had scarred her? They spent weeks, divulging autobiographical reminiscences. A voluble exchange of confidences, beginning at any time in the day and ending next morning, reinforced resentment, nurtured suspicion, fed envy. So totally uncapturable, irredeemable, were those separate years before their union, that uncaught time wedged them into enmity. In wrathful finality, they broke their engagement, like a not-valuable but over-fragile vase, into fragments that time would scatter in the fury of abandonment.

II

To fill the gapuum, time liberated some elapsing years, spacing a lengthy interval between their separation and the misfortune of their again meeting. Each had meanwhile married: Henry had an unjealous wife, and Sue a trustful husband. They had repressed any memory of each other.

Love had retreated underground, where an opposition government practiced legislation until the counter-overthrow would have restored the thrown. Like a suppressed neurosis, their love, in phantom shadow, kept formulative its ever-growing process. Like a nocturnally maturing mushroom that springs up overnight, their love, in subterfuge, grew up to a ripe health. The magic was being stored up, to be released by reality's flinging their bodies together in the entanglement of chance. Then Love would fatally emerge, well nurtured by its rich excursion into Hades, or Lethe, an immersion into restorative repose. Like a giant brought back to life, transformed from a dwarf who had first gone to sleep, this Love would lift vital muscles, at ten times the force of its former intensity that fell asleep.

Sue and Henry remet, ten years later, at, of all vulgar places, a bus stop crowded with returnees from the theatre. Sue and her husband; Henry and his wife: having evacuated neighboring theatres, both plays ending at the same mass-produced instant. So sure was their impact of rediscovery, Sue's husband and Henry's wife recognized with instantaneous immediacy that a drastic alteration had invaded all four lives: a radical reversion to the past for Sue and Henry; and fateful submission to this unalterable fact, in hushed acceptance, by their now non-mates. Swung into the general irrelevancy were some small children: who, not the issue of Sue and Henry's union, were now among the items that didn't matter. Adjustments were liberally made: Henry and Sue set up an apartment together; and fell apart, over those ten intervening years shared only by the irony of mutual infidelity. They must be rooted out, and rigidly redeemed.

(Real title is placed after end of story, where it belongs: it would be premature here.)

I

It was time for love to announce itself. Bob had learned to be forthright; he had designed his character from within so that the outside mask facing people was charmingly blunt and bold, as his successful style in social life, and he had made it work, people were taken by it, he got his way with them. Hie soft toughness was persuasive, it was the right line; and he always kept to it. He had been a fair-haired bachelor among women, but for some reason he was now feeling pure love for someone recently met, Lila. To keep it from her as a mystery strategy was not his ploy. More in keeping with his cultivated personality was to proclaim it outright—not to an intermediary confident, but to Lila herself. Then it was her responsibility to reject him, if that would be her decision. Let her be the one, in full knowledge of the contents of his heart, to decide him fate. This was manly and honest of him, as he understood it, thrusting an abrupt burden on Lila's startled shoulders.

Their one meeting had been at a party, she guardedly escorted by her date. They had stolen some side moments in quick talk while the date had become disengaged by a distraction. The one notable transaction had been Bob's scribbling of Lila's phone number upon so sudden a request as to catch Lila with her prudence down, shocking her out of choice. This was the number he was dialing.

"But I'm already in love with the man you saw me with at the party, I'm living with him, it was sheer accident that he didn't pick up the phone instead of me. It's flattering to be told that you love me so soon, but it's rude too to force me to tell you never to phone again, leave me alone. I'm already committed to the one I love, in due time we'll be married, there's no room for you, you tried to storm the issue heedless of my own state; now that you're informed, act accordingly, give me up, don't bother me. It's no fault of mine that you conceived a headstrong passion on the spot, I didn't lure you on, I only met you offhand and suddenly you rape my emotions but I won't let you, you have no right to impose unwanted love when my whole situation is unreceptive to you. Is that clear?"

They managed to hang up mutually, and Bob was left to ponder on this rare failure of his. Was her decision irrevocable? Might not time reverse it, in his unhurried haste to win her in patient eternity? Lots of time was available for waiting, if his mood should keep rate with this rather distant prospect that had for its aim the culminating attainment, by the long-range plan, of Lila whose current obstinacy would gradually give way; since statistics suggest that sooner or later all affairs or marriages must bust up or at least become cracked. It was a waiting game that Bob would embark on; Lila now was purely represented love. Would time steal *that* image, too?.

II

While the years passed, Bob compiled consulted statistics on the length of marital or other intimate relationships in the contemporary America of New York City among a certain kind of white intellectual people whose group category included Lila and her now husband, her same escort who was her date at the party Bob had met her at and remembered as their so far only meeting on this their solitary earth. Statistical classifications by type revealed that it would be soon, according to tho well-computed average, that Lila and that husband would find their way to the parting of tho ways as constituted by the laws of inevitability upon the average mean projection. This would occur, since it wasn't Bob's custom to be wasted on futile prospects with unreturned investment. Success was his very *being*, as lived. It would come about. Thus it was so decreed.

Bob still loved Lila with unabated purity, his soul had been kept clear for her, it was now only a matter of time's decay ripening her willing availability for Bob to pounce on in culmination of his toiling patience. A few years had elapsed, and once every year Bob had phoned her up, gently and forlorn, but hopeful. On all those phone occasions, Lila had proclaimed a thriving, happily-suited marriage, and Bob had to hear that unwelcome declaration with mutely stoical fortitude, and ever-temporary renunciation for another while of his heart's dotage. The game was spoiling for his revenge, and on that anticipation he supported a stubborn optimism, Lila one day would be his, alone. Her current love had already lasted too long. He would have his waiting rewarded. The waiting game, like cat-and-mouse, had its calculated result, on foreseen odds of the ultimate perfection of triumph in the ripening dawn of events once the long laborious night would wend its eventual way and proclaim Bob's heralded sun at last by giving way, as all things must, to time's stealthy battering. *Penelope* won at the end, didn't she?

She won out. But oh, how much time, how much of a lifetime's worth? The steadfast heart was not kept up with by the skin's fading, all the decay that body is known for. Bob still had some prime left, but how much? His life's Lila would be won, but after what wait?

Oh hope, and its sad vigil.

III

How odd, now that ten years had passed, that Bob still should love her; He already would have forgotten her if he had early attained her. It was by delay itself that love's longevity was perfected, on the principle of the inaccessibility of the dear one and her consequent exaltation as a prize longed for in heights of frustration by depths and degrees of despair, granting her exalted worth by measurement of unflushed ideal aged and honed at loyalty's fanatical rate and worshipped for a private tradition; made sacred for an object. Thus stood Lila for Bob, in time's waning.

By time, also, Lila happened to get divorced; She was saddled with a child, which Bob would be saddled with, but true love knows not any impediment. Thus it so happened, that Bob in time, as it turned out, but by course of *slow* time, tortuous time, Bob had his will, and became the second husband to Lila once a decent period had intervened to let the divorce proceedings pass away.

Bob had attained his goal; once attained, his goal was no more, and now his love stopped dead, barely after the wedding celebration. Fate had prolonged him to an ironic twist. He had got what he wanted, then it palled on him, on the scarcely hesitating wings of immediacy. All things come to them who wait. But by then, they're tarnished goods.

His heart's desire had been won. Success had crowned his tragedy pure, thanks to time's spoilage. Lila was detestable, had; who had been so glorious, unhad. Waiting had paid off: and Bob was still paying.

After a little while, their marriage broke up. Bob joined the ranks of middle-aged divorcees, and now he's looking for a new mate. A plain old affair will do, a marriage isn't necessary. Love had not proved well, so he discarded it, as an impediment to the game: it obstructed things.

(Title, following; story's end, now follows, in two paragraphs:)

BOB WAITS, AND WINS; THE WAIT WAS LONG INDEED, BEFORE LILA BECAME HIS. HIS WINNING SOURS HIM, AND ABRUPTLY HE'S LOST. WHAT WAS THE WAITING FOR?

BOB HAD BEEN OUTLASTING; NOW IT WAS HIS TURN TO BE OUTLASTED. ALL GETS RESOLVED IN A BITTER CONCLUSION, TOO BITTER FOR ANY MORAL TO BRAVE. THE STORY, THEN, HAS NO MORAL. BUT LET'S PITY BOB; AND WHO KNOWS ABOUT LILA'S FEELINGS? THEY'RE NOT EVEN INDICATED, AT THE END, SINCE BOB'S SOURNESS OBSCURES EVERY OTHER THING, BY THE SORE GRACE

OF CONCLUSION: EVEN HIS FORMER IDOL, LILA, THE GLORY AND THE DREAM.

THE SET OF MENTALIZED JEANS

When I was in love with Jean, I carried her with me wherever I went. But now I must qualify "carried." I took her along with me, in my mind. She was *in* me wherever I went. Her echo or her image, there she was, in me.

Now, that was one thing; one *her*. The *other* her was the physical Jean, the one who carried herself about on her own two real legs, no matter where she went, or whatever she did, or for whatever reason. That was the Jean-in-the-flesh as it were.

Descartes once said, "I think, therefore I am," in the French of that day. What a brilliant insight! It applied to Jean, as well. Whenever she thought she was.

But *I* thought about her, all the time, as well. So she *"was"* a second time—by virtue of *my* continuous thinking of her. I took her about with me. I carried her wherever I went.

But what when we weren't apart? What when we were together, Jean and I? There was the real Jean on her own two legs, walking alongside me; and there was the *other* Jean, also, walking inside me, or even lying down —she kept a separate life, within me.

The two Jeans. When I stopped loving her, she was only one. Then she became two again, when a *new* man loved her. But the second Jean was quite different than the *former* second Jean: in a new man's head. He loved and imagined her differently, being different than me.

The *real* Jean was slightly different when loved by him, compared to the way she was when she loved by me. She was slightly older and had gone through more recent events—including him.

She gets rid of him now. A new man begins to fancy her. *Another* "second-Jean" is born: fully formed, already; a *third* Jean.

Jean as seen; Jean as is. Jean as she *was* seen. Jean as she was.

All those Jeans. In all those minds of the different men who loved her. And the aging Jean of herself. Her consciousness through years.

The dead Jean. The different men all dead, who thought differently of her. The not-existing to herself. The not-existing to anyone else. The absence equally of existence and its different forms of thought.

Jean in whose mind? The non-Jean. And the non-thought-about.

AFTER ALICE—NOTHING

Without intending to (for she was really kind and had no malice) Alice ended me as a confidently passionate emotional being. I invested my whole treasury of love in her, my life savings, my total resources; and zoop!—down the drain they went. I came up bankrupt, ruined, a petty-survivor. Then Alice lost her importance. But Importance itself had lost all meaning. I was empty of significance-creating vitality. I exist on a calm, flat, and even plain. Alice can never happen again. The lesson so lessened me, I have no more to learn.

DIVORCEVILLE

THE WITHDRAWN REVELATION

How I used to love Masie!

Why not any more?

It's over. She's in my past.

Was it long ago?

Between long ago and recent.

What happened?

We loved each other.

Did you get married?

You're rudely invading my privacy. It's none of your business.

But you were the one who brought her up, that you loved her.

Was I? I forgot.

You piqued my curiosity.

Oh. Sorry to mislead you.

It was intriguing. You loved each other.

You're right.

Can you say what happened?

No, it's gone now.

Come on. Divulge.

You're urging me? Forget it.

But you seemed about to confide in me.

Well, I withdraw that.

Why'd you change your mind?

Never mind. It's my mystery.

What a change of heart!

You're right. It *was* a change of heart.

Oh, do tell!

If you have heart, stop inquiring.

Sorry to be so intrusive.

Oh, that's all right. Forget it.

THE "MARITAL CRISIS" DIALOGUE

My wife is being hyper-critical of me.

What does she unfairly accuse you of?

Neglecting her. Lacking empathy and compassion for her. And occasional rudeness.

Do you angrily retaliate? And defensively exonerate yourself of blame?

Of course. That virago!

Has the argument occasionally flared into heated exchanges that enter into divorce suggestions?

Of course. Where there's smoke, there's fire.

Well, how will this resolve?

Mutual hatred.

Doesn't sound like ideal marriage.

Hardly.

At the current status, does divorceville appear to be your future residence?

Yes, and good riddance.

Would she miss you?

Sure, like I'll miss her.

Then reconciliation sounds like a solid compromise.

Please. Could you be our moderator?

BEING TESTED

Do you cheat on your wife?

Never. If she catches me, she may divorce me at high-cost alimony, to virtually liquidate my financial resources.

So it's that penalty that keeps you from infidelity's temptation?

Yes, but I love her anyway.

Isn't "anyway" a cheap motivational preventative against betrayal?

Yes, but my intentions are honorable.

If you could *get away* with your wife not detecting, would you do that dastardly act of disloyalty?

(Indignantly:) Never! What do you take me for!?

I'm dubious.

Don't be. Take my word.

No, you have too many words, whose ambiguity gives me suspicion.

Well, cancel your friendship with me.

FIGHTING A MALICIOUS RUMOR WITH INCREASING INDIGNATION

I heard a rumor that you beat your wife.

That's completely erroneous! My indignation rises high: Who's the culprit who started this multiply collective lie?

It went in sequence from one mouth to another, from one pair of ears to another. The origin is hard to trace.

Those lying cowards, hiding behind the flapping curtain of social density! I never laid a hand on my wife except to help her into a taxi and to hug her for amorous reasons that are nobody else's business, so they better keep their nose out of it.

You maintain complete innocence despite the malignant charge? Everybody's asking.

Quell this pestilence!

It's already gone too far. The whole neighborhood can think about nothing else but to spread that vocal disease that plagues our district, whereby other districts laugh at us with mocking merriment.

If the rumor is getting out of hand, I must helplessly search for the source.

The rumor includes a clause.

What are the vile contents of this so-called "clause"?

That your very wife has registered complaints against your violence.

(Apoplectic:) I'll strangle her!

Is that a plea for innocence?

No, for justice.

But what is justice?

Ask me another time. I'm too angry now.

IS THIS A LITTLE LIKE TIT FOR TAT?
YES, SOMETHING ALONG THE BITTER LINES OF THAT.

How's your marriage going?

Not so good. It's not rolling.

At least you're still together?

No, she's already left me.

What happened between you two?

She met someone else.

Was your marriage on the rocks?

Yeah, another man had intervened.
He came rollicking in-between.

Is it curtains for you and her?

Our whole status is one big blur.

How sorry I feel for you!

Well, it wasn't my fault.
Her love fled from me,
speeding to the other guy,
with whom she's replaced me.

I had thought you and she were a fixture,
but now I have to draw another picture.
Have you accepted the new reality?

Partly. Not in its totality.

So you still cling to hope?

No. I'm fed up being a dope.
She's welcome to this new guy,
so from her I'll swiftly fly,
while meeting someone else by and by.

Is this a little like tit for tat?

Yes, something along the bitter lines of that.

A CHANGE OF PRESSURE

Love between two people is like a heavily weighted valise which, when carried by them both above their heads in an equal distribution of its weight, isn't at all taxing; but when one withdraws her support and the other is left holding the burden, it becomes unbearable for him, so unbearable it crushes him, he can't hold up under it, he sags into a heap, it crashes him down, with sheer tragedy's weight. And grief lies heavy over him. Nostalgia remembers the lightness of having a partner. The *shared* burden was no burden at all, it was a pleasure! And the pleasure has just come down to earth. With malice.

THE NOCTURNAL REVERIE: LOVE, GRIEF, AND DEATH. THE LAKE UNLIT. WHAT HIDDEN JOYS ARE BURIED IN THE PERMANENT BLACK?

Long ago, I once had a girl friend. God, was she beautiful! No need to ask me if I loved her. She was the exact matching piece of my heart, where she fit so snugly, it was hard to tell whether my heart altered its elastic size and adjusted its shape to fit her, or whether it was she who turned flexible to conform to my heart's tailor-made dimensions for her. Or maybe there was no adapting necessary, maybe an accident or miracle brought together exactly the heart to fit exactly the girl. It was a perfect pairing, the most impossible likelihood of combinations making the unlikely come true through the fortuitous circumstance of coincidence. For a spell of a year, she was mine, and I belonged to her. Paradise became a normal daily recurrence, bliss a commonplace, and the regularity of the ideal made me assume it for granted. I had her, and it seemed as normal as breathing. Only with the grief of her departure did I come to my foolish senses and learn what an empty life of misery it was when void of that true darling. I woke up, to despair.

∞

She left me, I was left. I couldn't stop her. She went. No preventing her. There was only me. She flooded my mind. The more she was physically absent, the more weighed her image-burden on my dark lake of reflection.

The midnight woe. The morning grief. The love that won't let go. The saddest of suffering. The lonely image on the lake. The woods receive its echo. The faintness of dusk. She abides, to remain. Her haunting spell. Her enduring presence. Her wider absence than the world has opening for when all space is spread and time can pour its gallons through. High and deep and wide: she can't be hidden.

She never returned. My night is closing. I've used up my dawns. No dawn to greet me. Between this closing night, and there not being a dawn, where can my traveling so go? It flutters up to her. But is she there? Such technicalities don't occur. Such mere facts can never matter, any more. What means only an *outcome*? All was contained by the *journey*. The longing feelings on the human solitude.

The darkening lake, void of its monthly moon.

Love dies, with the lover. The lover is its container. The vessel is broken; the fluid pours out.

The lake in its stained journey.

The lake unlit, even by its poisoned cloud.

A QUIET MEMORY OF THAT PLACE, WHERE I PLACE THE THEN COMPANION OF THAT TIME

For a little while, my soul dwelt in Ireland with my pretty fair; then the time moved slowly, and left me *here*, with only my body.

WHAT'S LEFT

She gave me love; then took it away. Where was I to find her substitute? Where stood her double in the whole outside world? The need was for her, and she was no type. Deprived of that archetype of her solo single kind, I was uniquely damned for the whole land of hope. That's the state she left me with: to carry it as far as death. Death completes the heart's heartbreak.

A PERSONAL TRAGEDY

When she returned my love, she represented the fulfillment of every dream; when she abandoned me, she represented the disillusionment of every dream. The second state succeeded the first state and remains to this day. It seems unlikely in be replaced.

WHAT TALKING ABOUT LOVE ARRIVED AT (OR ENDED INTO.)

(Man and woman. Man speaks first.)

You're the last person in the world I want to talk about love to.

I won't accept such an insincere insult.

But it's only too true, considering that you're the very *first* person I want to talk about love to; and the world being round, it curves into a whole circle back in on itself, causing the very last person to merge with the very first person, and all in your person. You're then first and last, and always were, though it took the current moment to confirm it.

What love do you want to talk about to me?

Mine for you.

You seemed to be hinting around; I suspected so. All this roundabout, indirect rhetoric. Now you're able to come right out saying it. Now I know where *you* stand.

And where do *you*?

I stand out of it. This talking of love has come to an end: full circle. I turn around, my back to your love. I walk out on it.

But my love follows you about.

Around the world it goes, the circular world. But time will slow it down, you'll see.

(Time goes by. There's no more love, and still less to talk about.)

TOO TENDER FOR REMINISCING; TOO PRESENT TO CALL IT PAST; TOO LOVING FOR YOUR ABSENCE NOT TO BE CONVERTED INTO—GRIEF, LONGING, SADNESS, SORROW: A SPURNED LOVER'S TRADITIONAL SALVES

There were those days when we were together. Those days that truly were. Imagination may have embroidered them, but it didn't invent them. My body was slightly younger then, but other than that it's the same body as now. *Today's* version of my body, though, is extremely remote from touching you. Your memory is alive in it, and a habit of response. But you're not here to respond to, you're not real to replenish *image* with some objective light of day. You don't renew yourself. The *mind* feels you, but you're unsummoned to touch. I'm passing along a similar landscape to a one *we* used to be familiar with. Imagine what's revived! Lacking the key element, you, to fulfill the need to repeat it in identical atmosphere, It was just the same time of day, at a very similar season. A town like this one, with mountains behind it, while traveling, with road and traffic and people never to be seen again after glanced at once. It was us together doing the experiencing: you were part of it. You were the element present then, that's missing now. The scene's repetition is incomplete, just by the fraction of you. And with that emotional difference, my heart is laden,

Grief is your absence. What are you doing? Why don't I join you? It does me no good to be bereft. What patient wisdom is taught by it? How to endure melancholy? How to love without having? How to live starving, with feasts of remembrance?

We're not still together because you don't still love me. That's the earth of the reason. But romance goes begging.

How long can I carry our joint love alone? When shared, what a light burden! Now I must bear it, without your assistance. You've thrown it over: it tilted, but I still carry it. It cripples me. It's an unbearable brunt. It was borne by two. The survivor doesn't survive.

My view of our love is conservative. You look back on it. I suffer to sustain it. It's all of you that remains. Why should I shed it? I cling to the idol of you, the love: and symbols must do, lacking the objects they were created by. My heart is a cult of you. The deity is lost; but the devout must worship. And trembling prayer, in place of the one prayed for. Religion substitutes for life's joy. Would I love you so much, if we were still playing together? Acting *with* you is not a love *for* you. Absence feeds love. But at intervals, we *were* back together. Now, your absence is prolonged. Must it be unbroken? Am I doomed?

ANGUISH IN GOING THROUGH LOVELY EVENTS WHEN SHE'S NOT HERE TO SHARE THEM WITH ME. CAUSING THESE EVENTS TO BE HATEFUL. CAUSING ME TO PERVERSELY WISH THAT *UN*INSPIRING EVENTS WOULD TAKE PLACE, TO MAKE ME *PLEASED* BY HER ABSENCE. TRYING TO MAKE A *VIRTUE* OF HER ABSENCE, TO LESSEN THE ANGUISH OF THE GORGEOUS THINGS THAT *COULD BE*, WERE SHE HERE.

The anguish I felt! Everything good I experienced become tainted and anguished by the haunt, "Oh she would so have loved it, had she been able to be here! It would have been lovely to share this with her."

To the point where I felt actual relief—less torment—when I experienced dull, uninteresting, distasteful things. For then I would have this golden consolation: "Ah, it's just as well that she *wasn't* able to be here: this way, she's able to avoid these banalities." And I would congratulate myself on the good luck in her being too indisposed to share these unglorious events, which it sufficed that I alone should endure them.

So I found myself *wishing* that things were less beautiful; less idyllic, less lovely. And my heart would break—with anguish—when these negative wishes did *not* come true. For then the anguish, "She's not here—how she would have loved . . .," whatever it was. "The waste! She *could* have been sharing this with me. This lovely thing was *meant* to be shared by us."

Romantic anguish. And how would I make it up to her? By writing this? My belated attempt at the futility of sharing?—thus uniting us through regret? More incentive, for bonds to be.

I CAN'T GET HER BACK, HOWEVER HARD I TRIED. FOR MY PAINS, MY LOVE FOR HER NOW PERMANENTLY OUT-STEPPED TIME; THE HEART HAS WRAPPED HER IN A FILMY COAT OF IDEAL; MY PHYSICAL FAILURE TO RE-GAIN HER HAS STRAINED THE MIND IN SUCH STRESS, THAT IMMORTALITY IS APT RECOMPENSE, MARKING HER IMAGE FOR MY SOUL'S ASCENT BEYOND THIS TEM-PORAL FRUSTRATION FOR HER BURNING LOSS THAT CROSSES ALL THE WORLD OF MY WILL TO END ITS FU-TILITY IN A GRANDEUR OF SUBLIMATION, THE HEROIC TRANSCENDENCE OF ROMANTIC GRIEF

Love overcomes all obstacles? But it can't overcome the one unconquerable obstacle: the insufficient reciprocation, the non-requital—to the point of indifference or aversion—on the part of the one loved. Muster all your forces, rally all your reserves, bring up reinforcements in the rear, to the summit of your very strength, employ all your eloquence and worldly goods, recruit powers even yet unused, learn new stratagems; appeal to the occult on the magic possibilities of superstition, or to the scientific on the sound basis of marshalling every knowable fact in the harness of ruse, deception, or intricately formulated plot and the ingenious inventiveness of scheme toward the sole end of winning the one you love. And if she doesn't love you, she doesn't love you: she'll give her love freely to another, from the independence and self-realization of her choice. Persuasion is futile, and every practical device is in vain. With relentless onslaught, you fail. Wage your ultimatum of all offenses, in the mastery of all skills, toward the single goal. Be dauntless, and persevere past all persistence, never take no for an answer, try and try again, never despair, clutch hope like the key of survival itself, with heroically conclusive courage and indomitable will. Endure a repulsion, and attack again: utilize qualities excelling superhumanity itself to mythical proportions found only fabulously in the superlative: and *still* fail; and fail because: "She doesn't love you." For you're weakly dependent on *her* will: and by inclination, she rejects you; or with reluctance; regretfully; or she once *did* love you, and has resolved to forget; and romantically, it's your *tragedy*: for *her* it's "tragic," but not to that extent; or, for a time, she enjoyed your company and found it a rewarding relationship. But it went no farther than that. For you, it went *disappearingly* far, beyond sanity's measure of renouncing her and being reconciled to the loss. The grief is yours: and the love is still throbbing hot, preserved by the grief, contained within grief's skin, transforming grief to itself. She refused you: finally. No, that's not acceptable: being bereft begets a non-forgetting; her *image* is enshrined. It's all of her that you have left; love sanctifies it, to the ultimate of significance. Despair brightens the weeping; the soul's tragedy is heightened to unbelievable poignance; and the whole ordeal is yours, the suffering that intensifies experience to memory. You have been very romantic about it. You will never get over it. The heart is distracted into recovery in the succession of new events that overlay a later tissue on the old one; but that dear, fond, tender, remote little thing, you've lost beyond the physical boundaries of living experience, Permanence has ideally replaced her; the *love* for her is what remains, now that, by free will, she chooses not to turn up again. Love prolongs her short stay in your life, or your life takes her on to the mind, beyond cell decomposition and decay in your matter. The heart will outwear the bones, and what is your heart but the lonely replica of her, commemorating what was. Her time with you has lasted; then time disintegrated, or died into a vibrating clock. You were desperate to regain her. At futility's point, despair replaced desperation. And now, how devout! She's gone into your glory. And how finely embalmed she is!

THREE WAILS OF GRIEF

1. SLEEP'S REACTIONARY RAGE

I woke up crying for you. Even yet my sleep has not accepted your departure.

2. MY SAD EXPLANATION INTERPRETATION THAT REPLACES SOMETHING INCONSOLABLY LOST

She couldn't support the weight of loving me. She felt relief in leaving me. And the relief eased the love away.

3. TO SOMEONE WHO DROPPED *HER* SIDE OF THE "BARGAIN"

Spring is here, and I love you. On my side our love is kept alive, My unforgetfulness is not mental, but emotional. My heart is our permanent museum.

TOGETHER STOPPED

There's no mental interpenetration. We're completely separate entities. We get together only physically, meaning superficially.

We're not sympathetically extending into each other. That was once, but not now.

We're apart except for perfunctory habit. Meaning, we're well apart.

CODA

DON GIOVANNI'S FAVORITE OPERA

In Spain, that country, practically a peninsula, in the southwest corner of the famed continent of Europe, Donna Elvira was kicking up an angry fuss, claiming that Don Giovanni had abandoned her, which was true, and the Don knew it. She screamed loudly, and he put a finger to his lips and whispered "Zitto," meaning "Hush," "shh," "quiet," in Italian.

(Why Spanish noble people were speaking in Italian is a mix-up, and it's easier *not* to explain a mix-up, just as most difficult things are easier *not* to do or say. But to return to the principals concerned:)

"Look, Donna Elvira, despite your love for me I reject you. I *already* made love to you. Why repeat with the same woman what can be more energetically begun with new (and the synonym for 'new' is 'more interesting') women? I'm a Lothario, stud, Casanova, a legendary Don Juan, already. So with my reputation, it's *easy* to seduce new women. If women *weren't* attracted to me so universally, Donna Elvira, then I would stick to you faithfully and loyally for a whole married lifetime, since it would be futile to wander.

"I would resign myself to contentment with only you, if other women found me dull. On the contrary, women love me sooner or later, I find, once I make the appropriate gestures and speech formation. Diversity and variety are dished up to me, thereby. Who but an angel or eunuch could resist this flattering quantity? So pity me my good fortune, which shoves virtue aside. I'm fallen, since so many desire me. Forgive me this extraordinary fault. Now, leave me alone. A lady waits for me, even now. I must be no more than romantically late, for our passionate meeting. It bores me to be every lady's only, since nobody is an only for me. It's unjust—but on whose side?"

∞

Donna Elvira was left to weep alone. Her weeping is copious. It's her only means for still retaining Don Giovanni, since the intensity of her tears symbolically approximated the man she grieved for. Each tear glistened full, and before exploding, contained his dear vanishing image, as though the full bulk of him was locked inside.

A hysterical religious association occurred to Donna Elvira's mind, between her adored hedon and the martyr Jesus Christ who died in advance to give Don Giovanni liberty to sin. She connected her fled lover with the universal Saviour, and this connection, strictly personal in its creative invention, converted her grief to ecstasy for a while. This was her imaginative triumph over her bereft state: *unadorned* reality was thus improved upon, and a desperate comfort plucked. This would fortify her for despair's inevitable return. She would quaff this cup of bitter solace, to choke back her bile of wrath whose pitch craved death of self or betrayer. Uneasily, she would be tidied over. Her religion-tempered rage would renew itself, but perhaps at a blunted point of violence. Christ assisted her *now*, at her most critical danger. He came in Don Giovanni's image, with divine love. He brought the appeasement of sublimation. Its perfection was in its timeliness. Meanwhile, the *real* Don Giovanni rode gallantly to his assignation. Unknowingly he left behind Christ in his stead. Thus be played at least two roles at once, in different ladies' hearts.

The plains of Spain gave way to his horse's hoofs. He rode with proud regality. He would have an adventure. The following morning, his servant Leporello will be rejoining him. They'll go to his castle, where nearby will be a wedding celebration of some peasants. Don Giovanni will attend. He epitomizes democracy.

∞

His clandestine nocturnal escapade was with a noblewoman, Donna Anna, in the gardens of her father's great estate. They meet, hug, and kiss. Don Giovanni then makes a pass at her, but she considers his advance rash, and coyly demurs with proud dignity. "I'm engaged to Don Ottavio," she declares, "so don't dishonor me." Don Giovanni prepares to disobey.

He drags her onto her porch looking for a likely place of privacy. Nearby is the greenhouse, where it's dark. He abducts her there, intent upon rape; she struggles, but cooperates to the extent of not screaming. Her resistance is partial, yet physical. He has to maul her, and does. Their breathing becomes hoarse. It's a very strenuous scene. Luckily, it's unspied upon. It's fruits are sin: they hastily nibble upon it, and then cram. For Don Giovanni, it's an old story: he's blasé under his ardor. For Donna Anna, this is new. It means marriage, at the least. Don Giovanni has usurped her fiancé. So much the better.

Her fiancé, Don Ottavio, is just an empty tenor. But Don Giovanni is clad in magic. She purrs up to him.

But the Don is now bored; he's had her already. He prepares to leave but she clutches hold of him, with the eagerness of a slightly soiled bride, Their voices rise to argue his with "Let go," hers with "You're staying!" A servant overhears, and rushes to report his finding at such an irregularly late hour to Donna Anna's patrician, noble father, nicknamed "The Commander," for he's used to lord it. He comes rushing to the rescue, with upraised sword, having ordered his servants to remain behind; for his daughter's allegedly sullied honor is his affair alone, as an outraged father smarting to revenge it. The challenged Don Giovanni laughs at the older man, but has the prudence not to take the challenge lightly.

Donna Anna flees in terror. In self-defense, Don Giovanni sticks his sword blade into the living "Commander," and withdraws it from the dead "Commander," turned redder with the change. Don Giovanni escapes. Donna Anna returns, with that magically appearing insipid tenor, Don Ottavio, to survey the horror of the "Commander's" fallen state. Donna Anna and Don Ottavio exchange revenge arias culminating in a duet. The plot thickens, the music spreads, grows wider, it's a masterpiece. Mozart is achieving immortality, to be conferred on his characters too, for being in it. What an opera!. Day succeeds night, it's a new change of scene. Peasant gaiety. A rustic wedding, in old Spain.

Don Giovanni is looking in on it. He's attended by his servant, Leporello. They're a pair of rascals, though of uneven status.

∞

Leporello had been chafing a smoldering revolt of discontent at being an oppressed "servant." Don Giovanni was so inconsiderate! He got all the glory and the goodies, the women, the food, the fun; while Leporello, for all his servile loyalty, had to play the deprived buffoon always at his master's beck and call. Well then, Leporello had the choice to quit, so why didn't he? He would be the worse off for it. The economic situation in royalist Spain of that century was not splendid for the penniless; nor was the job outlook full of juicy choices. So, begrudgingly, Leporello stuck to the Don: at least, his master was more interesting than any other master. Just to observe him was to be in awe and in admiration of so adroit, so in fact diabolically skilled, a seducer of girls. It was an ideal situation for a voyeur, should Leporello be one. He wasn't one by nature, but he became one, with such an enthralling master to vicariously identify with in endless amorous adventures. So Leporello smothered his discontent, to keep his post, and be consoled by his station of chief assistant to a living myth. All that took place in Spain, which was a musical country located in the composer's brain. Mozart by name. The dancing music hasn't come down yet.

It's poised in the endless air. And its airs put on new heirs, for posterity.

∞

The scene is a little peasant village close by the castle by inheritance of the opera's great hero. A pre-wedding celebration is taking place, with dancing merriment by the rustic swains and their humble womenfolk. Featured in the foreground are the two principals of the affair, the bride- and bridegroom-to-be, by name Masetto he, and the sweet Zerlina she. They know their station in life, which is low. But they can have their animal joys, like any farmyard beast, once the ceremony has been legalized and their nuptials solemnized by the moral priest. Then they could forget their daily rounds of hardship by nightly nudity in the round, to ease the day's labors by toils of nocturnal delight. Anyhow, that was the romanticized vision, which assumed an endless feast of prodigious potency: a widely painted myth, to deceive the innocent and beguile away their pedestrian bachelor hopes and maiden trustfulness by illusions too good to be true—or else (which is just the same) too bad. So the couple aspires to their wedding state. Now the complication shall arise—the aristocratic invasion of their innocence by the cynical Don, with the trusty Leporello smirking at the rear. The revels dwindle in interruption, while the noble but abrupt guest lightly questions the betrothed pair. He's bewitched by the bride, by his practiced mechanism of professionalism in the disruptive art of interfering with others for the sake of some erotic sport and the inflamed games of vanity. Don Giovanni plots to steal Zerlina away from her intended, to entice her from the bridal path for some rare spice of distraction. His ploys are too much for her, and she succumbs, for his wiles imitate sincerity to her bedazzled eye. He dangles before her the promise of raising her state from peasant girl to grand lady. His whim becomes her mirage. She's won, or won over, and Masetto is already abandoned. The latter is furious—but powerless. It's the Don's lordly privilege, and Masetto is forlornly resigned. He's been tricked—his bride ravished away, by a cunning betrayal, abetted by Leporello, who diverted Masetto while the Don's flirtation with Zerlina approached the boiling point. But then bad luck slips Zerlina from the villain's hearty grasp, as Donna Elvira, pursuing her betrayer in the shrill hysteria of her piety and the dogged devices of her persistence, intervenes: just in time; she warns Zerlina off that notorious rake before the peasant girl's fall was consummated into a fact. So Don Giovanni's foiled, and the angry lover has to flee the scene before Donna Elvira's righteous assault of platitudes. Leporello is secretly glad. His master has been spoiled, and the servant's envy gloats at his failure. All this moody intrigue, to the rise and fall of music sublimely steady in racing through all the moods. Mozart traces the scene with an infallible ear, to sprightly measure.

A few times, the tenor voice of Don Ottavio suddenly emerges solo from a climbing-up-and-down chorus of alternating characters alternatingly combining, and bursts loose with golden richness and light wonder. It lingers, long after the whole opera. But so too does the whole opera, long after its last memory audibly resonant in chambers suddenly piquant and illumined, spontaneously reissuing whole spells and chords, fiery with sequence. The opera is over. It's about to begin. The same characters now a few centuries old. The curtain rises, as the overture ends. Enter Leporello, solo. His throat throttles. The words sing out. Hours later, the final chorus, and the full orchestra. The latest ending, till the next beginning, somewhere. They can't ever stop it. Reputation excels in repetition. New performers, to carry on our grandest ghost. Dragging along its used-up plot. The silence dances, drowned to bits by the sounds that ache, novel but familiar, a drama set to music. Or music filled out, on a few bare bones of theatre in the crude. Bland pegs, for hats rarely plumed, to an insane vocal flourish. Logic, overwrought. Sense, sewed up in heard thought.

Marvin in October 2022. Photo by Colin Myers.

Marvin Cohen is the author of many novels, plays, and collections of essays, stories, and poems.

His shorter work has appeared in over 100 magazines and books, including: *Ambit, Antaeus, Assembling, Center Magazine, Cricket Addict's Archive, Essaying Essays, Extensions, Harper's Bazaar, Hudson Review, Monk's Pond, The Nation, National Camp Director's Guide, New Directions in Prose and Poetry, The New York Times, Plays from the New York Shakespeare Festival, The Pushcart Prize, Quarterly Review of Literature, Salmagundi, Sun and Moon, Transatlantic Review, The Village Voice, Vogue (UK)*, and *Wormwood Review*. Most recently, his work has appeared in every issue of *Exacting Clam*.

His writing ranges from the experimental to fable; from poetry to prose; from internal dialogues to playscripts; from art criticism to cricket fandom; from humour to philosophical essays, and from aesthetics to surrealism (he says "if people say so then it must be true").

His work has been performed on radio and theatres in the USA and the UK, including readings at the Poets at the Public Series.

Born in Brooklyn in 1931, Cohen has described himself as one who has "risen from lower-class background to lower-class foreground." He studied art at Cooper Union but left college to focus on writing, supporting himself with a series of odd jobs, from mink farmer to merchant seaman. He later taught creative writing at various New York colleges, including The New School, the City College of New York and Adelphi University.

For a long time, Marvin Cohen has lived in New York City with his wife Candace.